GW00630585

THE
OPEN PEN
ANTHOLOGY

A LIMEHOUSE BOOKS PUBLICATION

Edited by Sean Preston
Design by Katrina Clark
Managed by Bobby Nayyar

Typeset in Adobe Caslon Pro

First published 10.03.2016

ISBN 978-1-9075-3623-6

Limehouse Books
Flat 30, 58 Glasshouse Fields
London E1W 3AB

limehousebooks.co.uk
openpen.co.uk

Printed by Short Run Press.

Distributed in the UK and EU by Turnaround.

THE
OPEN PEN
ANTHOLOGY

EDITED BY SEAN PRESTON

LIMEHOUSE
BOOKS

CONTENTS

INTRODUCTION

For reasons too preposterous to trouble us here, I am writing this introduction to the Open Pen Anthology below a stegosaurus. Or, more precisely, beneath the skeleton of one that has been strung up in an entirely un-Jurassic fashion, thagomizer all a-dangle, in the vaulted roofspace of the Ronson Gallery in London's Natural History Museum.

Precious few, if any, of London's institutions appeared fully-formed. Most owe their genesis and survival to the vision, tenacity and charisma peculiar to a single soul: an individual who believed in something, and who gathered around them material that reflected that outlook – unaware, perhaps, at the outset, just how great a significance the consequences of their efforts would assume. The collection that provided a foundation for both the Natural History Museum and the British Museum, for instance, was gathered together by a physician from Ulster, a Dr Sloane (he of the Square), whose interest in naturalism propelled not only his medical career but also his collecting habits, resulting in a bounty of specimens that on his death would be bequeathed to the nation. From dictionaries to hospitals to parks to choirs, the story of London is the story of single individuals starting with modest means and big ambitions, getting on and making things happen.

Sean Preston, the Harris-rocking founder and editor of Open Pen literary magazine, is someone who gets on and makes things happen. The book you hold in your hands serves as excellent evidence of that fact, but any back copy of the Open Pen would do. In these last moments before you treat yourself to the cornucopia of ripened hand-picked prose within, consider, I double-dare you, the audacity it takes to launch, grow and sustain a quality print magazine at any time, and especially in an age that is spread thin and digitised, with the economy staggering about clutching its chest and trying to find its tablets. To have reached the point of publishing a first anthology is a considerable achievement; to have done so while fostering nothing but warmth, respect and camaraderie among the growing Open Pen family, and without compromising the values of literary openness and ease of access, requires a special personality.

1

Of course, if Sean remains true to character (and naturally he will), he'll be horrified at the suggestion that these accomplishments have been anything other than a *team* effort; and it is true that the magazine, every time it appears, is a little miracle of collaboration. Nevertheless, at root, this book, and the London publication whose name it shares, are here because, some years ago, one person decided to ignore the odds.

Which returns us to this anthology of writings, to which you are most welcome. It is shaped by the writers whose words await you, and by the Open Pen team, who know what's good; its production is possible through the generosity of a host of readers and enthusiasts too numerous to name here. To all concerned, thanks is owed. The result is a success that is emotionally resonant – as you will see, it is by turns powerful, moving, comic and angry – and manages to pleasingly stimulate the little grey cells.

But I see this collection, like certain other collections before it, as representing something bigger, too: an early step on a long journey into the future. Which is an exciting place to be headed, for the future is immense, and, for the dreamer, full of undreamed-of possibilities.

Even with his far-sighted view of the world, I'll bet Dr Sloane would have been thoroughly surprised to glimpse how posterity would remember his labours. But not half as surprised as the stegosaurus.

N Quentin Woolf

South Kensington
January 2016

FOREWORD

I forgot to bring any paper, so I'm writing this on the back of a coaster instead. It should fit because my handwriting is very, very small, and the coaster is square, so I won't have to write round and round and round and round, into some warped, illegible vortex. Some people think my handwritten words look like mouse droppings, while others, certain uninformed persons, believe it points to a psychopathic nature. But you're hardly going to ask a deranged, psychotic person to write the foreword to a published literary anthology, are you? What sort of a book would that be?

It's difficult to find a coaster with a plain side these days. Most of them are covered front and back with dull, clichéd advertising. None of it is readable. It's basically just wallpaper. Of course, a lot of supposedly readable fiction is the same. A waste of the space it's written on. Plenty of those long, chunky, space-wasting novels would be better off as beer mats. Rather than taking up room on library shelves, or in shops or warehouses, you could use them to rest your drink on. At least you wouldn't need to lift your glass so far to your mouth. The coaster I'm using today is for a lager brand. It's a brand you've heard of, but I'll spare you the tedious details, only to say that, like other mainstream lagers, it's completely tasteless. It's the same old shit, one might say, merely arranged in a different pile. Personally, I prefer a drink you can actually taste. Ales are good in this respect, as are whiskies. Have you tried absinthe? That stuff can alter your senses for real, and not just the taste ones. Writing, I suppose, is similar. Most mainstream stories are bland and easy to digest. You know what you're getting, and you can blindly wade through them without any need to actually engage your senses. This Open Pen collection is different. These pieces weren't chosen for their mass-market appeal. Quite the opposite. They're stories that set out to take risks and be different. They're more like a shot of absinthe than a pint of boring lager.

I really hope it has a launch party, this anthology, with one of those free bars. We won't need coasters like this one because you tend to hold your glass or bottle at those things and stand around. Maybe the contributors will attend, and I'll get to put faces to writers. But I don't want to meet them. No way. I don't want to ruin everything. Most likely I'll stand next to the drinks table and neck lots and lots of interesting tasting drinks. The contributors, I'm sure, are most interesting themselves, but talking shop isn't one of my strong points. I'm a bit of a social wipeout, truth be told. Better to read their interesting, sense-provoking stories with a likeminded drink. From what I've learnt, most authors are keen to give me a wide berth anyway.

There's not much room left on this coaster. Perhaps if I…

One of the bar staff has just smashed a glass and we, the gathered pub patrons, all whistle and cheer. Why? Why do we always do this? Perhaps it's because, when things are quietly drifting along as normal, you simply need someone to smash things up. Cheers to that!

Francis Plug

D.E.A. (Minor)
by Will Ashon

The Penitents of Camber Sands weren't nuns, they just liked wearing black. Nor, thought Travis, between blows, were they exactly penitent. He was trying to focus on the issue of taxonomy in the hope it might distract him. As none of them had ever played an instrument, never mind a gig, you couldn't really call them a band, though that was how they self-defined. *Gang* was the word that sprang to mind, as his mind bounced off the floor, but he didn't want to encourage them. It occurred to him that he should ease off on the classification and concentrate on escaping. Unfortunately, classification was what he did. He couldn't deny there was a brutal, driving rhythm developing as they kicked him that he found *thrillingly primal*. Though he still preferred the diminuendo that occurred as they lost interest, and the long, silent coda after they left for the bar which reminded him of the echoing sound of a grand piano's last chord in Studio Two at Abbey Road.

When he was sure they weren't coming back, Travis staggered to his feet and tried to compose himself, find a little dignity, despite the gigantic beer stain situated front stage right of his crotch. A few people looked at him without looking at him and he shrugged and smiled. He used to think of it as a winning—if slightly shit-eating—grin, but these days it split his face open. He was a Cheshire Cat who had lost his powers, floorbound, forever invisible. Travis pulled the scraggy overcoat round him. Fifteen years back, when he found it in a now-closed vintage store in Camden, it might have been cool. He wasn't quite ready to give up on the idea. That was the thing about clothes—the way you decayed inside them, matching their increasing tattiness with extra weight and tired eyes. He tried not to think about it. He tried to steer clear of his reflection.

All things considered, Travis was rather pleased to have been attacked. He could have done without the bruises and the incoming headache, but on the other hand, it had been a good few years since anyone had cared enough to kick the shit out of him. In the old days he'd always had to be careful at gigs—wary, coming in late and staying at the back of the room with a wall behind him, keeping an eye out for this or that offended band member or overprotective superfan. What bliss it was to be a music journalist back then! How powerful they had felt, how young! All-expenses-paid trips back and forth to New York! Free T-shirts! Listening parties! Free hoodies! That afternoon putting all kinds of things up his nose with the bass player from Ned's Atomic Dustbin!

It was more than just getting old. The world had changed, objectively, and was none the better for it. You couldn't go around saying the Internet was shit, but the Internet was shit. He remembered how excited he'd been when one of those music websites had set up in the States and offered to pay him a dollar a word for a column about the gig scene in London, which he could knock off in less than an hour. He kept remembering it, over and over again, while he was making tea, while he was typing away on his laptop, while he was doing a phone interview with some electronic-music producer or other living in Scotland or another cold place who he wasn't interested in anyway. He tried to remove it from his head now as he peered through the door and into the bar area, worried about where the Penitents might be. It had been great and everything, but he didn't want any more. He wanted a pint.

*

Travis began to worry about his ribs. This was a little later, after imbibing the gaseous yellow piss they served in a malleable plastic beaker for a fiver a pop which, contrary to expectations, had done nothing to improve his mood. It hurt to breathe. He thought he could make out a whistling sound, much like a dying balloon, that shouldn't be there. He imagined that laughing would be agony but he had no reason to laugh. He was also limping and there was a dull throb in his lower back to complement the dull throb in his head. He had no one to talk to and didn't want to talk to the few people he knew at the festival, even if any of them were here now, which they weren't. There were still almost six hours to fill until The Fall were due onstage and if he carried on strolling around he was bound to bump into the Penitents again, or Paul Lamb from the bloody *Guardian*, who he still thought of as the intern from *Sounds* and who he frequently fantasised about beating to death with a heavy shovel. In his current condition, he would be unworthy of the task.

He went back to the chalet and found his roommate, Chris, was already there. He and Chris went back a long way, though they weren't friends. They had been billeted together by the festival organisers at the end of separate and independent, semi-successful campaigns to blag free tickets. Chris was tall, badly dressed in a different way to most ageing music journalists, with an eidetic memory for band members and B-sides, for synth names and samples, which Travis would have found threatening if Chris were not such an appalling writer. He would be better used as a database than a prose stylist, and as there were now databases full of exactly this sort of information, he was functionally redundant. Chris was huddled beneath a blanket, kneeling in front of the electric fire, which he had neglected to turn on, the light reflecting off the thick lenses of his glasses as he angled his head up towards the new entrant. He spoke through gritted teeth.

—Fucking cold.

—Maybe turn the fire on . . . ?

—Doesn't work. Gave us a dud.

—Oh, well, maybe we should . . . ?

—Gave us a dud *on purpose*. Fucking fuckers.

—What you mean on purpose? We'll just ask them to move us.

—Already did. There's *nothing available*. Should've seen her face. Loving it.

—What, you mean they . . . ?

—*On purpose.*

It took a moment for Travis to process this.

—Shall we have a cup of tea then?

—Can't. Kettle's broken.

—I might have a shower . . .

—No hot water.

—Shit. And you reckon it's . . .

—*On purpose.* Yeah. Definitely.

—Shit.

They paused for a moment, unsure where this left them, then Chris remembered his manners, one winged arm flapping out.

—You wanna share some blanket?

—Ah, no, you're alright. I can get my own.

Chris shook his head gravely, his eyes very big behind their lenses.
—Only gave us one.

*

Huddled there, trying to pretend he wasn't, Chris very close, his
breathing rather too laboured for comfort, sure now that at least
one rib was cracked or even snapped, Travis kept worrying away
at the mystery of the Penitents. Now that the adrenalin spike had
dissipated, he found himself more scared than intrigued. He had no
idea how he had merited the kicking. They had come at him very
fast and without explanation. Secretly, he hoped they had recognised
him, somehow remembered and objected to his lacerating attack on
the third Sonic Youth album, but deep down he knew this wasn't
true. The Penitents, Chris told him when he mentioned them, as
casually as he could, were a bunch of new mothers, all well into
their thirties, currently on maternity leave from jobs in the City or
high up in the civil service, here at this holiday camp to listen to
grungecore and relive some version of riot grrrl they never actually
took part in. That was nostalgia for you, he thought: not as good
as it used to be. He'd hope they might score some bad skag, but it
seemed unlikely at a Pontins. And anyway, in all honesty, he wished
them no harm. He only wished they'd attacked him where more
people could have seen. Though not enough to merit a repeat.

The sense of threat at least made crouching here with Chris
seem bearable. And to be fair to the guy, he did generate a lot of
heat. The problem would be tonight. The Fall were headlining, and
he was writing a review for fk1dk.com, a new music website he
despised and who wouldn't pay him for his work, but whose name
had proved instrumental in getting him a ticket. He could hardly

afford to miss it. He knew it was ridiculous but he still harboured the hope that a byline on fk1dk.com might somehow reignite his barely smouldering career. On the other hand, he knew the Penitents would be there, too. Everyone would be there. The only reason for spending a wet weekend in November at this holiday camp was the hope that Mark E. Smith might die onstage so you could say *I was there*. The thought made his ribs hurt a little more. Hopefully they would be down the front, beating up middle-aged men in the mosh pit, and his time-honoured skulking technique would prove successful. He had to be careful not to stand too near the bar, he thought, and also to make sure the bar wasn't between him and an exit. He could perhaps use Chris as some sort of point man or decoy or even sacrificial lamb, if the worst came to the worst. Chris had a kind of slaughterhouse vibe, Travis thought, like the younger brother of a member of Devo left behind in Akron to work shifts in an abattoir. He should get him some white wellingtons. Or green, maybe. Something easy to hose down.

His phone rang in his pocket, and he cursed as he tried to tear it out from there—an impossible task with his legs bent, so that he struggled upright, the blanket caught over his head, Chris complaining about the draught, and the insistent repeat of Kylie singing about how lucky she was, muffled but distinct enough to set his teeth on edge. It had been like this for a month now. His nephew had put it on there as a *hilarious joke* and he had no idea how to take it off again. He was forced to pretend it was ironic and was surprised by how often this worked. All the same, the tune itself had drilled its way through his self-control, thin shatter lines running out from it in every direction, so that when he heard it he wanted to stamp on the fucking thing and only the lack of funds with which to replace it acted as a leash upon those dreams. He dropped it when it finally propelled itself free of his unbecomingly skinny jeans, striking Chris's head with a satisfying crack before thudding down onto the lino, where he scrabbled to retrieve it, frantically swiping at the screen with his index finger, the ancient software struggling to keep pace.

—Hello?

—Theo.

Theo being Travis's real name, the one he bore before he transformed himself into a *hip young gunslinger*, it could only be his mother, who had never made the adjustment, or his wife, in a mood with him about something. His *ex*-wife. It was constantly surprising to him how hard he found it to hang on to this fact, as if it were an extremely smooth rock slathered in butter, on which he balanced, naked, also covered in butter.

—Hi Kate.

—Sid wants to talk to you.

—Oh. Oh right. I'm a bit busy now.

—It'll only take a minute.

—Yeah, but . . .

—You were meant to see him this weekend, Theo. Surely you can spare a minute?

Her voice thrummed with ill-concealed irritation.

—Okay.

Hesitation as the phone was passed over, quiet voices talking just offstage, then . . .

—Ah?

—Hiya Sid.

A pause, snuffles, some deep breathing.

—Mama.

—No, it's Daddy, Sid. It's Daddy.

—Mama.

—Daddy. It's Daddy, Sid. Say Daddy.

—Mama.

—It's Daddy. Say Daddy. *Daddy.*

The breathing receded, more unintelligible chat, then Kate.

—Thanks.

—That it?

—He's your *son*, Theo. Call me when you're back.

He tried to respond but she was already gone.

*

What did it all mean? What the fuck did it all mean? He had to ask himself that. He had to ask himself that most days. The answer was never satisfactory, but somehow always less satisfactory when in a room where beer adhered your feet gently but insistently to the floor. He never felt less likely to escape than at these moments.

The Fall were just starting up. Chris had shouted the line-up in his ear but he didn't recognise any of the names and wasn't sure whether it was the same band, partially the same band, or a completely different band to when he'd seen them play back in May. He narrowed his eyes and nodded his head roughly in time with the beat and tried to decide if it was a good vintage, or terrible, or absolutely one of the greats. He wasn't sure. They sounded quite tight but it was hard to be certain if that was good or bad. Mark E. Smith staggered on from stage left and started hollering into a microphone. Disappointingly, he looked in excellent health. He seemed agitated about something and danced as if a small terrier had a hold of his trouser leg. Travis recognised the song but then again didn't. He took out a notebook and thought about making some notes, but he didn't want to put his pint down. Anyway, Chris would be able to provide him with the set list and so on—better just to *feel* it, to think of a classy turn of phrase or two and leave the details till later. He made a chuggy face of the sort he felt Mark E. Smith would appreciate if he were somehow to pick him out in the crowd. He was pretty sure Mark E. Smith would not pick him out in the crowd and was grateful for this. He whirled his arms in tight little circles and tried to feel something, or to fake it, anyway.

Travis was so caught up in his own performance that he didn't see her approach him, nor hear her first attempt to engage him. As a result, he only became aware of her when she tapped him gently on the arm. This, and the sight of her standing so close to him, was enough to send a spasm of fear through his body, so that his pint, still almost full, moved upwards and toward him as he leapt back from her, stung, and found a new though very different home, across his shoulder and upper arm. She moved in on him and he tried to get away, lurching back into the wall and slapping at her hands in panic, a small space forming around him as the crowd stepped away, trying not to look, smirking and raising their eyebrows and nudging each other. It took him another moment or two to realise she wasn't trying to attack him, that she had her hands raised and anyway was alone. Travis stood, his own hand behind him still feeling for the wall, breathing hard, cold beer soaking through to his shirt. She bent down and picked his notebook out of a puddle of drink. It seemed she was trying to say sorry.

*

13

They sat outside the venue on a bench next to a partially rotted white picket fence and a small, shrubby hedge. It was very cold now that the sky had cleared—their breaths clouded up round their faces as lost, dissipating souls—but Jenny didn't seem in a rush to get back inside. She had bought Travis a pint and a whisky chaser to replace the beer he had spilt and to apologise for the beating, which, it turned out, had been a case of mistaken identity. The Penitents, Jenny explained, were bound together by a solemn oath to revenge themselves on the men who had wronged them. Martha had mistaken Travis for Janine's ex-husband, apparently a renowned ligger but also something of a lothario, so Travis didn't feel all bad. Janine had missed the trip with flu and they had only realised their mistake when they rang her to tell her of their proxied victory. It turned out the ex-husband was there with her, looking after their son.

Despite the pain he felt at having not been recognised after all, Travis had decided to take it in good heart. He'd even bought Jenny a drink back—a double—trying to look like he wasn't checking how much money he had left. She was quite *cute*, he thought, unsure if it would be insulting to tell her so—dressed in Docs, all in black, with the tacky cut-down Ramones T-shirt and the serious, slightly cross-eyed look of someone who wanted to get things right. She was younger than him, probably quite a bit younger, he thought, when he thought about it, then decided not to think about it. The Fall had either thundered or blundered on (he would have to ask Chris later) while he and Jenny—much like the man onstage—shouted at one another and pulled exaggerated faces. Travis had taken it for flirtation, and his grin nearly reached his ears.

Just when he thought his vocal chords might finally give out, she had invited him to join her for a cigarette. He couldn't wait to get outside. He shot what he took to be a wry smile at Chris and guided her to the exit. He was sweating so badly the beer no longer showed. He was too old even for The Fall, which was like being too old for Beethoven. Travis had given up smoking eighteen months or so back, replacing his fags with an ugly looking e-cigarette, of which, on the whole, he was inordinately fond. He found now, though, that he didn't want to get the contraption out in front of Jenny, the feel of it in his pocket both baroque and penile. Instead, he stole one of her roll-ups and unleashed great plumes of smoke into the air as he tried to impress her with hints about his career in music and the people he knew. It was best to stick to hints. Jenny herself did something so boring and worthy he forgot what it was almost as soon as she told him, in fact even as she told him. He wasn't in it to learn about housing policy. She sat close to him on the bench, shivering slightly, and his arm snuck out along the back of it—his hand, holding his wet notebook, flapping and revolving at its end, unsure of what to do with itself.

—So you never told me what happened with yours.

—My what?

—Your bastard ex.

—Oh.

—I presume you've all got a bastard ex.

—Oh. Yeah. Yeah we have.

—So?

—You don't want to hear all that.

Travis didn't, but then again he did. He liked to think he wasn't so bad. It was appropriate to seem caring. He looked her right in the eye, his head tilted down.

—Go on, honestly.

—He left me. After . . .

There was a pause, and Travis sensed it and could have stopped it but he motioned her on, a character in a cartoon just starting down a ski slope.

—He left me after our daughter died.

A certain shrinkage occurred somewhere deep inside him. He couldn't help see an ambush, all over again. He glanced up quickly, for help or another surprise attack.

—Oh. I'm sorry. I . . .

—Our little girl. Maisy. She was only tiny. She was really premature, really early and they, well, they couldn't, she didn't, she didn't make it through.

Jenny leant into him then and she was crying, quietly, shaking, the tears tracking gravity down her face. Travis didn't know what to say. He put his arms around her and rubbed at her back and looked up at the cold stars above them. His ribs were throbbing. He returned his attention to her, his arm already stiff and uncomfortable. He knew it was wrong to think it, but he hoped he might be in, that this tragedy would present him with opportunity. She carried on crying and he tried to make a sympathetic sound: a strange, strangled gurgle. He waited for as long as he could and she kept on crying. He wanted to believe in his decency, and to achieve this he needed to postpone his own need. He could see the open pages of the damp notebook over her shoulder. He had written something there, a single word, and it took on, at this moment, the utmost importance. Try as he might he couldn't read his writing. Back beyond the door, the music rumbled on.

Dawn Into Night
by Will Ashon

She awakes into the projection of retrospective wrongdoing. It begins with the taste in her mouth, the way her skull presses in on her brain, the unfamiliar smell of the room, the clamminess of the sheets. It's the norm, though she still pretends that it isn't, this lack of norms. The slippages are coming almost daily now—and *daily* no longer makes sense. Her future and past swill together to the point where they become indistinguishable. Her present is just something she lives through in the vicious comedowns between the two—the long, painful moments when she has the time to try and put them together again, to reassemble the narrative from the memories and visions floating round in her head.

She thinks she might puke. That's the first and clearest clue to her own wakefulness. She doesn't want to open her eyes. There's something horrible about opening her eyes, as though none of this can truly be said to exist in quite the way it does until she sees it. That her witnessing it in some way *makes* it. Basic quantum theory, really, though she's aware it's a misuse. That the clothes scattered on the dirty floor don't exist until she sees them, nor the floor either. That the blind doesn't rest wonky in the window frame until she blinks at it. That the cup by the bed—its interior surfaces tanned brown by tea, a cigarette butt floating in the remaining liquid—is put there at the opening of her eyes by the opening of her eyes. That she herself, seen as if from above—tangled up in the stinking bedding, tired, cross-eyed, defeated in some fundamental way—is a figment of her own imagination. And that he is, too.

No, she doesn't want to see him, that's certain—lying behind her back, the air moving in and out of him like the last machine in the last factory in some dying industrial heartland. That's the worst part of the whole project. For a moment she tries pretending he isn't a man at all but a panther, waiting there for her to move: an animal, its whole body tensed, its head low between its shoulder blades, its entire being ready to pounce when she tries to turn, ready to eviscerate her, to end this ongoing stupidity. She wants that to be true. But any panther which sounds like this would've lost its teeth long ago, a milky-eyed zoo beast destined to pace the same tiny space pelted by lolly sticks. When she herself breathes, the air moving up her nose seems to push in on her brain, exerting a tiny but distinctly uncomfortable pressure on the front underside of her cerebrum.

She thinks now that she will indeed be sick. She can stay as she is and risk doing it in the bed where she lies, or she can open her eyes and look for somewhere better—a sink, a bin, a shoe, even—while making the act itself still more inevitable. It's no choice at all. You have to be seen to have tried, that's the thing, even though by not moving she is trying harder. She'd done it once—vomited in the bed—and the man she'd woken with had actually chased her, half-dressed, from his flat, called her a skanky bitch and taken a swing at her. He had missed, more through luck and incompetence than any innate slipperiness or skill on her own part, though as he stood cradling the fist he had accidentally punched the door frame with, he did indeed blame her, as if her failure to be punched was, in his mind, a final proof of her perfidiousness. This had caused her a certain amount of amusement later, though not as she ran down the street in a T-shirt and pants, holding her clothes in a random bundle across her tits, hoping he had broken his knuckles.

She opens her eyes. The room is much as she expected. She doesn't recognise it, exactly, but it's familiarly unfamiliar. Although they always vary in myriad subtle ways, they are also all basically the same—small, pokey, smelling of damp or sweat or something worse, with badly assembled furniture already beginning to break down again, returning to dusty woodchip and strips of wood-coloured plastic. Some are neat, some less so, but they all give off the same stink of loneliness, a laptop never too far from the bed, its browsing history clogged with porn sites. There was a time when she woke in better rooms. She doesn't think it was in the future, though the fact she can't be sure is a brittle kind of solace.

Darkness impinges on her vision. It is coming from below, as if her personality has cracked open somewhere round her chin and is seeping her essence. She wants to rub at her eyes but is afraid to raise her hand. She tries to lever herself up onto an elbow as slowly as possible, searching for a middle ground between the energy expenditure required by this gradualism and its benefits in terms of spewing. Of course there is no middle ground. It seems impossible she has slept. She is sickening for something. Her bones feel hollow and thin, as if the marrow has been sucked from them while she lay snoring. Even as she pulls herself up, her eyes are looking for a suitable receptacle, checking for the exact location of her clothes. She can't rely on them being there. It's a complex process, this transubstantiation—littered with inconsistencies, an ongoing and depressing defeat for her continuing faith in science. But her pants are there in front of her, and a T-shirt she doesn't recognise, which will do as some sort of covering if she can make it out of the room and stagger to find some distant, hidden bathroom.

The first retch comes—inevitable, so that she finds herself prepared for it. Her system is only warming up and it's not enough to fill her mouth. She holds it there, burning slightly, her face a bag for her own poisoned juices, and looks—quickly, efficiently— for somewhere to deposit it. She is hoping for the perfect home to present itself but knows she'll settle for less. (She always settles for less.) Nonetheless, her ingenuity impresses her. She snatches a supermarket bag from the floor, ties the bottom—with its holes to prevent children suffocating themselves—into a tight knot, then empties her mouth on top. Secures the handles carefully, thoroughly, making sure there will be no chance of leakage, and swings the package from her index finger for a moment before lowering it to the floor. Seeing it sitting there stirs something in her mind, a memory trying to break free of the mulch but not getting so far that it shows itself.

As usual, the act of being sick offers its own relief, the queasiness receding, her mind feeling lighter and less smeared. She remembers her only friend at the academy, T, who loved to hold her hair, seemed to live for those moments when she stood over her, attached to her ponytail, rubbing her heaving back and droning quiet reassurance, as if talking to a horse. She'd never been keen on reciprocating, but luckily T never got as sick as her. It wasn't something you could choose or unchoose. It was just what it is. Or what it was. Or what it would be. It's hard to keep tabs, all things considered.

She shudders, the sweat which has covered her prior to the evacuation evaporating off her skin and leaving her cold, naked and bony, sitting on the edge of a strange man's bed. She cranes, involuntarily, and looks at him, her latest host, although she doesn't want to. He is still asleep, that's the main thing—younger than she would've bet on, a couple of spots on his forehead and one at the corner of his mouth, eruptive and scabbed. His chest above the sheets is very white, a faint blue translucence between the moles and further acne. It appears to be hairless, or almost so, and she finds herself trying to assess whether this is better or worse. His lungs continue in their full and unhealthy interaction with the room's air and she doesn't think he will wake too easily. She reaches down and plucks the T-shirt from the floor between thumb and forefinger. It hangs lank and somehow more lifeless than a T-shirt has any right to be, as if it had been shot while flapping up beneath the ceiling. With a certain amount of trepidation, she moves it nearer to her nose and sniffs at it. Unless he smells of damp carpet, it doesn't smell of him. He could smell of African lilies for all she knows. She leans forward and pulls it on, the world turned red and fleshy as it snags over her head, just long enough that she returns to that dowdy room with relief. Escape! If she didn't feel so awful she might laugh.

Shaking, over-strung, she pushes herself up onto her feet, happy to find the T-shirt—a comedy affair with a punchline she can barely read, let alone find humour in—is big enough to cover her crotch. She checks the bed again, caught unawares by a sudden, unlikely wave of affection for this stranger. She can't imagine him as an autonomous adult, as someone's sexual partner, only the son of some mother sat worrying in a small house, fearing for his welfare. She can almost feel that mother's hands turning over one another, rubbing and squeezing at each other's digits, until she looks down and realises they are her own.

She has a brief window before the vomiting will start in earnest, and little time to decide what to do with it. The sensible choice would be to exit the room and find the toilet, fall to her knees and wait there by the stinking, unwashed bowl for what is to come. Instead, she steps carefully through the detritus on the floor and moves round the bed, her eyes scanning through the junk. She is looking for his jeans, it turns out. She didn't know until she saw them, which makes their discovery feel somehow more important. She stands over the twist of faded denim and watches the boy again, keeping her eyes on him as she lowers herself slowly into a crouch, her hand walking over the trousers with the blind deliberation of a crustacean pulled from the deepest ocean trench. She finds the belt buckle and her left hand clamps over it, deadening any sound, while her right inveigles itself into the pockets. Her face changes from feral to dreamy, a slackening of the muscles at the edge of her mouth. Going through people's stuff always does it for her. She's almost giddy for a moment, watching him, as her hand comes out with his wallet, her thumb rubbing across the leather, feeling its thickness and heft. Only when she has flipped it open does she glance down, her thumb now scanning the interior, running down the steps of the cards, nudging them up and then back down, one after another.

When she finds his driving licence she pulls it right out, checking the picture to make sure it's him, then squinting at the date of birth. She stands up again, her inner ear playing a trick on her eyes so that she sways and almost falls. She looks at the date again, as if she might have misread it, looks at him. Can that possibly be right? She has no idea. She tries to remember the year she was born but it seems to have gone. Everything—data and self, objective reality and soul— is leaching out of her and away. She stands, the wallet in her hand, hanging at her side, and looks round the room again, pretending it contains clues. And it does, in a way, just not the ones she wants.

Eventually, feeling defeated by the task and then defeated again by this defeat, her shoulders fallen back into their slump, her blood thick with toxins, nausea washing in like an ocean tide, she resolves to submit to her body and find the bathroom. In preparation, she takes another look around the forlorn room and the idea comes to her unbidden. What if she were to stay? Sort out or replace the blind, pick up and launder the discarded clothes, hoover, open a window, collect some dandelions from a nearby wasteland and arrange them in a glass of water? She could buy some paint, turn the walls a happier colour, replace the bulb with one generating higher wattage. She could wash the sheets or go down the market and buy a new set. While she was there she could find him some new clothes, get him some spot cream. The world is plastic, endlessly malleable, if only you have time in it, if only you can free yourself from being free of it, of dropping into and out of these shabby tableaux. Or so she has been led to believe.

As she replaces the wallet she decides she will try. Perhaps the secret is to stop running. She will find the bathroom, clean herself up, then come back here, climb into bed with him and wait, her face close to his, until he wakes. It doesn't matter whether he wants her there. He will find her there. She will kiss him as he opens his eyes, she will smile and grab his cock, and by the time he knows where he is it will be too late for him to shrug her off. Why not this one? What's the point in waiting? What does waiting even mean? She feels worse now the excitement has quickened her pulse, but better, too. She will not drift. She will not permit herself to drift. She will stick to time like a barnacle on the hull of a freight ship.

She allows herself one last look at her man, her partner in life. He doesn't repulse her, though she knows he might be at his best asleep. She tries to think of a compliment to pay him and consoles herself that if none is forthcoming this is due only to her ignorance of him and not the man as thing himself. What colour are his eyes? It doesn't matter—she can still say, 'You have lovely eyes.' And if her hand is on his cock, is moving on his cock, he won't care, anyway. That much she knows. That much she's certain of. It's unlikely she has woken next to a romantic. That will have to be her job.

She can feel all the sickness moving now, finding its focus in her throat, so that it becomes hard to think of anything else, to do anything but wonder what it was she ingested to achieve the effect. She has never drunk alcohol in her life, never tried recreational drugs, so has nothing to compare it to, only its own repetitions and reiterations. Juddering, she moves towards the door, eager to get it over with and return. In her haste, her knuckles hit the wood, a knock making the room instantly silent, disturbable, and she turns to see whether he'll wake, ready to scuttle back over to the bed if he does, to kiss him and catch his penis in her hand, to own him or be owned by him. He hesitates—a fraught parenthesis, a snuffled, snorted interlude—then carries on sleeping. The clock by the bed has stopped and she knows the stillness holding her is unnatural. She breathes and feels her body move one notch nearer to vomiting. Quick but careful, she turns the handle and pulls the door back. When she was young she liked to pretend she was from another world, that she could shuffle chronologies, rewind and redo in the nick of time, place herself—miraculously—beyond the remit of falling anvils. Somehow, though, now that powers unimaginable act on and through her, she always ends up here.

THOSE WERE THE DAYS WHEN INSTEAD OF ASKING STRANGERS, "WHERE ARE YOU FROM?" YOU'D ASK, "WHERE HAVE YOU BEEN?" THEN SIGH AT THE ANSWER AND LOOK BACK AT THE MUD, WHICH IN THE DRY SEASON WAS LIKE FLAKY COMPACTED LEAVES AND IN THE WET SEASON LIKE SHEETS OF BROWN PAINT SLIDING PAST YOU, MAKING YOU FEEL DIZZY LIKE WHEN YOU WENT PADDLING IN THE SEA AND IT RUSHED BACK THROUGH YOUR FEET: "THIS DEAD CITY, THAT DEAD CITY."

Smoking in the Library
by Peter Higgins

Mister Buckley said, 'Someone [pause for dramatic effect] is smoking.'

Without hesitation (I'm just a naturally witty guy, I guess) I said, 'I'll get the fire extinguisher.'

Mister Buckley didn't laugh, and I was not surprised; he just stood there, with his turd-brown tie tied too tight (thin end longer than the fat end) and looked at me like that was exactly the kind of thing a facetious young buffoon like me *would* say, *was*n't it?

Then he tilted his head back and sniffed the air, affording me a really excellent view into his nostrils, all hairy and mysterious. I turned away. I didn't like Mister Buckley.

'Yes,' he mused. 'Someone is definitely smoking. In the Reference section, unless I'm very much mistaken.'

There had been a time when I'd been dully impressed with Mister Buckley's ability to ascertain, not just that someone was smoking or talking or eating, but precisely where in the library they were committing these offences (he was always right). But that time was long gone. Now I just half-listened to him, and thought about other things: my naturally witty line about the fire extinguisher, for example. I could use that, couldn't I? I imagined a cartoon showing a man sitting in the Library, smoking beneath a *No Smoking* sign, while a Librarian blasted him with a fire extinguisher. Perhaps the book he was reading would be displayed to the viewer, so that its title added something... something like... how about-

'I suppose,' said Buckley, and my train of thought jumped the rails and tumbled into the ravine, killing everyone on board, 'I suppose it's only to be expected, until people get used to the new regime.'

'Well, yes,' I said, 'I suppose. But even so, we've put signs *every*where, and we've been ann*oun*cing the new regime for the last six *months*.'

It's unbelievable, isn't it, that smoking was ever allowed, anywhere in New York, let alone actually inside the New York Public Library? But, hey, the past is a foreign country, am I right? Like, they eat different food there, and have different money and they talk a different language, and no-one has a cell phone, and you can smoke in the library. There was a cartoon in that, wasn't there, somewhere? I could use that. Couldn't I?

Old Man Buckley skulked off, no doubt wondering why he had ever hired me. It was almost eight PM – we'd be closing in a half hour. Outside, beyond the large, high, black windows, New York was waiting for us.

I lost sight of Buckley as he turned left into Periodicals, but I could hear him, saying to David, poor Library Assistant David, 'If you have the time to read them, young man, you have the time to put them away, which, I need hardly remind you, is what we pay you to do.'

Could I use David in a cartoon? Why hadn't I thought of that before? Alone at the counter I grabbed some scrap paper and a pen and drew him in the stacks in his usual pose: one hand holding a book, the other busily scratching his rampant acne. It was easy and fun and cruel. I was bored out of my mind.

What was happening, I wondered, in Blackfoot, Idaho, right

now? What were Jen and Tyler and Carl doing, right now, back home? And Tyler's Awesome Sister?

That was how he introduced her to us - he actually said, 'And this is Chloe, my awesome sister.' So that's what I called her for the rest of the night – Tyler's Awesome Sister. And she was kind of awesome. She was younger than us by a couple of years, but she seemed much more confident and, I don't know, wiser, I guess, if that doesn't sound totally ass-hole-esque. She had this thick black tangled-wool hair and all night I couldn't help wanting to touch it. She was all small and quiet but not shy, more like she knew just exactly what to say and she was biding her time, waiting for the exact right moment to say it. The rest of us were babbling and joking and ribbing each other all night, but not her.

We were staying up all night on the edge of the Blackfoot reservoir to get drunk and count the stars.

Tyler played a few tunes on his guitar – he was pretty terrible, really - and Tyler's Awesome Sister sang something without anyone having to persuade her or cajole her, she just sang this one song, one I'd never heard before.

It was excellent, it really was, sitting around the fire beyond midnight, forever, all wrapped up in blankets and laughing, and Tyler explained to everyone about how I had managed to get myself a job with unsettling ease at the New York Public Library.

'The one on 5th Avenue?' said Carl.

'No,' I said. 'The other one. One of the other ones. The one on East 23rd street, near 2nd Avenue.'

'OK, so, not the one with the lions outside,' yawned Jen. 'Not the one that's in all the movies.'

'Has your one,' said Carl, 'been in any movies?'

'Not so far as I know.'

Cue Tyler's Awesome Sister, saving my life: 'Sure it has. *From Brooklyn to Broadway*. Remember? When he runs after Mia Farrow, right at the end.'

'Oh,' said Carl, 'Cool.'

'You're the guy,' said Tyler's Awesome Sister, turning her sleepy midnight eyes at me.

'I am?'

'The guy who wants to be a cartoonist,' she said. 'Right?'

'Well,' I said, 'I guess.'

'Have you had anything published?'

'Shit,' said Tyler. 'Don't you read *The Coyote*?'

'Nope.'

'Well,' I said, 'you're not missing much, actually, to be honest.'

'Jesus,' said Tyler, 'always putting yourself down, man.'

'Sorry, Tyler.'

'Stop apologising, man.'

Silence for a while, with just the sound of the flames cracking. Much later we headed back up the hill, with dawn going from being just a feeling to something you could almost see, and Tyler's Awesome Sister shivered, and said, 'Where will you be living?'

'Oh,' I said, trying to come across all nonchalant and cool, 'There's this place in Brooklyn. With Brian and some friend of his. It's not much, but anything's better than staying here.'

'Really?' she said, blinking at me.

'Oh. I didn't mean–'

But I did, didn't I? I did mean. Anything *was* better than staying here. And so we walked up the hill, and didn't seem to have much else to say to each other, and then she slowed down and let her brother catch up with her.

The place in Brooklyn turned out to be a literally unbelievably small one-room apartment. I was last, so I was on the floor. Steve had the couch and Brian actually had a bedroom, with an actual bed in it, the spoiled bastard. I literally could not believe an apartment could be so small. It was three floors up from a nondescript office that I soon became convinced must be a front for a private detective agency. God, how I longed to become embroiled in some wild case being investigated down there. Trudging up the ratty stairs to the roachy apartment, holding my breath against the piss smell for as long as I could, perhaps at last I would be mistaken for someone else, shot at, kidnapped, handed a suitcase bulging with cash, entrusted by a mortally-wounded blonde with ensuring the safety of her twin sister, forced to defend myself against an unknown assailant and discovering, as much to my surprise as to his, that my hands were lethal weapons.

My only real excitement, it felt like, was getting the regular rejection letters from the *New Yorker* and, of course, actually reading the *New Yorker* every week in the library (I couldn't afford to buy the damn thing). Imagine my bitterness and envy and awe and admiration and anger at seeing just how good all the cartoons in it were, every week, how much better they were than mine, damn them, Jesus, when was it going to happen? When was one of those letters going to not be a rejection? But you could always tell, even before you opened it, just from the slimness of the envelope, or its somehow hangdog air, its total lack of urgency, that it was a rejection: Thank you so much for your submission to the *New Yorker* magazine. I regret to inform you...

Mister Buckley said, 'Does anyone else smell cigarettes? Periodicals, I believe.'

Caught up in my own troubles (the latest issue of the *New Yorker* had disappeared, and I had not yet read it, and it was not fair) I just stood, staring at the windows, until Buckley said, 'I'd go and deal with it myself, only I'm a tad on the busy side.'

'What?' I said.

He indicated the little old lady he was helping: a regular customer with a habit of forgetting which large-print Harlequin Romances she had already read.

'And David,' he continued, sighing a little, 'is of course nowhere to be seen.'

'Leave it to me, Mister Buckley,' I said, with what I hoped was an air of brisk efficiency. Why did I hope that?

I trudged to Periodicals. From behind, I could only see the smoker's short straight red hair. She sat, and smoked, and had red hair, and she looked terribly small and alone, on a table meant for twelve. She wore a corduroy jacket the colour of dried blood.

'Miss,' I said, 'I'm sorry, but you can't smoke in here.'

Now I could get a good look at her, and I saw that her eyes were green and large, and her lips were painted the same colour as her jacket, and her skin was pale and she had quite a few freckles, on her nose and cheeks, and on what I could see of her neck. She leant back, pointed her mouth at the ceiling, and breathed out an alarmingly large cloud of smoke and said, 'I know. Isn't it awful?'

'No, miss, I'm sorry, but you'll have to extinguish your cigarette.'

'But, I only just lit it.'

'Perhaps you'd like to go outside,' I said. 'And finish smoking it?'

'Oh, I don't think so.'

'Then I'm afraid you'll just have to put it out.'

Her area of the table, I saw now, was littered with what I had to assume were her things: a paperback book, pinned open under her left hand, but also acres of other flotsam: a lipstick, another lipstick, an MTA card, a bus timetable, an unopened letter, an opened letter.

'Would you like one?'

'I don't smoke,'

'Why ever not?'

'Well,' I said. 'No willpower.'

There was a pause. Then she laughed. Her laugh was raucous and not in any way musical, and, like the cloud of smoke which was still hanging over us, too large to belong inside this tiny person.

'Miss. Please. The cigarette. I'm afraid I have to insist.'

'Oh, well, if you have to in*sist.*'

She took one last puff, created one more cloud, little brother to the beast that was only just evaporating above us and then she did something that I had only ever seen someone do in a movie: she licked the tips of the thumb and index finger of her left hand and used these to extinguish the cigarette. It hissed and died. She tucked it behind her ear.

'I once,' she said, 'actually set fire to my hair, doing that.'

'You ought to be more careful.'

'More careful? Rather than less careful? What marvellously sensible advice. I don't know why I never thought of it before.'

She smiled, and her autumnal lips revealed surprisingly small teeth. I wanted, more than anything at that moment, to know how those teeth tasted, how it would feel to bump my own teeth against them and then withdraw, as we both laughed, taken aback by our own abandon, and then unable to resist starting all over again.

'Would you like to come outside,' I said, 'and, I don't know, get a coffee? You could finish your cigarette, too, I guess.'

She rummaged under the table. What was under there? A rape alarm? A gun? Her boyfriend? Her boyfriend, holding a gun? Pointing it at my chest? Just her purse. Her colossal grey-black purse, into which she now proceeded, in thoughtful silence, to sweep all her stuff, all her items, all her belongings, all her junk.

She slapped the bag shut, reversed the chair away from the desk, and stood up – the top of her head reached to just above my nipples. She said, 'OK, big guy.'

I walked behind her, watching her really excellent legs in those green tights she was wearing, trying to look like I wasn't looking at her legs. Old man Buckley and David were both busy at the issue desk as we breezed past and, to my mild but nevertheless palpable surprise, her purse turned out to not be full of stolen library books, and so she didn't set off the alarm, and so we managed to escape without incident.

And then we were outside and I can still remember the bright sunshine and faultless blue sky of that cold dry November day. We sat on the only bench that wasn't occupied by drug-addicts or homeless people or the dead.

'Oh,' she said. 'Weren't we supposed to be getting coffee?'

'That was just a ruse to get you out here and stop you smoking in there.'

'So,' she said. 'Apart from working in that gosh-forsaken heck-hole, what else do you do?'

'Oh, well,' I said, 'I draw *cartoons*.'

'Oh, well,' she said, with the ironically patronising air that I would just have to learn to live with, if we were going to get married. 'You draw car*toons*. Like in the *New Yorker*?'

I swallowed. 'Well, that's the-'

But she interrupted me (I'd just have to learn to live with that, too) and said, 'There was one last week by Roz Chast – she's my favourite. Hers are more like little stories or crazy thoughts or just random craziness, and I love her characters' wild hair, don't you?'

It's a perhaps regrettable fact that, if pressed, I could recite – word-perfect - the captions to at least thirty of my favourite *New*

Yorker cartoons. I wasn't going to tell her that, of course. Jesus, I didn't want her to think I was some kind of a-

'If pressed,' I said, 'I could recite the captions to at least thirty – possibly forty – of my all-time favourite *New Yorker* cartoons. Word-perfect.'

Ignoring this, or perhaps just stunned by it, she opened her purse, rummaged around, found a cheapo purple lighter, took the cigarette from behind her ear, lit it, and inhaled. Then she offered the cigarette to me.

I took a drag, and we both sat for a moment, the perfect silence broken only by the howling police cars, the screaming air-brakes of badly-maintained trucks, the barefoot lunatics shrieking about The Lord.

'God,' I said, in my best hard-boiled world-weary-detective voice. 'I love this crazy town.'

She didn't smile (at *all*) but she did at least say, 'That's a good line. You could use that.'

We sat and smoked for a while, feeling terrific in our own little self-generated cloud of pollution.

And then she did something truly surprising. She dug into her purse again and extracted the latest issue of the *New Yorker*. My eyes widened. I said, 'How'd you get that out without...?'

'Excuse me?'

'Without setting off the alarm?'

I was seething with rage and wanting to laugh at the same time, but mainly I was just seething with rage. She had had it all the time, in the library, and had then somehow managed to steal it, walking along right in front of me. Unbelievable. She must have torn out the security tag, the little gizmo that the busy and careful and conscientious librarians stick into the books and periodicals in order to prevent them being stolen by wayward, rebellious, careless, thoughtless, gorgeous-

'What alarm?'

'In the library?' I laughed, trying to inject a note of amusement. Trying to lighten the tone. But it was too late.

'It's not the library's copy. It's mine.'

'Yeah, sure,' I said. 'Sure.' But I knew she was right. It was far away already, and getting further away all the time: her cigarette-and-shampoo-and-old-books-and-coffee-and-lipstick smell.

'What? I don't *steal* from *li*braries.'

I looked closer at the *New Yorker* in her hand – jolly painting of Riverside Park in a fall breeze, brown leaves flying around, moms with kids in strollers. There was no tell-tale library stamp on the front or little sticker in the bottom left hand corner saying *NEWY*. She was right, of course. She didn't steal from libraries.

'Holy shit,' I said. 'I'm sorry.'

'Good.'

'Sincerely. I'm really sorry.'

'Good.'

'I can't tell you how sorry I am.'

'I don't doubt it for a moment.'

I stood up, feeling hot and clammy, and told her I had to get back to work. She didn't look like she was going to argue.

Later, a few hours older, and a great deal drunker, I sat at the "kitchen" table, and drew a cartoon. So, OK, there was this middle-aged couple walking down the street, unperturbed, while behind them there raged all this: storm clouds, lightning, Godzilla eating the Bridge, a line of high-kicking chorus girls standing impossibly on the side of the Empire State Building, the Chrysler Building turning into a rocket and blasting into the sky. And the middle-aged guy says to his wife, 'God, I love this crazy town.'

It didn't quite work, though, so I tweaked it and did it again and again all night, (I made it King Kong instead of Godzilla, but that interfered with the Empire State Building, so I put him on the WTC – those were the days - one foot on the top of each tower) until it was as good as I could get it, until it just worked. I sent it to the *New Yorker* magazine. Three weeks later I got a very nice letter, rejecting it (of course) but praising it, also, suggesting ways it might be improved (as though they had no idea how long I had already worked on the fucking thing) and suggesting also that, if I did manage to improve it, I should send it again. They looked forward to seeing it. Along with one or two other of my cartoons, if I had any. I should send them to the guy who had written the letter, rather than to the standard address that all the other losers sent their stuff to. I was in. No, I wasn't. I was almost in. Calm down. Jesus.

I wanted to call someone and tell them. Call who? I didn't know. Call Tyler? Yes, maybe. Call Tyler and tell him to tell his Awesome Sister? Brian and Steve? Yes, I would tell them, but would they really understand? Who would really understand?

A couple of weeks after that I was in the Library, still absurdly high from my not-quite-acceptance-but-not-quite-rejection-either from the *New Yorker*. Mister Buckley said, 'Do I smell smoke? Someone's smoking.'

'I'll go and see to it right away,' I said, in my best professional library tone.

Was it her? Would she be wearing the corduroy jacket, the green tights? Had she seen my cartoon in the *New Yorker*? No, dummy, because it had not been published, but they at least had some of my stuff, now; I had sent them some of my stuff in response to their request for me to actually send them some of my stuff. I hadn't sent it, yet. But I would send it. Very soon. I just hadn't sent it, yet. I'd been crazily busy. And I couldn't quite decide what stuff to send them.

'Sir?' I said, hiding quite successfully my utter and total disappointment at the simple fact that it was not her, but him, just him, just some guy smoking in the library, and it was my job to tell him the bad news. Perhaps he would put up a fight. Were my hands lethal weapons?

I told him he couldn't smoke in here and he almost died of embarrassment and apologised so much that I almost died of embarrassment. I suggested he go and finish his cigarette outside, but he was already gone, dashing up and out. On my way back to the Issue Desk I spied David, scratching his neck in General Fiction F-K, deep in *The Dead Zone*.

'David,' I said, without pausing, without even looking at him. 'If you have the time to read them, young man, you have the time to put them away.'

The Gloves
by Peter Higgins

My route is always the same, every day: I cycle along main roads down towards the park and then I take the old canal tow-path for about a mile. This is the best part of my journey: no traffic, apart from a few other cyclists, and a few dog-walkers and some children slouching towards school. The old canal path runs behind the new flats and the timber warehouse and then, towards the end, when it's almost time for me to rejoin the main road, I enter the underpass. This underpass is a little dip beneath the dual-carriageway; it's dark and damp under there. I always pick up speed as I approach to make sure I get through as quickly as I can. I have vague concerns about youths, vagabonds, standing on the road above and dropping things on unsuspecting cyclists as they pass underneath. This has never happened, and I do not know how or why I ever got the idea that it would. But I still cycle through there as quickly as possible, my shoulders tensed, ready for anything. Nothing ever happens. On the way home nothing happens either.

And then, something changed. I was cycling to work as usual, and it was a rather good morning for it – sunny and dry, but not too warm. I was actually looking forward to work that morning, as I knew my boss would be away all day, and this usually meant things would be pretty easy and hassle-free. I provide IT support for a small charity in an industrial estate off the Old Kent Road (we do things for refugees and asylum seekers).

I swept down the high street, across the junction by the library and then into the park where I joined the canal tow-path. Nothing very exciting to report so far: a few other cyclists, all of us in our bright yellow tops, and with bright yellow covers on our backpacks, with their brand names in black block lettering: Hi-Viz, Hump, See/Be Seen. I approached the underpass. Without really thinking about it, I put on some speed, changing up to top gear as the road dipped down, pedalling hard, clenching my shoulders up towards my ears.

On the left, in the little dark cranny where the underside of the bridge met the ground, there was a large bundle of rags or rubbish, about as big as a man. It flashed past in the corner of my eyes and then it was gone, and I was out the other side, coasting up the short incline and preparing myself for the sharp bend a hundred yards ahead.

All day at work I thought I had stopped thinking about the bundle of rags or whatever it was, and then I would start thinking about it again. As big as a man. Easily as big as a man. Lying tucked against the sloping inner wall of the bridge, where usually there was nothing but litter, and puddles, and weeds.

Pretty soon it was time to go home. I stopped at the little Sainsbury's to pick up a few bits and pieces. I was planning to make a lentil and feta salad for dinner – I'd found the recipe online during the day. To imprint my own personal touch on proceedings, I would make the dressing with lime juice instead of lemon juice.

I cycled home, feeling the tension build as I approached the underpass. The man-sized shape was still there, but different. Now it was sitting up, and holding – but not drinking from – a golden can of Special Brew.

The salad was a success, though I say so myself. The lime juice worked perfectly. I took the printed-out recipe, crossed out 'Juice of one lemon' and wrote in 'Juice of one LIME!' and filed it away with my other recipes.

The next day's cycle journey was again uneventful, until the underpass. The shape – the man – was still there. He was lying down again. It was now impossible to not look at him as I cycled by, no matter how fast I went. Equally it was now impossible to mistake him for anything other than a human being. He was gone in a flash and I was out in the sunshine and moving on, but, again, I thought about him throughout the day.

That evening I took a different route home, not because I wanted to avoid seeing him, but because I had a few errands to run, which diverted me from my usual route. The next morning I was back on course, and he was there. I think he waved at me. Or perhaps he was just raising his golden can to my health, toasting me.

All that day at work my mind wandered (or cycled) back to the underpass. Would he be there that night? And the next morning? Yes, he would. He was there. He became a new fixture, a new landmark on my journey. As I approached the underpass each morning and each evening, I didn't tense up because I was worried about some lunatic dropping a brick on me from the bridge above, I tensed up because I knew the homeless man would be there. And he always was.

Some mornings, especially if I left home earlier than usual, he would still be sleeping, and I would breathe a sigh of relief. On other occasions he would be sitting up, his back to the curving wall, his legs straight out in front of him, his epic trousers, his incredible shoes. And don't get me started on his black overcoat and his collection of swollen bin liners, three of them, perhaps four, and a few Tesco carrier bags, and a scarf that had once been tartan but which was now just the memory of tartan, over-written with layers of filth.

The seasons were changing. Summer was hardening into autumn. It was getting colder. I noticed one morning that he was holding his hands under his arm-pits. His Special Brew can was on the floor. I could see my breath as I cycled towards him. Yes, it was getting colder, all right. As I approached, picking up speed, he took a hand from a pit and waved. His grin, his teeth, his tongue.

How old was he, I wondered? What had happened to him? Had he fallen, as they say, on *hard times*? What had he been, before being a homeless person? What was he now, apart from a homeless person? Was he religious, did he have opinions on anything, did he ever read books or newspapers? What did he like to eat, what did he miss from his old life? I tried to put myself in his place, and all I could imagine was that homelessness would take over one's entire existence, narrowing your focus until all you cared about was getting through the day, the hour, the minute. No point planning ahead, or thinking about the past, for that matter, or thinking about much of anything. Special Brew and a lot of bags full of useless trash.

I tried to concentrate on my work. It did not require much concentration. It was easy and I was quite good at it. I realised, one day at lunch, as I sat in the supermarket café, that I ought to do something for the homeless man. I was pricked by guilt at the comfort and ease of my life in comparison to his. I ought to do something for him. Of course I could just toss a few coins his way, one morning, or one evening. That would have been easy. I would just stop my bike, get off, and lean down and give him some money. Yes, but then I would have to actually interact with him. I couldn't just toss coins at him as I cycled on my merry way home, without stopping, like some kind of pope from the dark ages, bestowing his blessing on the wretched of the earth without ever having to actually deal with them. Could I? No. I would have to stop, and lean my bike up by the same wall he sat slumped against, and I would have to say something to him. He might then say something to me. I would have to listen to him. I would have to hand him the money. Perhaps our hands would touch. I would have to make sure I didn't flinch or grimace, if that did happen, or even if it just looked like it might happen. And what would I say to him? And how would I speak to him? No doubt I would slip into the same mode of speech which I used for tradesmen: whether it was the man at work who came to grumble at the air-conditioning, or the bearded teenagers to whom I paid colossal sums to service my bicycle, I addressed them all in the same way – a kind of bluff no-nonsense heartiness coupled with liberal usage of the word *mate*. Yes, I could already hear myself: *Bit of loose change for you, mate. Take care. Cheers.*

It was getting colder. One morning I thought it might actually snow. This was early October suddenly. It didn't snow, but I realised I needed to get myself some new gloves.

That lunch-time I stood in the supermarket looking at the rack of men's gloves. This was an enormous supermarket. They sold everything. Which was fortunate, as there were no other shops anywhere nearby that sold anything useful, apart from a place that specialised in sofas, another one that sold kitchens, and another one that did nothing but hire out power tools.

I grabbed a pair of fleecy gloves and bought them. I also bought the ingredients for tonight's dinner – some lentils and cherry tomatoes and red onions and a bottle of decent-looking Shiraz that was on special offer.

That evening, my rucksack bulging heavily, I cycled home. My new gloves were warm and snug. I came round the sharp slow bend, and began to approach the underpass. Of course, he was there. He was standing up and stamping his feet, no doubt in an effort to keep warm. I noticed, for the first time, his terrible grey-and-yellow hair that reminded me, somehow, of cigarettes.

At home, I was busily making my dinner when I realised: *of course*. I could buy *him* some gloves. And maybe some thick socks, too. No point giving him money. He'd only spend it on Special Brew.

The next day I entered the supermarket with a spring in my step. I grabbed some black, very warm-looking gloves, a pack of five pairs of thick black socks and a rather snazzy blue wool hat with a red bobble. I was queuing to pay for these when I was suddenly assailed by doubt about the hat. It seemed suddenly inappropriate. I dumped it in the racks of sweets by the checkout, and just bought the gloves and the socks. All afternoon I thought of my journey home. Would I lean my bike against the wall, or just let it drop to the ground? I would lean it against the wall. Would I have the stuff – the gloves, the socks – in my rucksack, or in a separate bag, maybe hanging from the handlebars? In my rucksack. Or, in a separate bag, in the rucksack?

And what would I say? I would say nothing. I would just stop, take off my rucksack, open it, get the gloves and socks out, and hand them to him. Neither of us had any need for chit-chat. A simple wordless transaction, between two decent gentlemen, one of whom had just had better luck than the other, that was all. I tried to imagine us swapping places, as in the kind of film they probably don't make any more: the poor penniless outcast and the middle-class office drone, through some movie magic or other, are each forced to experience the other's life, and of course they both learn a thing or two along the way, and find that they have more in common than perhaps they first thought.

What would I be like if I were him? And how would I feel if someone - some stranger - decided, at random, to give me some gloves and some socks? Would I be grateful? Or would I be angry, humiliated? Would I throw them back in his smug clean soft middle class fat face?

Was that what was going to happen to me, that evening? I took the gloves and socks from my rucksack and stuffed them into my desk drawer. I took them out again and looked at them for a while. I peeled the price labels off. Was I worried he would be offended by how much I had spent, or how little? Should I have gone to a more expensive shop? Should I have bought him the hat as well? Should I just give him some money? Should I just cycle past him, as I always did? And, of course, everyone else always cycled past him, too. I had never seen anyone else stopping to help him, or give him cash, or dress him in nice new socks and gloves. He wasn't my problem. Or rather, he wasn't *just* my problem.

I closed my eyes and saw him, toasting me with his can of Special Brew. Stamping his feet against the cold, or perhaps just out of some unspecified anger or frustration. What did I know? Nothing. I knew nothing. I knew nothing about him or his needs. I knew nothing about his life, his experiences. I knew nothing.

I put the gloves and socks back into my rucksack. It was time to go. I got into my cycling gear, put my rucksack on my back, snapped my glow-in-the-dark cycling clips round my ankles, and donned my helmet with the little red light on the back. I stood in the car park, just staring at my bike for a moment, before unlocking it and setting off. I cycled slowly, self-consciously. I don't know why. Eventually I approached the underpass.

It was empty. He had gone. I slowed down. I stopped. He was not there. I stood astride my bicycle, breathing hard, my toes just touching the ground. I looked at the ground. I looked at the wall. Nothing. Not even an empty can of Special Brew. Another cyclist zipped past, his flashing white light at the front, and then his flashing red light at the back, disappearing, gone.

That night, I hardly tasted my food, although it was delicious (halloumi in chilli oil with a green salad and chunks of quite excellent sourdough bread). The next morning I set off, with the gloves and socks still in my rucksack. I was sure he would be there, he would be back, back from wherever he had gone, and I would be able to hand over my gifts. It was another bright but very cold day. The underpass was empty.

I kept the gloves and the socks in my drawer at work for some time. I thought about taking them to a charity shop, but the nearest one is miles from my office and getting there and back in my lunchtime would be, frankly, a pain in the arse. This morning I threw them away in one of the huge bins they have here, round the back. I must say, it's a real load off my mind.

I WENT TO HIS HOUSE TO GIVE HIM BACK HIS TONGUE. I DIDN'T KNOW I'D STOLEN IT, AND DIDN'T REALISE I WAS IN POSSESSION OF IT UNTIL IT BEGAN TO STINK OUT THE BACK ROOM.

THE KITCHEN HADN'T CHANGED. NOT EVEN THE MUGS. HE POURED MY COFFEE AND STARED AT THE TONGUE ON THE TABLE. DRIED, LIKE OLD BARK.

"THANKS", HE SAID, "BUT I'VE NO NEED OF IT NOW". HE SAT ACROSS FROM ME. STILL HUMBLY BEAUTIFUL. EYES STILL TOO KIND. REACHING INTO HIS MOUTH, HE PULLED A LARGE ROOT FROM HIS THROAT. HE PLACED IT ON THE TABLE. IT TOO WAS DRIED AND SHRIVELLED.

WE STUDIED THE DEAD THINGS, SIPPING OUR COFFEE AND TEA. "MAYBE IT WAS TIED UP FOR SO LONG THAT THE ROOT STARVED", I SUGGESTED.

HE NODDED, A LITTLE DISAPPOINTED. ONLY A LITTLE.

"THOUGH I DID ENJOY IT IN THE MORNING," I LAUGHED, LOOKING AT THE TONGUE.

HE STARED AT IT, CONSIDERING REVIVING IT. HE THOUGHT ABOUT CUTTING A PIECE FROM THE MORNING AND WRAPPING IT LIKE A TOURNIQUET AROUND THE OLD ROOT AND TONGUE. "YES," HE BLUSHED, "THEY WERE GOOD TIMES."

"SO WHY DID YOU NEVER SAY YOU WANTED MORE?" I ASKED.
"BECAUSE I TRIED TO BE GOOD."

WE SIPPED OUR DRINKS.
"SO," HE PAUSED, "WHY DIDN'T YOU TELL ME?"
"IT WAS EASIER TO BE CRUEL,"
"SHAME," HE SAID, CARRYING THE DEAD THINGS OVER TO THE BIN.
"YEAH," I SHRUGGED, "IT WOULD HAVE BEEN NICE, BUT EVEN NOW YOU BITE YOUR TONGUE."

THE TONGUE   LISA FONTAINE

The Grudge Elephant
by Darren Lee

Sarah bought Michael an elephant. It was meant to be a surprise.

She had spent a whole week wrapping it; a task that proved next to impossible because the elephant kept moving and trying to free itself from the constraints of its packaging. She had left the trunk till last, leaving a small space in the shifting mass of brown paper to enable the animal to breathe.

Sarah hoped that Michael would not question her absence during the hours she spent gift-wrapping it. She need not have worried; he had been sat on their sofa, oblivious, his two red eyes staring into a space beyond the flickering of their television screen.

The day of the elephant's unveiling arrived and Sarah could not contain herself as Michael cautiously approached the large writhing gift.

"I bet you can't guess what it is!" she said.

"It looks like an elephant," he said without a hint of gratitude. It made Sarah want to slap him, and not for the first time.

Michael used a stepladder to climb onto the elephant's back so he could untie the large ribbon that garnished the gift. The elephant occasionally rustled in its paper cocoon but on the whole remained docile throughout the ceremony.

It took Michael half an hour to successfully unwrap the beast.

He stood, exhausted, wiping the sweat from his brow. "It is an elephant," he said in between breathless gasps. "What would I want with an elephant?"

"It's one of those new Grudge Elephants," said Sarah. "I saw them advertised. I thought it might help cheer you up."

Michael was still catching his breath; by way of thanks he smiled warmly back and Sarah noted that it was the first time he had smiled in a long while. Her annoyance with him evaporated.

She handed him a large book with words written on the cover in a solid and authoritative font: *BARBAR Industries Model S-12: How To Get The Most Out Of Your Grudge Elephant In 73 Easy Steps.*

"Is it electric?" asked Michael. "Do we have to plug it in somewhere?"

The elephant shifted uneasily.

Sarah went to look for the box of attachments and she returned with what looked like an oversized cycling helmet connected to a much smaller one by a length of vacuum hose.

"I saw it in the advert. You put these on- you and the elephant," she said. "The larger one is for him"

"Obviously" said Michael instantly regretting slipping back into his usual sarcasm. He began flicking though the elephant's manual:

Congratulations on purchasing your very own Grudge Elephant™. It has been genetically created to absorb any user's ill feelings of anger and regret. Depressed? Frustrated? Elephants never forget, but you can! Why not let your wrinkly friend carry the load? Scientific studies have proved that just half an hour of Grudge Elephant™ use every day improves life quality by sixty-seven percent, leaving you free to be happy and enjoy a carefree life.

Michael was overcome with gratitude and he felt a small pang of shame at not realising how bad things had been. He decided he would have to make it up to Sarah somehow. He reached for her hand and a laminated quick-start guide fell out of the manual and onto the floor.

"Let's try it now!" said Michael as he eagerly grasped his helmet.

Sarah scanned the guide and summarised for him; "Simply attach the brain wave transmitter to your head, check the emoting pipe for obstructions and attach the other end to the elephant's patented Grief-Receptor-Helmet™."

Michael strapped his helmet on. He was nervous, but found it comfortable and reassuring. Sarah stood on the stepladder and performed the tricky process of attaching the Grudge Elephant's own headpiece. Satisfied, she checked the connection and told Michael that they were ready to begin.

"It's important you concentrate hard on what's troubling you," Sarah continued. Michael was spoilt for choice; the restless daily grind of depression had settled firmly in his stomach like a sack of billiard balls. He tried to think of where all his problems began and his sadness began to bubble away inside him; as soon as it began to boil over he hold Sarah that she could switch the machine on.

The helmet throbbed and lit up brightly as it gently read Michael's brainwaves and vacuumed the regret from his body. It oozed down the hose and began to transfer everything into the Grudge Elephant's helmet. Michael felt the subtle hum of the electrodes massaging his temples. He pictured the office; countless missed deadlines, shortfalls in figures, pointless appraisals and unwarranted tellings off. He felt the mist slowly ebb away as he exorcised all his negative feelings, regrets over things not said and opportunities he had missed.

The elephant experienced a brief moment of confusion before his genetic engineering kicked in and its brain placidly accepted all the bad parts of Michael's CV.

Just when the elephant thought he had assimilated everything, there remained one final image; it was Michael as a small boy, running around in the family garden with an upturned goldfish bowl on his head imagining that he would be a space explorer when he grew up.

Sarah turned the machine off and asked how he felt. There were tears falling down his face, but they tasted less bitter than usual, sweeter, like relief.

"I feel... better," he said, "let's try it again."

The next phase of the conditioning began. The elephant suddenly grunted as it began to flush Michael's memories from its system; it reared up, trumpeted and promptly expelled them onto the shag pile in a steaming heap of dung.

Sarah had noticed a distinct improvement in Michael's outlook on life since the arrival of the Grudge Elephant. He was less tired, the furrows of his forehead had smoothed and the murky aura that followed his every move was dissipating with each therapy session. He was slowly turning back into the man she had fallen in love with- youthful, optimistic and full of hope.

Michael would begin the day with light elephant usage, dispelling any restless night-time dreams before the day ahead. When he returned from work, there would be more vigorous use of the pachyderm.

Sarah had only one rule; tidying the elephant shit was Michael's problem. He accepted this as a fair price to pay for the return of something approaching happiness and the couple's garden gradually became heavily manured with mountains of droppings that went on to form valleys and canyons of safely excreted angst.

Michael began to look at the world as if it was brand new and it was only then that he realised that Sarah had also been desperately unhappy. Michael felt guilty at the burden his sadness had placed upon her and by way of thanks he proposed that she should give the elephant a try herself. And so, after an initial reluctance she too became a fervent user, and their social lives became spent whiling away the hours connected to the gift. Their friends were turned away and appointments were missed in favour of transferring their cares over to the beast.

Having spent weeks plugging themselves into their large house guest, Michael and Sarah had began to regard themselves as experts on the use of Grudge Elephants. Michael eventually threw the bulky manual away with the re-cycling

Had either of them bothered to read it the instructions in any detail they would have found the section marked *"Care and Maintenance of Your Grudge Elephant"* particularly useful. They were in such a state of renewed bliss that they failed to observe that the elephant was beginning to visibly ail; its in-built docility had given way to lethargy and finally apathy. As well as its regular bowel movements the elephant also needed further cleaning and without the right kind of attention residue memories built up in its mind like lint clogging a clothes drier. It would lie in the corner of the room, morosely staring out of the window, its sighs of frustration misinterpreted by the couple as nothing more than a natural trumpet call. The elephant's brain was turning into a misshapen stew of Michael and Sarah's half remembered neuroses and anxieties; it wanted to be far away from the petty problems of humans. In the elephant kingdom there is no fragile love, no disappointment and no want.

Michael and Sarah also began to deteriorate. Since there was only one headset they would squabble over whose turn it was to be treated. They became impatient with each other, snapping constantly and without realising it they had become trapped; the more they used they elephant the more they argued, the more they argued the more they used the elephant.

Meanwhile the elephant in the room trumpeted its blues while no one cared to listen.

Michael had begun to leave work earlier so he could race Sarah home and upload his woeful working day into the elephant straight away. Sarah had the same idea and when Michael burst through the door he would be dismayed to see her already there, lying on the sofa, pleasantly tranquillised. The elephant would slowly turn to look at Michael. The pleading look in its eyes was misread by its owner; what Michael understood as *"I know-she's on it again. Can you believe the cheek of it?"* was really *"I can't go on anymore. I am dirty. Please clean my mind."*

On one day Michael made it home before Sarah, and with only seconds to spare. He heard her key in the door as he was putting on the helmet. He grabbed the switch as she was crossing the threshold and turned it sharply to maximum upload. He had only been exporting his grievances for a few seconds when he felt Sarah's hands try to shake him from his clam stupor.

"It's my turn. It's always my turn first after work!" she pleaded as she tried to undo the straps around the helmet.

Michael began to squirm wildly in an attempt to shrug her off but Sarah's fingers danced around his head trying to grab the straps and wrench them away. He tried his best to curl up into a ball to avoid her nimble hands while firmly clasping the helmet down on his head. The force caused the electrodes to press down upon the veins in his temples. The sensitive connection was amplified, both by the proximity to Michael's synapses and the simultaneous challenge he faced uploading the day's events while fending off an angry partner.

The elephant began to scream, but this did little to dissuade the fighting couple. They were locked together and wrestling as if for dear life.

Sarah tried a different tactic; she couldn't wrench the helmet away from Michael but she could start to pull at the wires and connections to see if she could tap into the machine herself.

Michael's wrestling was losing momentum as he gave himself over to feeding the elephant. Sarah saw her chance and yanked hard at a wire protruding from Michael's receptor. It came free and he groaned. Sarah had removed half of the mechanism, plunging him suddenly into both past and present. His body was still in their living room but by the bookcase his mind's eye had conjured the office; the violent gurgling of a water cooler and a photocopier menacingly vomiting forth hot steam and sheets of A4 paper.

Sarah eagerly grasped at the wire; at one end was a small electrode that she stuck onto her head. Her brainwaves instantly mingled with Michael's and a strange sensation overtook them both; their thoughts conjoined and they could both see what the other had been sharing with the elephant. They shuddered and jolted at the sensations seizing their bodies; grief, anger, loss and disappointment crashed over them in waves; this was what elephant had seen all along- two scared people, falling apart, lost together and with no-one to talk to but an elephant.

The elephant itself could no longer cope. Its system was clogged with their collective anxieties and the input from two sources began to cause what it knew would be a fatal overload. It began to creak, its grey hide slowly expanded, stretched tight, and then without further warning the elephant burst.

Michael and Sarah were showered in a violent explosion of blood, shit and meat.

The couple sat dazed on the floor. Lumps of pachyderm blubber fell down their faces and into their laps. The smell was excruciating.

They both looked at each other dumbfounded. There was nothing to say.

Michael reached out towards Sarah and they both held each other tightly as the mess began to congeal around them.

The last thing the Grudge Elephant saw before it combusted was an image retained from that very first day; it was a small boy playing in a garden on a hot summer afternoon, a goldfish bowl on his head, racing around, arms flailing, living the spaceman's dream as he fought off imaginary aliens and the gradually approaching darkness.

Mickey Awful
by Darren Lee

Fade in.

We open on a pub toilet. Not just any pub toilet; this belongs to *The Pub That Time Forgot*, hidden down a Dickensian London street where the looming shadows of tower blocks cast a two fingered salute to the gentrification of the capital. Empty, save for the last surviving regulars, this drinking den has been fossilised, a relic of times gone past, and the little boy's room is simply a frigid pissoir periodically frequented by grizzled old men with beetroot complexions. They piss quickly, hacking yellow phlegm, not washing hands, all too eager to get back to their pints and their tabloids.

A barred window is permanently wedged open in lieu of air freshener; it allows a cold breeze to blow through every nook and cranny in the simple hope that germs can be frozen in their tracks.

Other than the miserable locals and the mould around the cisterns the only sign of life is the urinal's flush; a East End Niagara Falls that threatens to spill over from the ceramic trough and onto the cracked floor tiles.

Michael had been given better dressing rooms.

He wanted to complain. In the first series he had been given a trailer to prepare for shooting, but although his series had been recommissioned the production budget had been ruthlessly shaved. His producer had explained the cutbacks, but Michael didn't see Quentin making any sacrifices of his own; he would be in the next room with the crew, setting up some shots of the bar, vaping away, a grande skinny latte in one hand and a fawning runner in the other. Michael was left to the Arctic cold and the reek of stale urine slowly corroding his nostrils.

It was time to get into character.

He hunched over the sink and turned on the tap. The plumbing groaned into gear and he gazed into the tepid water swirling down the plughole. The process began with the routine of limbering up his vocal chords. Michael exercised his jaw, contorting himself as he chewed on an imaginary piece of gum that swelled inside his mouth until his face ached and he could no longer work his tongue and jaw around it.

He spat into the sink and began to loop his tongue around a verbal twister, taking care to annunciate every syllable. The words flowed upwards from his diaphragm, and with great dexterity, emerging as pitch perfect Received Pronunciation, the default accent of the drama school graduate. He spat again and his saliva mingled with the water from the taps, forming a small islet of gob as it swirled away.

Michael flashed back to a decade before and his first elocution lessons, Dame Sybil, the smell of lavender on her breath, her advice echoing in his ears with perfect, upper-class English: *"Michael, you must break free. Let the words dance on your palette. The rrrrrrain in Spain falls mainllly on the pllllainnn"*

Michael repeated the phrase and gobbed again, imagining his old acting teacher clinging for dear life on the raft of vanishing spittle. He also visualised his accent disappearing down the drain, being swept away into the dark vortex, cast out, leaving behind a vacuum for a new voice to inhabit; a fictional dialect full of aggro and dropped aitches, the lazy facsimile of London speech commonly known as Mockney.

Stage two: Michael ran his hands under the tap and then through his hair, slicking and spiking his mane until it made him look younger, tougher, aggressive.

The last stage of his transformation was to glare in the mirror, wave goodbye to the actor Michael Dalton and inhabit the shoes of the thing he hated the most, his worst, but most successful creation: Mickey Awful- celebrity geezer, the star of *Slag, Screws* and *Shooter*.

Quentin rapped on the door to let Michael know that they were ready for him.

Michael spat for one final time, not with saliva, but with sharp words that he machine gunned at his reflection: "HoldyerfuckingorsesI'mfackingcoming!"

Mickey Awful turned off the taps and strutted out of the Gents' with a cocksure swagger, as if he owned the fucking place.

Minutes later, Mickey was locked in a staring match with a ravenous cross-breed called Frankie. Frankie's pedigree was indeterminate, part-Staffordshire Bull, part-Baskerville. Mickey couldn't tell where the dog's muscle stopped and his fat begun. The mutt resembled a swollen testicle, an angry ball with slavering jaws, jaws that were eyeing up Mickey Awful with relish.

"He likes you. I can tell," said Lenny Wright, offering Mickey a tobacco- stained hand. Mickey shook bravely, not breaking character for a second, even though it felt like he was a grasping at a bag of stones. Despite this strength, Lenny was pinched thin, a craggy, calloused whippet of a man, with salt and pepper hair and booze-blossomed skin. His eyes were light blue and piercingly aimed at Mickey. They glinted with ambiguity, impossible to tell whether their owner was happy or about to tip over into an angry frenzy.

Quentin was still busy with the finishing touches, supervising the camera angles and checking the sound levels before they started recording. They had easily found a quiet corner of the pub in which to film; the place was dead and they had been spoilt for choice.

Frankie continued to eye Mickey greedily before Lenny tossed him a pork scratching. The morsel sat in front of the dog, lying on the odd squares of threadbare carpet masking years of stains and bullet holes of cigarette burns. Frankie eyed the food expectantly and when Lenny clicked his fingers he began to wolf it down without a moment's pause. The awkward silence between Mickey and Lenny was punctuated by the crunching of rind in Frankie's mouth, a brutal reminder of the canine's awesome potential as a man-mauling bollock on legs.

"Screws was on telly last night," said Lenny. "I got a biriyani in and watched it. 's alright. 'though that scene when you shived that bloke in the showers seemed a bit fake... the way the blood flowed, that wouldn't have happened. Nah. Not that way. You should have got an expert in or summink," he paused before adding a hasty "You were good in it though."

Mickey thanked Lenny for the complement, executing a perfect Thames Estuary "Cheers bruv!".

Thus a fragile rapport was established between the drama school graduate and his interviewee, the professional psychopath.

Quentin sat behind the monitor, his hipster haircut peeking out like a fox's tail from behind the screen. He gave Mickey the thumbs up and they were ready to go. For the next hour, fans of *Mickey*

Awful's Hardest Geezers would be treated to tales of underworld beatings, anecdotes of extortion and lascivious torture, all wrapped up in the name of factual entertainment. This week's episode: Lenny "Nails" Wright, called so because of his fondness for hammering spikes into people who crossed him during the sixties and seventies. Quentin had specifically asked Mickey to draw attention to the holes on the bar where Lenny had attacked a loan shark in '78. Sure enough they were still there, like a holy relic, right next to Frankie's bag of scratchings.

"Watcha!," said Mickey to the camera, suppressing the last remnants of Michael firmly into the background. "I'm Mickey Awful and welcome to annuva gangland story. Tonight I'm with the legendary Lenny Wright."

Legendary was stretching it a bit; they were nearing the end of the second series and the Hardest Geezer barrel was being well and truly scraped. They'd began with some proper tough-cases, all household-name Robin Hoods or feted sociopaths, but by the time Quentin had found Lenny Wright they had already began to lower their standards to anyone who had once in the same room as the Kray Twins. Given this downward spiral it wouldn't be long before Mickey would be interviewing anybody who had once fought in a pub car park, or had been dared to shoplift once as a teenager. Giant cracks were starting to appear in the programme's format and Michael longed for something meatier to earn his crust. However, the contracts for yet more episodes were being negotiated by his agent; Harry was a shrewd businessman who was always keen to point out Michael didn't pay the bills, Mickey did.

Michael often remembered his youthful dreams of greasepaint, iambic pentameter and the glare of the footlights; just a few of the right auditions under his belt and he could have been in Stratford-upon-Avon instead of Stratford, London. Instead, he listened to his agent when a change of career goals were suggested; something more urban and gritty, more "street", a film by an up and coming crime director that had the dubious title of *Slag*.

Michael endured the audition by pulling every cockney hard-nut cliche out of the bag. Despite his ironic mocking he won the lead role, the part of wide-boy Terry Cant, and thought nothing of it; the one thing lower than his fee was his expectations. A change of name was suggested to go with the new image, a thespian nom-de-plume that would be forgotten as soon as the film hit the cinemas, just for a bit of fun; and so it was that Mickey Awful was christened.

No-one could have predicted that the coke-adlded film school reject at the helm would turn out to be a genius after all, and for a brief period of time Mickey Awful became an iconic figure. The poster for *Slag* regularly jostled for space on the walls of student digs in between Withnail's inebriated scowl and Samuel L. Jackson's glistening jeri-curls.

Despite the fact that Cant was killed off at the end of the first movie, Mickey was brought back for two more films. His resurrection was never queried in the underwhelming sequel *Cant's Revenge*, but by the time the *Slag* trilogy concluded with *Get That Cant!*, Michael was beginning to tire of his screen image. His agent was always one to favour the lucrative, and so a brace of similar roles were thrown at Michael/Mickey's feet. The films had titles like *Shooters, Villains, Blaggers*, and the aforementioned Screws, as if more than one word would be too much for their target audience to cope with. Each one performed with diminishing returns until Mickey was forced to turned to TV, thus *Mickey Awful's Hardest Geezers* began to clog up the arteries of the television schedules. The show had been moderately popular, fuelling talk of a fourth Cant film to surf the trend for re-booting tired old movie franchises; so far Harry had been tight-lipped on the deal.

He was trapped; no-one knew who the real Michael Dalton was; the RSC would never come calling, they'd be no BAFTA fellowships or lunches with Branagh at The Ivy, instead Mickey Awful blazed a trail through the dregs of the underworld, glorifying mid-level thuggery for the masses. Michael cursed himself for the sin of playing along with the charade and every new episode saw him further condemn himself to the purgatory of spitting his dreams down the plughole.

Mickey warmed up the show by asking Lenny to describe, for the audience at home, the moment when he nailed a suspected paedophile's feet to the floor.

"Yeah," said Lenny. "Saw this nonce hanging aht by the school gates. Acting all weird. I thought, I'm not having that. Don't talk to me about kiddie fiddlers. The lowest of the low. I'd thought I'd teach him a lesson, y'know nail 'im to the floor. I start on his feet and he's screamin'- y'know, help me!, help me! That sort of fing."

Lenny began laughing as he relived the moment in his head.

He continued, "I was about to nail his cock to a fence before he only goes and tells me he's the fucking headmaster of the place! So I apologise like, anyone can make a mistake y'know, and I remove the nails with my claw-hammer, but the ungrateful fucker only calls the boys in blue."

Lenny threw another scratching at Frankie.

"Put me away for three years it did," he smiled ruefully. "Just for doin' my civic duty."

Mickey laughed, pretending to almost fall off his bar stool. He giggled with fake bonhomie: "Great story bruv!"

From behind the camera Quentin silently agreed. He began to

story-board the inevitable reconstruction in his head: jump cuts, crisp cinematography, menacing sound effects as Lenny raises his hammer and brings it down in slo-mo with the grace of a ballet dancer. Very Scorsese.

Lenny relaxed a little, glad to see his tale had amused everyone. Frankie was looking up at his master, his beady eyes pleading for another yarn.

"'Course, I done much worse. But nuffin' they could pin on me at the time," and with this Lenny settled firmly into the role of gangland raconteur for his appreciative audience. Mickey remembered to snigger in the right places, namely the most salacious episodes of Lenny's career. It was difficult for him to work out if the gangster's tales were true; he was sure he recognised them from a few movies, but he nodded along enthusiastically empathising with his interviewee, tacitly corroborating as if to say *"Yeah, I know what you mean. I threatened to cut someone's hands off once too! It's a bugger when they scream so loud isn't it?"*

Michael would have hated this, would have had flashbacks to the hard kids at school, surrounded by a phalanx of sycophants grinning their way through their leader's every exploit. But fuck what Michael thought, while the cameras rolled Mickey Awful was centre stage, smiling along, pleased that the day's shoot was proving to be such a piece of piss. Easy peasy.

Lenny began to wind down, his frank confessions neared the present day, taking on an air of secrecy, as if those witnesses involved were still active or hadn't yet been threatened into silence. Mickey knew the tone from experience, Lenny was entering territory where he might have begun to incriminate himself; this was Mickey's cue to wrap things up, to break out the usual question that rounded off every programme.

"So Lenny," he asked. "What does the future hold for ya?"

They had reached the conclusion of the programme, the point where the villain usually showed their only flickers of remorse, the moment where they temporarily redeem themselves by forsaking their previous lives, stating their intention to leave the world of larceny and GBH behind them, retire to the Costa Del Sol or loiter the rest of their lives away grumbling in a bookmakers.

Lenny grinned. Mickey had seen the same leer on the mutt panting at their feet; both dog and owner looked like twins.

Lenny let Mickey in on the joke. "I'm diversifyin'," he said tapping the side of his nose. He clicked his fingers, summoning the landlord who appeared, harassed and saggy, a vision in stained polyester, looking like a darts player after a heavy night of projectile vomiting.

"You've met Ken yeah?" said Lenny. "This is his gaff. He's seen a few things over the years I can tell yer."

Ken snorted in agreement. The snort morphed into a bronchial tremor, loosening his forty-a-day habit into a pronounced gurgle.

"Ken's been looking after something for me. Ain't yer Ken? Bring it 'ere. Mickey and his fans want to have a butchers!"

Lenny winked theatrically at the cameras while Ken ferreted and rustled behind the boxes of out of date crisps. He produced a bulky object wrapped in a carrier bag. Just one glance was enough to see what it was; it wasn't Lenny's trademark weapon.

Lenny ruminated as he solemnly unwrapped the package. "I've been thinkin' that a hammer's too much of a... blunt object. So I got me this little darlin'."

He removed the last of the polythene wrapping to reveal a sawn-off shotgun. Tears began to well in Lenny's eyes as he cradled the weapon.

"She's stunning ain't she? I call her Stella."

Quentin gleefully gestured to the cameraman to get a lingering close-up.

Mickey stared as the firearm as she rested comfortably in Lenny's rough hands. He had been close to guns before, but there were all fakes made to shoot dummy rounds for the silver screen. This was the first time he'd been up close to something with such lethal potency. He tried to summon up the correct response, something that would acknowledge the awesome power that Lenny wielded, something that would reflect the intimate relationship his interviewee had with his beloved shooter, something profound and memorable that summed up one man's unbridled love for his beautiful, beautiful gun.

"Sweeeeet," said Mickey sucking in air between his teeth. "That's fucking sweet bruv!"

Michael Dalton woke up the next day in a cramped, single room at the Isle of Dogs' Happy Traveller. He had hardly slept, ignoring Quentin's advice to get an early night as they were due to meet two more loveable villains the next day. His body ached from the restless turning over, his fists felt tender after punching the limp pillows into submission. The hotel was another sign of the slow decline of Hardest Geezers; the first series saw them treated like royalty, staying overnight in plush hostelries, the ones that lived on the green and blue streets of a Monopoly board. He missed the king size beds and Egyptian cotton.

Michael made a quick inventory of his spartan surroundings: the travel kettle encrusted with limescale, the television stuck on one channel, the feint smell of wet animal hair, and beside him, lying on the bedside table next to the alarm clock, was his sleeping companion for the night- wrapped in her duvet of polythene. Stella.

Michael stared at the gun with the grim realisation that the events of the previous night had not been a fevered dream. He screwed up his eyes and reopened them to find the shotgun still there; only then did he realise that she had rested with her barrels pointed at exactly where his head had been. Michael cursed Mickey under his breath and pushed Stella out of the way, pointing her towards the empty mini-bar; in case of damage Quentin would be footing the bill.

It was Quentin's fault anyway; he'd broken one of the rules: *The Rule*. Back in the early days the production company had splashed out for a training course on dealing with dangerous people. They listened while a former SAS officer taught them the basics of self-defence and the cardinal rules of filming the potentially volatile. Michael would have liked to have thought this was out of concern for his own safety, but the presence of an insurance lawyer demanding signed waivers told him otherwise.

Michael learned a lot that day. Chiefly to show respect; a bruised ego on a hardened villain was as good as a death sentence. People like Lenny Wright wanted to walk down the street and have people recognise them again; wringing out the last drops of recognition from the dishcloth of life was all they had left. They looked at the new breed of gangs, and wanted to hang on to the good old days for as long as possible. In that respect, Mickey's programme was acting as the National Trust for ex-convicts.

During the course they were told, repeatedly, that there was one cardinal commandment that they broke at their own risk: "Never leave a trace," said their mentor. "Don't swap addresses, phone numbers, Whatever. Don't ask these fucking people to be your Facebook friends. Remember this -You never want the hear the words *We Know We You Live*."

This was the rule that Quentin had broken in front of Lenny Wright. The meagre crew had been packing up their camera equipment and Mickey was exchanging pleasantries before heading back to the diabolical toilets to morph back into the sanity of being Michael again.

Lenny was still enthusing about Stella and had become more candid around Mickey after the recording had stopped.

"I was finking about Post Offices, but most of 'em have closed now," he said as Mickey half-listened. "...trouble is you can't rob a post office with a dog and a hammer, so me and Stella are teaming up. Bonnie and Clyde"

The crew had already packed their things away, afraid that the camera equipment might vanish as soon as their backs were turned. Quentin tapped Mickey on the shoulder and interrupted "Same time tomorrow luv," he said. "We'll pick you from the Happy Traveller at 8am sharp."

Quentin realised his mistake and briefly grimaced before his slack jaw dropped further than normal, so low that it was almost scraping the tatty carpet. Mickey brushed the comment away, and hoped that Lenny hadn't made a note of where he'd be staying for the night. It was more likely that Lenny wouldn't even care, that he'd be spending the evening at home planning his fantasy raid over a pickled egg and Bake-Off.

Frankie rescued them from the awkward goodbye with a relentless stream of barking that scratchings couldn't calm.

"Think he needs a shit or summink," said Lenny. "Best be off."

"Thanks man. Laters," said Mickey, shaking his hand. He thought nothing of it at the time. Laters- that's how everyone says goodbye in Mickeyland. Besides, people always say "see you later" when they don't mean it. They don't think a man with a shotgun, a hammer and a ravenous dog are going to show up to their hotel room.

Laters. Bloody laters.

Flashback to the evening before: The TV in Michael's hotel room was stuck on a cosy, rural drama. He spotted a drama school acolyte in the cast, provoking a pavlovian torrent of jealous abuse towards the screen. The tirade lasted for several minutes and was so intense that Michael thought the banging on his door was the guest in the next room complaining about all the shouting.

The banging continued to the point where it couldn't be ignored. Michael got up from the bed and was rehearsing his apology when he heard a dog bark, a bark that he'd know anywhere.

Michael shat a brick.

"Mickey? It's Lenny mate, I need you to open up son."

Michael stood still and silent, hoping Lenny would think he was out.

"I know you're in there Mickey. I can hear *Emmerdale*."

Frankie barked again.

"I got Frankie with me," said Lenny.

Michael hoped Lenny hadn't arrived to crucify him, that his plan was something other than nailing him to the magnolia walls of the tired hotel room. A call to reception might have got them removed, but an aggrieved Lenny would either wait outside in the bushes, or head straight to Wapping to tell the papers what a timid pussy the real Mickey Awful was. Neither option was a good idea.

"I really need your help mate."

Michael detected a plaintive and panicked tone to Lenny's voice. There was audible desperation in the gaps between the knocks and Frankie's growling. Something was up.

Michael had little time to get into character. In a flash he mentally went through the transformation from middle-class artist to cockney spiv. No time for vocal gymnastics, not enough time to spit away the real him. Improvisation was required.

Mickey Awful slowly opened the door on Lenny Wright.

"It's gone tits up mate," said Lenny, grasping for breath. "Utter tits."

Frankie wouldn't shut up, so they fed him stale biscuits that were hidden behind the room's travel kettle. Without asking Lenny helped himself to a miniature of scotch from the minibar.

"I did it," said Lenny. "After I left you I was feeling all nostalgic and I thought fuck it- No time like the present. Went to find a post office, but most of them had closed down. Turns out there's a big one in Smiths' now. Fucking Cameron. Probably turning the old ones into luxury flats or something."

Mickey nodded, dreading what was coming.

Lenny tossed the empty miniature over his shoulder and immediately began rifling through the fridge for more. It was clearly going to be a long story.

"So I'm there in Smiths', checkin' the place out, you know, pretending to read the magazines, getting the lay of the land, when this spotty shelf stacker comes up to me and asks me to take Frankie outside. 'I'm sorry sir' he says 'You can only have guide dogs in here.' I tell him, I says, 'This is Frankie. We're inseparable. I'm not going to tie him to a lamppost so fuck off' Well, he didn't know what to do this... foetus. So he asks again, but even though he keeps saying 'sir', there's no respect in the word. None at all. And I'm not budging. My Frankie's a fucking awesome specimen. People would kill to have a dog like Frankie so he's not staying outside for anyone to nick. Over my dead body he is."

"..and so?" ventured Mickey.

Lenny shrugged. "Did what I had to. Nailed the little shit's hand to the wall, right in the between the Radio Times and the Vanity Fairs."

Mickey laughed, while deep inside Michael began to fear for his safety. Even worse, his guest was about to drink the mini-bar dry, and who was going to pay for that?

"So this little brat, he's like screaming 'ow!' and everything, and before I know it there's these two security geezers surrounding me. So I'm thinking at this stage that the robbery's pretty much off. But you know, I've got my honour to defend, there's no way Lenny Wright's going to be felled by a couple of bouncers in a jumped-up fucking newsagents."

Lenny patted Frankie, who had been slobbering at Mickey's feet throughout the story.

"That's where Frankie came in. I set him on the one closest to me and then, like a flash, I whip out Stella, and the other one shits himself. Some fuckin' security! Well at that point the noise got a bit too much," he sighed, eyes glazing over. "People knew how to deal with pain in the good old days, but every fucker's yelling and wailing, so I thought sod this, I'll rob summink else another day."

Another tiny bottle of booze disappeared down Lenny's gullet.

Mickey crumbled away in fear, leaving only Michael behind, hideously exposed, naked. He knew why Lenny was at the hotel: *Couldn't rob a Post Office, but I bet Mr Film Star's got few bob or two tucked away.* His eyes began to swell and puff, his brain trying to work out how to explain to Lenny that he was broke, that the best thief he knew was his agent, there was all the dodgy investments, and being seen at the best nightclubs didn't come cheap. He was staying in a fucking Happy Traveller for Christ's sake.

Michael was about to open his mouth, to start blubbing and

pleading for mercy when Lenny finished drinking the min-bar dry. From that moment on, all bets were off.

Lenny reached across and placed the weight of his gnarly palm on Michael's shoulder. "Truth is I need a favour," he said. "By the time I got back to the pub there were police cars outside, they were at my place too. Left their flashing lights on. I could see 'em from miles away. So I need to lay low for a while. Let this blow over."

"I...I...," said Michael, "I don't think you can stay here. The hotel has rules about overnight guests."

Lenny laughed. "This shithole? nah, I'm not staying here. Neither's Frankie. Stella though. That's a different matter."

Michael stared into space.

"It's just for a few days," said Lenny. "There's too much heat on me at the moment. If I get nabbed with a shooter it's over for me, but if they can't find any firearms I could probably talk my way out of it. Pretend I'm senile or somethink, Have the jury feeling sorry for me- *Poor old fella and his dog. He didn't mean no harm, just got scared.* Please Mickey. Just until it blows over. She won't be a bother. You can use her as practice, you know for your films. That one you were in the other night, you were good and everythin', but I could tell there was no way you held a proper gun before."

Michael quivered, bile rising slowly in his throat. A drowning man. A phrase flashed before his eyes; "ACCESSORY AFTER THE FACT" - what kind of sentence did that carry?

"The thing is, I know you'll look after 'er. I saw the look in your eyes when I got 'er out this afternoon. They glowed. We're not that different you and I. All we want is a bit of respect. A bit of worship. That telly twat, he don't give a toss about you Mickey. I could see him, sniggering at us when we spoke. You're supposed to be a film star, why ain't you in Hollywood?"

A good point, thought Michael; there had been a brief trip to LA a few years before. The big break Stateside. Henchman number 3. Kicked down a staircase by Stallone half an hour into the film. Only two lines of dialogue that were eventually re-dubbed by a different actor. Problems with the accent apparently.

Lenny continued, "Don't let yourself fade away. We could make them fear us if we wanted. I know we've only just met, but tell me if I'm wrong. We're disappearing down the drain, you and I. I'm going to go out fightin', so please, take a chance Mickey, I'm good for it. Just take the fuckin' gun. What do yer say?"

Lenny handed Stella's carrier bag over to Michael with the reverence of a regal ceremony. Michael looked down at the bag in his lap. His legs jitterbugged with nerves.

When he looked up again Lenny Wright had disappeared, only Frankie stayed behind. A whistle came from the corridor and before bounding off to his master, Frankie seemed to shrug at Michael as if enforce the futility of resisting.

Michael turned to the TV and spotted someone else from drama school. This one was playing a vet. Even with a hand up a cow's backside, he still displayed a greater range than Mickey Awful had done in his entire career.

He felt the strong desire to talk to his agent, to offload, do something, anything. There should have been some news about his recent auditions, and he'd been assured that a role in the Terry Cant re-boot was done and dusted. Michael wanted out, but he knew that Mickey would be eager to sign on. He wasn't fit for anything else. They both needed the distraction of a friendly voice with some good news.

Michael rang Harry, but the phone kept tripping onto voicemail. After a dozen attempts he gave up. He stared at the ceiling and seethed himself to sleep. Lenny was right- he deserved better. Things were boiling down to a complete lack of respect.

Satisfied that Stella was no longer pointing at his head, Michael went to the bathroom to get ready for the day's filming. He was late for breakfast but not hungry. He was distracted by the Stella problem and fear made a formidable diet. He had no idea what to do with the shotgun. He hunched over the bathroom sink, staring at his reflection. Mickey's Artful Dodger glint was beginning to flicker back and forth, blending with Michael's own features, erupting from his pores. Michael felt that he was laughing at him, goading him for being such a scaredy cat.

Michael ventured back into the bedroom. He gingerly picked Stella up, Mickey had handled many like her in his career, but they were harmless replicas. Stella was the real deal and he felt an electric charge through his fingers as he touched her, the same frisson that Lenny Wright felt whenever he cradled his beloved. The jolt sparked Mickey into life and the alter-ego took over, posing with the shooter, looking every inch the hardman. He snarled and postured, like a pound-shop Travis Bickle without the interesting haircut.

The silence of the room was disturbed by Michael's mobile. Its ringtone pierced through him, jolting him back to reality. He almost dropped Stella, but quickly laid her out on the bed before scrambling for the device. Michael expected it to be Quentin waiting in reception, hoping to ferry him to the next gangland assignation, but the caller ID registered that it was his agent trying to get in touch. Finally.

"Mickey luv! how are you?"

Michael winced; in the offices of Harry Forshaw and Associates he had ceased to be Michael a long, long time ago.

Forshaw carried on with a cascade of verbal diarrhea and flannel before Michael could even respond: "Listen luv, I've just heard back from the Cant people and it's bad news I'm afraid. They're going with someone younger for the re-boot. They were very grateful for all you've done and wondered if you wanted to do a cameo in the new movie. Perhaps planning the young Cant's father or cousin or something. Only a couple of lines. They say it'll be post-modern and ironic or something, keep you in the public eye. yes?"

Michael faltered. Sweating ice, his clammy hands struggled to hold onto the receiver. As much as he hated him Terry Cant was supposed to be a done deal. It was the role that had made him famous, that kept him working, the part that had birthed Mickey Awful into the world, and now Terry Cant belonged to someone else. Inside Mickey was raging.

The rest of Forshaw's monologue washed over Michael: "The series is not looking good either I'm afraid. Depending on ratings they might pull the plug on more, so make sure each episode is a winner eh? I'll see who we can get to return my calls. Don't despair luv, we'll get through this. A dry patch. It happens to the best of us. Oh, and while I remember that new VIP night club in Essex has cancelled your opening. Not enough tickets sold, but I'm guessing you could do with a night in. Toodle-pip!"

The phone went dead.

Michael sat the the edge of the bed, rubbing his eyes with his palms. He looked at his surroundings: The inane chatter of early morning TV in the background, the greying London sky outside seeping through the dirty net curtains, the empty minibar, the shotgun by his bed. It wasn't supposed to be this way.

He was Michael Dalton. He was Mickey Awful. He was Terry Cant. His alter-egos were dwindling in their twilight, and Michael felt nothing but disappointment at their demise, the way they were being treated, left on the shelf, forgotten. He had spent all his time acting out the roles that were expected of him, only to find his career had climaxed in nothing but regret and emptiness in a budget hotel.

Michael began to understand the villains like Lenny; the men who just wanted one more moment in the sun, their weathered faces demanding one more act of respect, because without their past they were blank slates, forced to confront who they really were. Shabby old men letting their attack dogs do the talking.

Michael stared at Stella. Other than his small bag of luggage she was the only thing in the room that he felt he had any true connection with. He didn't hear Quentin dialling him from the lobby, instead the noise of a raging Mickey Awful careered inside his head, bounding off the sides of his cranium in a blazing fit of screaming and thoughts of revenge. He'd show them. He'd show them all.

After a few minutes Michael got up and headed towards the bathroom sink to spit.

He spat and he spat and he spat.

Action!

Watch out- here comes Mickey Awful!

Tightly holding a shopping bag that contains something heavy and long, Mickey Awful tears through the hotel lobby, venom in his veins, capillaries pounding piss and vinegar. Mickey ignores the crew waiting to pick him up. The coffee swilling Quentin make a grabs for Mickey's shoulder. Mickey goes in for a headbutt, but switches to attack his assailant's latte hand, sending hot artesian java flying into the director's face.

Quentin drops to he knees and Mickey rams his hand into the screaming man's pockets. He grabs for a bunch of keys and heads out of the automatic door leaving the crew to help their writhing colleague.

Cut to security footage of Mickey Awful in the car park. From this angle we can see gunmetal barrels peeking out from the plastic bag. His is pace forceful, an alpha male searching among the four wheel drives and Smart cars for his getaway vehicle.

He sees his quarry, grunts and struts to space where the crew's van had been parked.

Cross fade to Mickey Awful behind the wheel of the van. Horns blaring, it kangaroos down the streets, dodging its way between the traffic, mounting the pavements and central reservations, performing an erratic ballet at the expense of its fellow road users.

Close up on Mickey's face. He's looking from left to right, as if he is searching for something specific. His face is determined, intent, brows furrowed in concentration. And then he sees it.

Cut to bank on the opposite side of the road. A small branch, not exactly Fort Knox, but a bank none the less, and more than enough for Mickey Awful.

Back in the van Mickey dramatically turns the steering wheel ninety degrees to cut across the traffic coming the other way. Tires screech, cars spin, the cum shot of airbags inflating. Mikey's van makes it through unscathed, and he mounts the curbside narrowly missing a lamp-post.

Split second shot of Mickey coming to rest. No time to waste.

Slow motion shot of Mickey Awful jumping from his seat, waving the carrier bag in the air. The plastic is whisked off to reveal Stella in all her glory. Cut to arty shot of the bag fluttering away in the breeze before coming to rest in the gutter. Pigeons disperse in slow motion.

Shot of Mickey's feet. Strong, sure steps, striding towards the entrance to the bank. Pounding music swells on the soundtrack.

Close up on the eyes of Mickey Awful. The music begins to mix into the hero's heartbeat. This is the moment the whole film has been heading towards. This is Mickey Awful's moment in the sun, his shot at respect, the climactic gamble that will show them all: the feckless agents, the narrow- minded casting directors who refused to give him the time of day, the directors who had moulded him into a star before deserting him, the aged villains he was forced to flatter on a channel no-one watched, the growling cock-compensators that the tired criminals paraded about, the media tossers behind the cameras, ladling out their gangster porn to the masses, the shit nightclubs where the even VIP area reeks of semen and vomit, the smarmy talentless pricks from drama school who arse-licked their way onto the goggle box, the Happy Traveller, Sylvester Stallone, William bloody Shakespeare for writing plays that Mickey wasn't allowed anywhere near, and top of the list- the wet, tiresome, feckless sell-out that was Michael Dalton.

Alarm bells ring. Shouts. Screaming.

Here comes Mickey Awful, gunning for all you slags!

Cut.

HE SITS ON HER BED.

THE WINDOW HAS FOGGED AGAIN, REVEALING THEIR SECRET MESSAGES TO ONE ANOTHER. SALLY. PAUL. SMILING FACE. PAUL LOVES SALLY.

THE FLAT IS SPOTLESS. SILENT IN HER ABSENCE. EVERY ROOM CALM AND ORDERED. HE LOOKS IN ON EACH ONE AGAIN, CLOSES EACH DOOR BEHIND HIM.

PAUL PUTS ON HIS JACKET, TAKES HIS KEYS OFF THE HOOK AND CLOSES THE FINAL DOOR.
HE WON'T MISS THE PISS-STINK OF THE STAIRWELL.

OUT ON GLOBE ROAD, THE WET AIR HITS HIM. THE RAINCLOUDS HAVE PASSED. IT IS A CLEAR, COLD AFTERNOON. HE WALKS PAST THE ROW OF DODGY SHOPS, THE KARAOKE PUB SHE HAD HER LAST BIRTHDAY IN, THE CAFE. HE PASSES OTHER WALKERS: A DRUNK; A WOMAN IN A BURQA PUSHING A BUGGY; TWO WOMEN CARRYING YOGA MATS. HE SEES NONE OF THEM.

AT VICTORIA PARK, PAUL STOPS ON THE BRIDGE. HE PRESSES HIS HIPS AGAINST THE IRON RAILINGS, BENDS FORWARD INTO THE FADING LIGHT. THE CANAL PATH BENEATH HIM IS ITS OWN, UNTOUCHABLE WORLD. A CYCLIST RINGS HER BELL AS SHE PASSES UNDER THE BRIDGE. A MAN WALKS HIS DOG. A COUPLE STROLL ALONG, HAND IN HAND. HE KNOWS SHE IS HALFWAY TO SCOTLAND ALREADY. THE SUN IS SETTING NOW. A PINK BURST OF COLOUR STRETCHES ACROSS THE EARLY EVENING SKY. PAUL WAITS AND WATCHES UNTIL EVERYTHING IS DARK.

Love in the Time of Ketamine
by *Xanthi Barker*

The day before he was supposed to leave, Huk cancelled his ticket to
Australia. "Fuckin' winter over there anyway," he told the television.

He didn't change his mind because of what Chortle said. That
kid was a prick, a hero, but a prick. He was good on a night out but
in the morning you wanted to break his skull. He wasn't going to go
postponing his dreams for that prick.

The day before, in fact pretty much every day since he was six,
Huk would've chopped his right hand off and eaten it to get the
hell out of that city. He wouldn't shut up about it. "I'm buyin' a
fuckin' car and drivin' to India," he'd say.

"Yeah?"

That could be Chair-Boy, it could be anyone.

"Yeah man. Soon as. Gettin' the fuck away from you morons."

"Fuck you, Huk."

"Fuckin' prick."

Those would be Chortle or Chris or Chair-Boy again.

"India'd be fuckin' sick man."

That'd be Dave, maybe Doo-Wap. They were the guys who
were going somewhere. They weren't K-head waster no-hope sleep-
through-your-own-fucking-youth losers like some of the heroes.

"Yeah man I'm gonna drive to fuckin' India, get me a kaftan, learn to make spirit gongs, re-align my chakras - and never come back to this fuckin' shit-hole. That bit's for certain!"

Some of the heroes laughed, some had forgotten what he'd been saying, some thought he sounded like a fucking square.

Chortle thought he sounded like a fucking square. But Chortle was a big guy - a super-hero. He was older than the rest, worked as a buyer for Harvey Nicks menswear, dressed like a fucking cucumber - cool as, man, cool as. "Platform trainers and a Westwood blazer? Yes my friend, I'm a fucking courgette."

Nobody bothered to disagree. Chortle got them the stuff. Had K coming out of his ear-holes.

Before Chortle came along they mostly just drank shit-loads. Sometimes they dropped pills or MDMA, snorted the occasional crap-filled line of coke. On a bad day they'd take speed, maybe, if they were desperate - speed was for junkies, losers, squares. The aim wasn't to speed up, the aim was to lose your mind, expand consciousness, whatever. Fuck man, what are you? Another fucking thrill-chasing *student*?

K hit them like acid in the '60s. It hit everyone. Your mind blown wide open and nothing but mania and music to fill it. You couldn't go to clubs without it - they were fucking boring without it anyway - and there'd always be someone there on it, bending their legs at impossible angles, dancing like they were breathing underwater.

No one batted an eyelid when the first person dropped through the other side into a K-hole and lay palpitating, dribbling and "Talkin' in fuckin' tongues man! Look at him!" It was hilarious, amazing, wild as Jesse James. You came back. You came back and someone had video-ed you on their phone and you watched yourself and you thought, man I look insane, man I can't remember that. I fucking lost it man. I collapsed into that hole in my chest where I thought my heart ended and flew straight through the floor, the roof, I don't know, I was alive and dead and nowhere and always and fuck man! Fuck.

I only ever took keys after that, but the heroes all took lines. Fat lines, like you'd take of coke. Fucking stupidly fat lines. Fucking idiots.

But I'm dead so I'm allowed to judge them.

Now I've got to tell you who I am, don't I? I was going to leave myself out but hey. I'm Huk's dead ex-girlfriend - hi there! The one who planned that trip to Australia. The one who he swore to we'd get out. When I died he swore on my ashes he'd still go.

It's funny, we always thought someone would die from it. When I spoke to the other girlfriends that's what we all said. Someone's gonna die. We weren't morbid. We weren't just sitting around shaking our heads and knock-knock-knocking on heaven's door. Any doctor who looked in on our nights-out would have said the same thing. I mean, I remember this night when I thought my arms were cartoon strips and they kept moving to scenes I didn't like so I decided to rip the pages out and draw my own ending. Who the fuck is writing this shit? I thought. I got a knife from the kitchen and a permanent marker and I was lying on the floor trying to keep my arm still when Huk came in and found me. He freaked out and grabbed the knife and must've shouted to Doo-Wap because soon they were both sat against the wall, wide-eyed and swaying, talking about how much I'd sketched them out. I didn't care. I kept picturing Huk's face. He'd turned *green* when he thought I was hurt. He was shitting himself. Because he thought I was hurt. That's all I was lying there thinking.

Where was I? Oh yeah - the heroes didn't think anyone would die. Heroes don't die, right? And they were right. It wasn't K and I wasn't a hero. Someone's got to laugh at that. I died two nights after a massive bender but that had nothing to do with it. We were all hanging at Doo-Wap's, watching a film, smoking weed, hungover as fuck. The film went on for four fucking hours. I would've gone to sleep, but I felt sick. Chortle wouldn't stop giggling. Really shrill, like a witch, right through the four fucking hour-long film. I started shivering and Huk pushed me off him, said it was distracting. When I started being sick he told me to go home and I burst into tears. "Jesus, fuck, all right!" he said, and got us a taxi to his.

The shivers and the vomit kept going all morning and all the next day. I hadn't slept. I kept passing out. I asked Huk to take me to hospital. He said no. Chortle was having a party that night. Bondage themed. Fucking creep.

I asked him, please, if he could at least stay in with me. He shook his head at his reflection in the mirror, fastening a collar round his neck. "You're hungover, doofus. That's all. It's always worse after a K-hole. I'm not missin' a party to nurse a fuckin' sick bird because she can't handle her drink." I said I thought it was something else. His grin disappeared. "For fuck's sake, Pipsqueak, it's not that bad. It's never that bad. You're always exaggeratin'. You're never as fucked as you say you are."

I shut up then. That was a mortal sin, for a hero. Being less fucked than you said you were. Like snorting talc or pretending to inhale. Like getting drunk on WKD. I scowled and booked my own taxi. He said he was trying to be optimistic. If I was truly as bad as I said I was, I'd be dying. So there.

So there.

Meningitis kills you so quickly, it's a joke. One second you're chatting to a cab driver and the next your're passing out on a hospital bed. Huk didn't know that meningitis has exactly the same symptoms as alcohol poisoning. Alcohol poisoning plus hypothermia. Neither did I. Goodbye, I said. No one heard me. The nurse had gone to look for a doctor.

The night before Huk canceled his ticket was a Saturday. A few heroes went to Doo-Wap's early and started doing K. Doo-Wap was at work. Huk invited them round. He had his own key. They'd all been out the night before for his leaving party so no one was exactly sober. Around six they went to Olean's for two-for-one cocktails. It's by the river and has one of the only all right views in the city. They sat in a line facing the water and sipped their Zombies and Mint Juleps and Mojitos. Huk leaned back in his filthy white plastic chair. "Ahh! This is the fuckin' life, eh? We're fuckin' sailin'. I'm gettin' a yacht, man, soon as I get to Oz."

Chortle tossed his head. "Course you fuckin' are."

Doo-Wap and Chris turned up about eight. Doo-Wap was pissed off. Someone had promised they'd wait for him at the flat. *His* flat, he said. He started picking on Huk. Chortle joined in so fast you'd have thought he started it. He must've been pissed about spending all the previous night toasting the bastard. Maybe they all were.

"You stink." That was Doo-Wap. It was true. Huk never washed. "My flat reeks of your fuckin' manure-stink."

"All right grandma! It's hard for me - keepin' up with your human standards." He clamped his teeth in a grin like Mutley's.

"It's not funny. I had to eat my dinner stewin' in your fuckin' sweat, basically."

"Why you tellin' me this now? When did you grow tits and turn into my mum?"

"When he fucked her," someone had to make that joke, it didn't have to be Chortle.

"Least he's not a puff like you, then, eh?"

Chortle rolled his eyes, shuffled in his seat. Everyone froze, waiting for his come back, ready with their gasps and high-fives. Chortle licked his lips.

"That why your girlfriend screwed me?" he winked.

I froze. I watched Huk's face. So did everyone. Fractal gasped. Nobody high-fived. I watched Huk's eyes. I wanted to see through them. I was rushing so hard I almost forgot I had no body and thought I was gonna be sick.

No I fucking didn't.

Chortle licked his lips again and moved himself up in his plastic chair. Huk's expression still hadn't changed.

I didn't. I swear I didn't.

"Oh please," he said, "as if she'd touch a cunt like you. You'd wet yourself if you saw what we got up to."

His lip curled. I could've kissed him. I couldn't. I could've smashed a glass on Chortle's head.

I didn't.

"Did you screw him or what, then, Pip?" he asked me. He drawled. It was later but we were both still fucked. I shook my head. It was shaking anyway.

"Course I fucking didn't," I said.

"Then what were you doin' in there?"

"I was in a fucking K-hole!"

"Were ya?"

Yes I fucking was. Yes I fucking was. I only took a key but I didn't see how big it was. He told me he'd do double.

"What's wrong with your wrists?"

They were dotted purple. I shrugged. Huk smiled and shook his head.

"Should get you a safety harness, shouldn't we, Pipsqueak?"

Chortle leant his head back, his eyes narrowing, then collapsed into a grin. "Yeah, maybe I would. Picturin' your face at the heights of passion's already got my stomach churnin'."

Everyone laughed at that. Even Huk giggled a bit.

"Fuckin' did her in and all, didn't ya?"

Fucking Fractal. The laughter stopped. Dave opened his mouth to speak but shook his head instead. Chortle plucked at his shirt. Fractal glanced from side to side, trying to catch Chris or Chair-Boy's eyes. They didn't look up. Doo-Wap whistled like a pin dropping. He kicked an empty bottle that had fallen to the floor and it rolled along the concrete and over the edge into the canal. They all watched it - turning, turning, turning, gone.

"See ya," spluttered Fractal.

Huk jumped up and screamed. "Fuuuuuck!"

The ducks exploded off the water. Even I jumped.

"Fuuuuuck!"

He screamed like a fire-bell. Doo-Wap started to laugh. He clapped his hand on Huk's shoulder. "Come on you big prick, let's get out of here."

They went to another bar, and another, and another after that, taking keys and then lines of K, their drinks spiked with MDMA. After midnight they went to The Balcony. Huk danced right next to the DJ, his hands on his head, his face, the walls. Doo-Wap chatted to some girls outside. Dave sat with Chris in the corner, smoking and frowning.

"Looks like fuckin' Jimmy Carr," said Dave, tossing his head behind them. "The bastard."

Chris looked over and sniggered. "Got your bird, did he?"

"Not my bird, is she? He's just a fuckin' creep is all. Tryin' to get her fucked."

They watched the girl stick her nose out for a key. She jumped and giggled and the guy's hips pinned her closer to the wall.

"Oi Bilbo!"

Chris and Dave turned round. Chortle sauntered over to Jimmy Carr and hugged him, leering down at the ginger girl. Dave shook his head. Then he turned and looked right at me, I swear.

"The cunt," he said.

Huk couldn't stop dancing, if you could call it dancing. He was shaking his limbs, holding onto the walls and shaking them. The DJ was getting pissed off.

"Huk's fuckin' gone man." Doo-Wap kicked the floor Dave and Chris were staring into.

"Fuck," said Dave.

"Fuck," Chris agreed.

Doo-Wap fished in his wallet for the wrap. "Let's fuckin' join him."

Huk woke up on the sofa with all his clothes and shoes on. His t-shirt was soaked. He pulled it up to his nose and inhaled, retched, shut his eyes as the images crowded down.

Dancing like Ian Curtis in front of the TV. The guys trying to play Mario Kart. He giggled and it turned into a cough, looked over and saw the top of the X-box was split open. The side of the TV was dented. He looked at his knuckles. They were scabby and blue.

K-holing in the middle of a house party. That was shit. This chick next to him who'd been giving him fuck-me looks all night shoved her face right up to his to check if he was breathing. That was the last thing - her smile twisting into a shudder.

Huk stuck his hand between the cushions to find his phone. His insides were shaking like he was sitting on top of a tumble dryer. He had to go home and pack. He had to book a hostel and a coach to the airport. He couldn't remember where he'd left his passport. He didn't know the time of his flight. The bookings were all in Pippa's fucking name. The tumble dryer turned up to full-power and he let his body rip into a scream.

Bad fuckin' vibes, he thought. Fuck it. I'm not gonna go.

That felt good. Decisive. Like stapling down his edges. Yes. Fuck it. I'm not fuckin' goin'.

I could've fucking killed him.

I'd figured it out, you see. What I was doing there. I was supposed to look after him, keep him safe, get him out. To complete the mission I'd messed up on earth. I was his fucking guardian angel, all right? And I wasn't getting out unless he did. I'd figured it out. Why the hell else was I stuck watching his every fucking move?

I was supposed to get him out. And he was still fucking sitting there. On the sofa, picking his nose. All fucking day.

Doo-Wap came out of his room about four with an apron on and started hoovering. He hoovered Huk. Some girl he'd met in the smoking area stumbled out of his room and laughed. Huk ignored her. She left and Doo-Wap sighed, threw down the hoover and pulled out a bag of K.

"Sneaky fucker," Huk laughed.

"Let's get 'em all over. Never-endin' weekend right? Give you a welcome back party or somethin'. Pretend we've blasted straight through 2012."

"Ascension party, eh? Yes Doo-Wap! We'll all bugger off to the astral planes on a great, fat cloud of K."

Doo-Wap laughed and started calling the others, telling them to get their arses back round there, saying he had a surprise for them.

After an hour, they started to file in - pale-faced, greasy-haired. Not looking so heroic now, are we boys? I thought. Chris rolled a spliff. Chair-Boy put the TV on. Chortle came last, carrying his beanbag and an arm-load of Kettle Chips. "Anyone up for a little Sunday special on me?" He shook his black velvet pill-purse in front of the TV. No one bothered to grunt beyond a yes-no-maybe.

"What's this surprise then?" Dave asked in the ad break.

"Huk's back."

"What? What you on about?" Fractal frowned.

"He's back, isn't he? Back from his big trip. We've gotta welcome him back."

"He never went anywhere you limp prick."

"What the fuck are you talkin' about?"

"You changed your plans then, Huk?" Dave turned towards him. Huk didn't respond. He was trying to look like he was in a trance. He had one hand down his pants and the other tap-tap-tapping on the arm of the sofa. "Huk?"

"What?"

"You not going to Australia anymore?"

"Am I fuck! Fuckin' land of squares that one. Goin' to London instead. Fuck it."

They smoked another spliff. Huk let his arm fall back down beside him. Chair-Boy started snoring. Some guy on *Takeshi's Castle* broke his leg.

Chortle wouldn't stop fidgeting. You could hear his sketchy breathing over the top of the TV. I thought he was pissed off they hadn't taken up his offer. Pissed he wasn't the centre of attention. Then the ads started again and he smacked his fidgety hand down on this thigh.

"You're not fuckin' it off 'cause of what I said, are you? 'Bout Pippa?"

Huk tried to laugh but he looked like he was choking.

"You don't wanna fuck your life up because of some flighty bird."

I stared at Huk, willing him to look my way. He didn't.

"You don't think I take anythin' you say seriously do you? Fuck no. Who do you think you are? My guru or somethin'. Fuck man. No fuckin' way." Huk kept swearing and protesting until it almost became funny. He started laughing. Fractal and Chair-Boy started too. Then everyone was laughing.

I wasn't.

I knew what he was saying.

I was in a K-hole. His face appeared like a blow-up doll at the bottom of a swamp. "How about now?" his voice warbled. His eyes were huge. He was licking my neck. Words swam away from me. I watched them. I couldn't speak. He lay on top of me, so fucking heavy I thought the floor was giving way. His hands were pressing into me, making holes in my skin. A white clump of powder dangled at the edge of his nostril.

"I dare you," he'd said, holding out the key. But I said it first.

"You wouldn't know how to fuck me if your grandaddy taught you!" I was joking. I was fucked.

"I fuckin' would too," he was laughing, he was joking. Where was Huk?

"Yeah right."

"Yeah, *right*."

And then I said it. "Dare you."

And he dared me the key. The biggest fucking key I'd ever seen. I couldn't breathe, I couldn't see, I couldn't move. An axe split me down the middle. The world cracked open. I couldn't scream. I tried to scream. I tried to shout but the words ran away. They moved, I watched them. I couldn't. He moved. I couldn't. His face. His heat. His weight. Everything spinning, melting, his voice. "Hey Pip-pip-pippa! Pip-pip-pippa!" Like he was bouncing my name on the floor. His face bouncing in and out of vision. "Hey Pip-pip-pippa-pippa-pip-pip-" Over and over like he had to remind me. Like he was stuck, bound, mad. His hands poking holes in my skin.

And then the feeling around my legs like they were liquid and all my insides were flowing out and the whole room was a pool that I had drowned in or turned into. *Sick, sick, sick, sick. I am drowning in sick and the world will be flooded.*

He pulled my tights up for me. I could move again by then. I didn't look. I thought there might be a hole. I thought my legs were bow-shaped, circle-shaped, Chortle-shaped. He grinned. His face through the swamp. He kissed me. I bit him. His flesh felt like jelly-fish, like poking a stick through a dead jelly-fish. He yelped and jumped back. "Fuckin' bitch!" His voice was whiney like a child's and I laughed. The floor was liquid. We were soaking.

"What the fuck just happened?"

"You fuckin' told me-" he looked me in the eye and shut up. "Your lips are blue, Pip. You cold or what? Fuckin' boilin' in here."

My body was shaking so fast the room looked blurred. I touched my skin. It was rough all over. It took me a minute to figure out it was goosebumps. My fingertips were white. I reached down to touch my legs. They were straight, hard, heavy, huge. I tried to poke my fingers through them.

"I'm gettin' Huk," he said, stumbling out the door. The walls were caving in.

"Pippa!" It was Huk. "Where've you been? Dave told me you

were K-holing. Dipstick. You OK?" His face appeared, bright, sudden, sharp, straight. It was an inch from my face. I could've kissed every pore. "He said Chortle did you in."

"No," I shook my head. "He didn't."

Yes he fucking did.

Huk sat up straight on the sofa, knocking Doo-Wap's arm off the back. His eyes flicked around the room, towards the door, down at Chortle's lap, up at his face. His shoulder's squared. His knees spread further apart. His lip curled. I thought he was gonna start on him. Smack him. Tear him limb from limb.

He didn't.

He laughed.

"Fuckin' serious aren't ya?" he said. Chortle smiled with half his mouth. Doo-Wap raised his eyebrows. "You know what that means?"

I knew what he was going to say before he said it and I would've shoved a bottle in his mouth to stop him from saying it, but I couldn't, and the words came pouring out of his mouth like ten-dimensional bullets and Chortle's eyes gleamed and I swear I almost exploded.

"She wasn't as fucked as she said she was! You know what that means? She wasn't as fucked as she said she was!"

"What the fuck you on about?" Fractal looked up from his phone.

Huk laughed harder. "Pippa. Couldn't shag for shit when she was conked. Chortle's just given me the key to my future!"

Chortle stuck his hands in his pockets and slid down in his chair. *Right fucking down, you prick.* Fractal and Chris leered from Huk to Chortle and back again. Doo-Wap shook his head and tapped his hands on his knees. Huk kept roaring it, the same phrase, "She wasn't as fucked as she said she was!" until Dave's face turned grey. Then he laughed that crippling, ripping, burp-laughter that hurt everybody's ears. And that's when I finally lost it.

"Yes I fucking was you arsehole, motherfucking-" I really fucking lost it. "I'm fucking dead. Dead! Dead! Don't you see that? Haven't you clocked yet? I'm fucking dead! How much more fucked could I possibly be? How much more fucked can you get? How much further do you want me to go?"

Of course nobody fucking heard me. None of them anyway.

Huk's laughter woke everybody up. Doo-Wap switched off the TV. He handed Huk a spliff, said "Welcome back, you prick," and stuck out his lighter. Chortle racked everybody up a line. Chair-Boy chucked Fractal's phone behind the sofa. Chris grabbed the spliff off Huk. Dave didn't move. He had to say something or he'd start feeling sick.

"You're a fuckin' pair of slimy bastards, the both of you." He got up, picking his cigarettes and lighter off the table.

"Where ya goin'?" Fucking Fractal.

"Real fuckers, you know that?" He buttoned his denim jacket and lit a cigarette.

"Fuck you, Dave." That bastard.

"See ya!" Fucking dickhead Huk.

"All right, all right, just sit down, man. Have a spliff. Chill. All right?" Doo-Wap waved the joint above his head.

"In fuckin' love with her, weren't ya?" Fucking Huk.

"Fuck you, Huk." Dave walked to the door.

"Gonna dig her grave up or what?"

"Jesus. Fucking. Christ. You lot are a load of fuckin' cunts, you know that."

"Oi, Dave. Sit down. He didn't mean it, come on." Doo-Wap blew on the end of the joint to get it lit again. Dave shook his head, walking to the door.

"I hope she's doin' OK up there."

Up there. Fuck.

Dave shut the door. Chris snorted. Huk giggled. Fucking idiots, I thought, fucking infants, fucking beginners.

That's what they looked like. Beginners. Like fucking crumbs off the end of a sandwich. Like prehistoric plankton. Like fucking *beginners*.

Their bodies blurred. I couldn't make out who was who, they all looked like washed-out jellyfish. Shapes and colours disappeared. Someone was tapping me on the shoulder. It seemed like they'd been tapping for ages.

"Come on, Pipsqueak, the parties going on up here. If you don't stop gawpin' we'll put you straight on the next plane back to that shit-hole."

I laughed because she was speaking like that to tease me. She sounded like a hero. My mouth wouldn't move to say it, but she sounded just like Dave.

Baby Faces
by Xanthi Barker

After the baby had left her body in a stream of salmonella badness, Alfie got dressed in a blue dress and rolled herself a fat cigarette.

Downstairs, Fen was waiting, leaning on the gate with his own cigarette dangling from his mouth and one foot tapping out behind him, frowning into the sunlight. He didn't even do it on purpose.

"All right, Steve McQueen," she said.

The triangle of neck and chest visible above his shirt glowed scarlet. Then he stepped over the bag of rubbish and picked Alfie up by the ribs.

"Ouch!" she said. "My boobs are still killing me."

Fen put her down. "You look happy," he said.

"I am happy," she said. "Aren't you?"

He dug a yellow Clipper from his top pocket and lit both their cigarettes. Smoke puffed out around the edge of his mouth and his eyes shut like a fish's. "Yehmf," he coughed.

In the front seat of Fen's hatchback Skoda, Alfie kicked off her shoes and rolled her seat back. Fen dug into his pockets and pulled out fists of crumpled fliers and pencil stubs, which he stuffed into the slot beneath the radio. "I almost didn't get her back," he said. "The guy in the garage said he should've failed her. But I said I've got to take this girl out. It's a big day. I said give me the certificate and I'll bring her back next week. I'll never go to another garage again."

Alfie watched the underneath of Fen's chin telling the story. The bristles of his sunlit stubble stuck out unevenly. There were lines she hadn't seen before like they'd been ironed into his cheeks. "He let you off," she said.

"I said I had to ask you a question."

"He thought you were going to propose."

Fen burst into wheezy laughter, his fists rising to eclipse his eyes. "He's a romantic, all right. He knew if I took her out today she'd be back there costing thousands next month straight."

When he turned the key, the engine meowed. Fen grimaced. Alfie gazed around at the worn brown seats, the sat-on climbing magazines in the back. The meow turned into a grumble then a purr and the car pulled away. Two kids walked past, pointed straight through the window and doubled over laughing.

"What's that about?" Fen said.

Alfie shrugged. "I hate kids."

They juddered off towards the main road. Fen chucked his cigarette and put another straight in his mouth. Alfie lit it for him. The car filled up with smoke and she drank it in like mountain air, getting hazy on nicotine and oxygen deficiency. If this had been last week, she thought, he'd be spitting his exhalations out the window and glaring at her, making sure she wasn't aiming for the funnels of second-hand smoke. Now they were both free to slowly choke themselves again. It was good, knowing it didn't matter much if you happened to die.

Traffic on the North Circular, deadlocked, like every car was stuck in the bitumen. Poisonous gases wafted through the open window and Alfie drank them in, too. Finally, they turned off onto the A4 and a car horn screeched behind them. Fen swore. His fists swelled. Alfie's stomach rumbled. "You know the worst thing," she said. "It's not the blood or the cramps or anything. It's the sickness. It's like food poisoning. Like imagine giving birth when you've got food poisoning."

"Shit," Fen said.

"Exactly. That's the only bit which made me cry."

"You cried?"

Alfie said nothing. Then Fen coughed, and it was his cough that embarrassed Alfie the most.

They drove past houses, tower blocks, sparse parks — an expanse of beige and rigid shadows. Alfie wondered how many babies, how many kids. How many little wails sounding right now, demanding nipples, peek-a-boo, new nappies. She patted her swollen stomach. Something about all this had meant her body did not belong to her, and not because it belonged to some half-formed froggy embryo. It didn't. It seemed more to belong to itself. Its shame was not her shame. Its greed was not her greed.

"I'm hungry," she said.

As if by magic, they pulled into a petrol station. Fen kissed her once on the shoulder then disappeared across the tarmac. He had a limp from when he fell off a roof last year. A metal pin in his knee. In his wallet there was a small plastic card that told security guards it wasn't a gun stashed deep within his bones.

Alfie climbed up so she was kneeling on the seat and looked at her face in the mirror. For six weeks, and now probably forever, it had been Fen's face too that stared back. Like how, when you saw the parents of a person, you couldn't unmix their features. They both looked like your friend, so they looked like each other. A bit sick, really, when you thought about it. Wanting to go to bed with the face you brushed the teeth of, squeezed spots from, tried not to notice decaying. But at least the reverse hadn't happened. It was still possible, for Alfie, to look at him and see only someone else. Some stranger with too-long hair and a wry mouth and a smell she wouldn't have minded inheriting. Would their kid have smelled like that?

Alfie was sure she still smelled like yesterday. She'd soaped and scrubbed but there was only so much you could do in one minute. The doctor said no more than that or you'll get an infection. No sex, either. It was like losing your license for drink-driving. Her gums were blistered from the sharp hexagonal pills and her stomach was regularly churning. It had not been pretty. And now when she smiled it was unnerving to think that that face had been inside her, had swum trusting as a snail across her belly, fattened itself on her blood, nestled down, and what had she done? Flushed it out.

See you later, pup.

She bared her teeth at the face which was also his face and then there was a click and a rush of cold air.

"Checking for rubies?" Fen said.

Alfie sat down and a Galaxy, an apple and a pack of blue McCoys landed on her lap. Fen sat down with his feet out the door and upturned a bag of peanuts into his mouth. Then he tore the wrapper off a Mars with his teeth, shoved half of it in his mouth and gulped.

"My first proper meal," Alfie said. "Thanks." She bit into the apple and juice sprayed across the car.

Fen hauled himself round, did his belt and turned the key. The car meowed again. They pulled back onto the motorway. "Check in the glove box," he said. His face was sparkling.

Alfie gulped the apple, did her belt and reached forward. The black plastic came away in her hand. She placed it on the floor. There in the dark, neatly packed, were four cans of Holsten Pils and a 50ml bottle of vodka. Alfie took out the bottle and clicked off the lid. It smelt like cleanliness. "You're a mind-reader," she said.

Then she said, "Where are we going?" while he said, "I love you," their words swapping person like kids playing hot potato so nobody felt the need to say anything back.

He was good at this kind of thing, Alfie thought, lugging heavy plastic coconuts at fake cans of beans. After all, he could spot grease-stains on windows from 900 feet, his bald manager's wave or wink from the same distance. He could've worked in a fairground, he had that easy way about him, charmingly elusive with his thoughts and plans. He liked meeting older men in doorways for a smoke and a beer, well — that was how Alfie always found him when she met him after work. His colleagues were all ancient. They had grandchildren and white hair and muscles like old ropey goats. They teased Alfie about her clicking heels and flimsy dresses. "I work at Jackie Queen's," she explained. "It's lady mwah or no tips." Alfie wore facts like a brodie helmet. She had many good reasons to believe telling the truth was often the best way to hide in plain sight. Jackie had been horrified by her billowing maxi-dresses, shroud-like shirts, recently, by the quantity of her new flesh. She was famous for her ruthless diet motto, *Let them eat men.*

Beside her, Fen cheered and Alfie's eyes focused again. He'd scored a hat-trick and won a sack of sweets. He jostled her against his ribs, smacked his lips on her forehead. Even the wily adolescent on the stall was impressed. He grinned while Fen ruffled his hair and accepted the bulging, bumpy sack. Fen untied the knot and told the kid to hold out his hands, then emptied a clutch of Haribo and Heroes onto the boy's clammy palms. The kid beamed and showed his gappy grey teeth. Alfie sensed Fen was about to invite him for a beer so she stretched up and kissed Fen's mouth hard. He went red again and swung the sack off the counter. "See you later," he spluttered.

"All right," said the kid.

They walked off towards the beer stall. Alfie carried the small fluffy banana and soft green ball he'd won previously. They found a bench and Alfie waited with the booty while Fen went to get some beers. But when he came back she was in a cold sweat and had to run back to the piss-stinking toilets four times before she felt OK to sit down. Fen sat waiting, passing his plastic beer glass from hand to hand, patting Alfie's shoulder between trips.

"You're a trooper," he said.

"You're at home," she smiled, "aren't you? You took me home."

He frowned at her. "I wasn't born in Thorpe Park, Alf." He paused. "Even if my mum would've preferred it that way." He laughed but it was thin, maybe just a bad swallow of beer.

"What d'you mean?" said Alfie. Her slurred words surprised her. She hadn't drunk in weeks. Well. She drank once, before Fen said the words, *Maybe I don't know*, and switched on that whole other future.

It had been like that. Four words. And then like a TV you hadn't noticed was in the room, full of channels you hadn't heard of, suddenly garbling out other worlds before Alfie could say she'd seen enough already. There were too many options she'd never anticipated — too many channels, too many TVs. Too many rooms. How were you supposed to choose a future if you didn't know any of the options?

Alfie had never met a man who liked children before. She

thought now that she'd never met a woman.

"I don't know," Fen was saying, "it might've been more exciting for her. Pushing a spinning teacup instead of a pram."

Alfie sipped her beer and nodded. They hadn't talked about families. How long had they known each other? A few months. What kind of time was that, to talk about families? Alfie would wait years, if it was up to her. Decades. Longer.

Whoever wanted to talk about families?

Fen, clearly.

Alfie could make do with the versions she made up. The people she pieced together from boring anecdotes, glimpsed photos, bitter asides. In Alfie's imagination Fen's mum was small and thin, a Fen with a narrower face and shorter hair, painted nails and court shoes and an Audi A3. Alfie was sure her voice was slow and boring, in the way some people's were when they thought everyone else was very slow and boring. She went shopping every Saturday at Westfield, Shepherd's Bush and had a salmon lunch with white wine in the oyster bar which had such sparkly clean windows that she was inspired to remember, for one moment, oh yes! she had a son.

It was a lot, Alfie thought, to have made up, when she couldn't right now remember Fen's mum's name.

"She loves roller coasters, bungee jumping, that kind of thing," Fen was saying. "She used to drive on the wrong side of the road for kicks, my dad said." He did that half-laugh again.

"Huh?" Alfie said. She copied his laugh.

"Yeah," Fen said. "That was the worst thing, the final straw. But she did it on purpose, he said."

"What?"

"Drove a mile down the A1 on the right, when she was pregnant. I mean with me. That was when he really lost it."

"Uh," Alfie said.

"She could've killed them. Us. Killed us." He beamed into his beer and Alfie felt confused. She watched him gulp the dregs and roll a cigarette. His hands were twitching, flicking the paper. Alfie reached over and took the tobacco pouch from him. She rolled her own and he lit them both, waving his eyebrows at her through the smoke. Alfie listened to the woman in her head explaining in a slow, boring voice, "Thad, I was simply looking for excitement."

Thad, Alfie had met. For half a second, because he'd been staying with Fen. He was like Fen exactly, but timeworn. If you put Fen's face in the app that aged people, the picture that came out was him. "Your dad lost it?" she said, too brightly. Fen shrugged. He looked confused about his expression himself, now.

Alfie was getting lost. Seeing it. It was a bad habit Alfie had, seeing things. Not like, seeing things, but like, seeing what people said instead of listening to what they said next. Right now she was seeing the young couple, basically Fen and then a thin spectre with nails — she couldn't use her regular Fen-mother version, because then really she'd just be seeing two Fens. *Three*. She saw the yellow and red pairs of lights trailing the motorway and the street lights lighting the car intermittently. The bizarre double-sense you get on a motorway of both flying and staying dead still. The rising vertigo as they soared into the traffic. The dad's hard fury. She was about to say something nice, or about to think of something nice she could say, but then her stomach gave a defiant churn. She felt her breath go.

"Um," she said, turned and dashed back to the toilets.

When she came back, she was ready with it, but Fen had already changed the subject. He was standing up with a secret look in his eye. He had two unlit cigarettes in his mouth and was holding two full cups of beer. "Better?" he said.

Alfie screwed up her face, took a cigarette and a beer.

"I saw something crazy over there." Fen pointed towards the Waltzer. There were some chatting dads with hats on, kids systematically poking each other's eyes, a woman with a bun and a crisp blazer holding tight her three-foot Spiderman's hand.

"What?" Alfie said.

"There's a guy taking bets. It's some escape feat. He'll be chained up in a coffin at the bottom of a fish tank."

They walked over and Alfie spotted him immediately. He wore only a pair of black lycra swimming shorts, diving shoes and a bumbag, into which he was stuffing people's bets. His hair was gelled up like hungry worms poking their heads through his skull. He saw Fen and Alfie approach and flicked an eyebrow, sauntered over.

Fen said, "We'd like to place a bet."

Alfie frowned. "Do we?"

"Shush," the man said. Then in a low voice, "Fifty quid."

"A hundred," Fen replied.

Alfie thought about that much money. She'd missed the last week of work. Jackie said, Sick pay? We're not civil service. Then she said, It's the man's money you want, not mine. She was nostalgic, Jackie, she tried hard not to move past 1980. Alfie's mouth curled up, imagining. "Fuck you," she said out loud.

Both Fen and the man looked at her. Her mouth opened in silent defense.

Fen hugged her against his side. "Big day for us," he explained.

The man nodded gravely, folding his arms. He sighed and his face softened. "I understand," he said. "Say no more. I can see right through people. S'my job. I'm clairvoyant, by trade." He gazed down pensively. Alfie and Fen followed suit. The man reached out and squeezed Alfie's forearm. She shifted an inch towards him. The three of them stayed like that a moment, not speaking. Then the man said, "Big decision. Same thing happened to me exactly when I was your age, so young really, you're what — twenty-two, twenty-three?"

Alfie said, "What?"

"Twenty-nine," said Fen, "both of us."

The man looked aghast. He stepped back. "Christ," he said. "Baby faces." A smirk appeared on his bony chin. "Well," he said. "Don't know what you thought, lady, you can't trick a man and expect to keep it." He chuckled, jostled his shoulder towards Fen, winked at Alfie.

Alfie felt her eyebrows shoot up. Fen frowned, stepped back. The naked man was glancing over his shoulder, jiggling a bit. Alfie and Fen looked at each other, both suddenly surprised they hadn't realised sooner this guy was nuts. Alfie turned to go. Then, "Actually," Fen said, "it was the other way round. I would've loved the baby. Alfie here would like to wait. Spread her seed, who knows? We're not all your blokey stereotypes, you know. Mate."

Alfie tugged Fen's hand. His face was going red again, but not in the usual way. His blush was uneven, puffed up. The man scowled, fluttered his fingers like a kid proving he wasn't scared. Fen's shoulders got broader. The man rolled his eyes. "So are we on for this bet or what then, *mate*?" he said.

Fen picked up the sack of sweets and swung around with Alfie planted into his armpit. The sack thudded against her back. He strode and Alfie scurried along, trying to keep up. His face was blotchy. The fluffy banana in Alfie's free hand looked choked. Fen said nothing. Alfie said, "Fen." They kept striding towards the bottleneck of the park, where crowds of people jostled to get from the food village back to the rides. Alfie's shoulder felt bruised where he was pressing it. Then she remembered it was already bruised where they injected her so the baby's alien blood wouldn't poison her own.

Beside the merry-go-round, they stopped. Alfie was out of breath. She sat down on a metal bench. Fen crouched. Tying his shoelace, Alfie thought, but then his head was between his hands. He was scratching and rubbing the hair above his temples. Alfie rolled two cigarettes, lit them both and held one out to him. "Here," she said.

Slowly, he stood up. "Thanks."

An ornate carriage sailed past them, followed by two golden ponies, a giant pumpkin, a cloud. Mothers and fathers with little boys and girls revolved in slow motion. "Look," Alfie said. "Are they part of the ride or what? Everybody looks so — permanent." Their faces were fixed forward, strained. She nudged Fen with her toe. "Want a go?"

Fen was staring back the way they'd come, rocking on the balls of his feet. When he looked around, his eyes were shrunken. "Go on then," he said.

They rode on the magic carpet, squashed together with their knees shoved to one side. Fen pulled Alfie's right leg over his thigh and ran his hands up and down her tights. The music was confusing. Kiss FM blasting over the looped fairy tale tinkle. Taylor Swift and Chris Brown vying for airtime with an instrumental version of 'Somewhere Over the Rainbow'. Their carpet moved up and down as the merry-go-round rotated.

"Bad traffic today, isn't it?" Fen said.

It took a moment for Alfie to recognise his joke. She laughed and said, "God I'm knackered."

"Sleep if you want," Fen said. "I don't mind. Did you sleep last night?"

Alfie looked at his ear. The long hair curled around it. She thought maybe she'd never looked at his ear before. There were freckles all along the top. "No," she said.

"Me neither," he said.

"Me neither what?" Alfie said.

He gave her a classic you-must-be-joking look and Alfie's mouth dropped, ready to apologise, but then it was right there, sitting on her, with its fat little arms and mucus. At the same time, Alfie and Fen screamed.

The guy running the ride came out of his plastic hut, his arms up ready to help, but when he saw them, he glared and spat, "No messing around," then went back inside the hut.

Alfie's heart was beating fast and she could feel Fen's too, pulsing through his stomach against her leg. He had twisted around in the seat to look at her, behind her, down by their feet. "Did you see that?" he said.

"Yeah," she said.

After a minute or so he said, "What does it mean?"

The question flew around with them for another six rotations and then there was a judder and a crank and they were released. Fen climbed out and Alfie followed. They jumped to the ground and stood there, shifting from foot to foot and watching a new set of people board the ride. When it started, they walked back to the food village and Alfie bought them more beers. They sat on their old bench without saying anything. Fen put his arm around Alfie and jostled her.

"Forget it, Alf, it was a trick of the light," he said. "Easily done, in this place."

"It's not that," she said.

"We're drunk," he said. "We've both been thinking about it. All the stuff you told me — it's grim."

"It's not that."

"You're amazing, you know."

"It's not that."

Fen gulped. He was usually so good at this, Alfie thought. He knew everything she was feeling. Or seemed to. It was like he had her thoughts provisionally downloaded. It was one of the things she hated most about him. "I don't know you very well," she said.

He put out his cigarette. He sipped his beer. "I know," he said. "But you will. Four months next week."

"Four months," Alfie repeated. "And still. I know exactly what our kid would look like."

Fen winced. "I hope it wouldn't've looked like that. Come on — it was a mirage, or something. Part of the ride."

"No," she said. She stared into her glass and her eyes traced the spiraling white froth. "Not that. It's in my face. It looks right at me. Its little face. It's your face." She sipped the beer than burst out laughing, spraying flecks of liquid onto their legs. "Why did you say that?" she said. "About it being one-of-a-kind? About the DNA? About what science says, how that exact kid will never exist again? You don't believe that, do you?"

"No. I dunno."

Alfie kept laughing. She had to put her beer down she was laughing so much. "Why didn't you say," she said, "if you wanted me to keep it."

"I did, Alf."

"Oh yeah."

He held her knee. "But you didn't," he said.

Alfie was laughing so much she couldn't pick up her beer. "Give me a sip," she said. "Help me, come on." Fen held his beer to her mouth and she slurped it. Then she sat up, took a deep breath and exhaled. "But when it was sitting there. You saw her. I dunno. I thought, like, I wouldn't mind. You know. If she stayed."

Fen nodded.

"I wanted her to stay, even. How stupid is that? A little ghost baby and I wanted her to stay."

She inhaled heavily again and her lungs filled up with Fen. He was close, his arm up around her. A klaxon sounded above somewhere and then a crackly man's voice explained they had thirty minutes until the park closed. Alfie stared at her shoes and the grass crushed and dying in the mud. She thought about her face, his face. How more than likely in a few weeks, they'd never see each other again. He'd get tired of her not hearing what he said, she'd get tired of his inescapable embrace, his knowing. He'd forget to call, or she'd forget to reply, or he just wouldn't ask, or she'd make an excuse. Her bed would stop smelling like him. His old men would tease some other woman about her shoes. And she'd still brush his teeth, wash his face, tie up hair around this strange new face, she didn't understand how it would ever go back, now it had lost its way of being her own.

She said, "It's funny though, it's just, what if I wanted you to stay?"

IT WASN'T HIS VOMIT. IT COULDN'T HAVE BEEN. HE WAS SURE. HE PUT HIS HAND TO HIS THROAT AND TOOK A STEP BACK ALONG THE HALLWAY. LAST NIGHT: TELEVISION, A GLASS OF WINE, DINNER ON HIS OWN, BED EARLY. HIS MEMORIES CRYSTALLISED, AND THERE IT ALL WAS. NOT A NIGHT THAT HAD ENDED IN VOMITING. BUT WHAT ABOUT HIS SLEEP? HAD HE BEEN ILL IN HIS SLEEP? THIS, SEEMING A MORE LIKELY EXPLANATION, BROUGHT HIM SOME RELIEF. HE TURNED AND WALKED BACK INTO HIS BEDROOM. THERE WERE NO MARKS ON THE SHEETS OR PILLOW. HE LEFT THE ROOM AGAIN AND AVOIDED LOOKING AT THE DRYING VOMIT. MAYBE HE'D BEEN ON THE WAY TO THE BATHROOM AND… HE TURNED INTO THE BATHROOM. PURSING HIS LIPS HE LOOKED INTO THE LOO. NO STAINS OR CRUST.

HE LOOKED IN THE MIRROR. THERE HE WAS, TIRED AND WORN AS EVER, BUT NOT ESPECIALLY ILL LOOKING. DISTRACTED, HE GAZED AT HIMSELF, EXPERIENCING THE FAMILIAR, TROUBLING WONDER AT HIS OWN AGEING THAT THE MIRROR ALWAYS GAVE HIM. AFTER A MOMENT, HE RALLIED HIMSELF AND TURNED AWAY. THE FACE IN THE MIRROR REMAINED THOUGH. WHEN HE'D TURNED HIS BACK ON IT, ITS FEATURES TWISTED INTO A LEER.

Waiting for a Hurricane
by Ben Byrne

I hate Florida. I really do. I used to pass through it so many times on the way to and from the States. The girl I thought I'd marry used to live there, though I'm not sure if she's living there anymore.

*

I was at Miami airport on a layover from São Paulo, where I'd been working for the week. As I wandered downstairs to the musty chill of baggage claim, a handsome old Hispanic man, arms folded, was staring absently at the luggage belt as a young woman and her family crept up behind him. The amber lantern flashed and the rubber belt slid into action - the old man spun around and they all whooped! He hugged his daughter tightly as a child flung itself at his legs.

I smiled and went outside into the warm, clammy night to smoke a cigarette. I always had a snippet of sentimental song going around my head whenever I arrived in those places, lingering, halfway across the world:

I wish somebody was waiting
I wish somebody was waiting
I wish somebody was waiting
And I wish that somebody was you.

No one ever was though, so I just stood there, smoked my cigarette and thought about her. She might have been forty miles away, dancing half-naked in front of the mirror in her parent's bungalow to German alt-rock, her small breasts twirling round and around. I went into the deserted lounge and spread myself out between two big leather armchairs. I put on my noise-cancelling headphones and opened the bottle of whisky I'd bought at duty free. The malt sent little shock waves around my brain and I took another swig. I sat there, suspended, as my chin began to bob into my neck.

*

We decided to get back in touch after a long time. A New Year's text message, a birthday email – we'd nibbled at each other like little fish, all night sighs and sentimental electronic scribbles in the ether. Finally, one evening, I faced the inevitable. I stretched out on my couch, a bottle of red wine mustered on the table, and called her.

"Well – hello," she said.

*

We had met at a show the week I moved to America. I was excited and high, she was cute and funny and relished the fact that I was English. We made a date for the zoo the next day but I woke up late, hung-over, and on the way, my cab nearly crashed in the fog. An hour late, I tried to call her, but I couldn't get through. Despairing, I floundered in anyway, hoping that I might just somehow spot her.

And then, somehow, I did. Standing in a pair of pink sneakers in the grey whiteness of the afternoon, watching the chimpanzees.

"Well – hello," she said, smiling.

She did most of the talking. She talked about songs she could play on the guitar, about stars she had interviewed for her website. She explained how I might have noticed already, but she was sometimes compared to a certain blonde pop star, whom I hadn't heard of, but anyway she had once slept with the band's guitarist one night after a show in Berlin.

By the time we sat down by the parrots, my head was pounding. As we smoked, she told me, conversationally, that she was now sleeping with her father's best friend. That they'd been on a road trip together the year before, and 'things had just happened'.

"When you spend time with someone like that," she said, "things can just happen."

"Right," I said, wheezing. "That makes total sense."

*

Hours later, ruby-mouthed and blurry-eyed, it had been agreed. I'd take a few days off, go to visit her at her parent's place in Florida, where she was living on her own for a while.

"There's NOTHING to do here, just so you know."

"I don't mind. It'll just be nice to see you."

"Nothing AT ALL."

"I don't mind."

"Seriously – there is Nothing. To Do. And everyone here is at least A HUNDRED."

"It'll be cool. It'll be fun."

"Uh-huh."

"So. What is there to do? Really?"

Her voice took on a cute, flippant tone.

"Well! We can go to the beach . . . and the old folks have their bingo at the club house on Tuesdays!"

"I haven't been to the beach in ages."

"Or – we can go to the Flamingo Gardens…"

"I'd love to go to the flamingo gardens."

"Ahhh! He'll go to the Flamingo Gardens with me!"

"They sound very picturesque."

"And just so you know, honey, there's probably going to be a hurricane, and we'll probably have to put up the hurricane shutters and have no air con for a week. Oh, it'll be dreamy."

"I can't wait."

"You have no idea what it's like. This is Florida. Seriously."

"It'll be fine."

"Huh."

*

I wish somebody was waiting.

I wish somebody was waiting.

I wish somebody was waiting –

And then – there she was. Floating across the tarmac outside the terminal in her dad's battered green Cadillac. She wound down the window. "I've gone around three times already, honey. You better get in before they arrest me."

I clambered inside and the car jerked forward.

"Ahem. You'll have to move my yoga mats from the seat."

I threw them into the back as we drove away from the decaying, heat-stained airport.

"And can you pass me my water bottle. Please."

I handed it to her and as the car veered toward the exit, I started to helplessly grin. I wound down the window, hot air blowing in against my face.

"Uhm, nye – nye – nye, honey, if you open the window then the air-con doesn't work."

I shrugged, still grinning, and wound it back up again.

The road led through a small beach town, the silver tripod of a gas tank looming over us. A billboard stuttered up, advertising the gun show, then another for Motel 6.

"Just so you know – if you need another place to stay," she said, smirking.

Then we were out on the freeway, the malls scudding by on loop of concrete and pastel – Taco Bell, Borders, Blockbuster, Home Depot, Safeway, Burger King, Blockbuster, Taco Bell . . .

A car in front of us swerved in and out of the third lane of the highway, a silver thicket of hair bobbing beyond the rear glass. She held her hand to the horn, but then put it back on the wheel, rolling her eyes.

"Jesus. Florida brain! I get it after two weeks of being back here."

She shifted lane, overtook the old lady, smiling sweetly through the window.

"Honey, if I ever get like that, you promise to shoot me?"

"Ha!"

A horn blared from the car behind us as we sailed in front of it.

"Ahem."

The country sped by. Retirement communities tucked away behind long screens of laurel and chain fence – secret, wistful pockets of milk and honey salvaged from the swamp, given names of lush, fragrant promise: Willow Grove, Emerald Pointe, Orange Blossom Manor . . .

All above and around them – the sky is vast, as if hoisted up on stilts a hundred miles high. Far away, where the tropical sky meets the flat land, snake tongues of lightning flicker and dance against the pinkness, as if tasting the salt in the warm, moist air.

*

We stopped at Safeway and I went around the aisles, cheerfully picking out meat and vegetables, stocking up with wine and whisky. We drove to the other side of the road, waved at the sullen guard, and she picked me up a security pass at the community office, written out in spidery handwriting by an ancient sun-wrinkled woman. We wound around the lane of the retirement village to her parent's bungalow, where her neighbors were sitting out in deckchairs, tanned and leathery as alligators. She waved and they squinted and nodded as she introduced me.

When we got inside, she turned on the air-con straight away.

"So what are we eating tonight? There's some mini-steaks in the freezer."

I cooked chicken with tarragon, and pasta. We ate side by side, at the glass table in the lounge, so she could see the TV. She finally seemed to relax. She put down her fork, and I noticed a twist of tarragon around one of its metal teeth.

"This is delicious."

She held up her misted glass of wine to me, and nodded.

"Cheers to you."

"Cheers."

"I'm sorry."

"For what?"

She took a sip.

"Thank you for coming, anyway."

"My pleasure."

"Right. Anyway. Ymm."

She picked up the barbarous remote control and changed the channel, turned up the volume.

Animated spirals and vortices were twisting jerkily across the Caribbean Sea. They stopped, went back, repeated, over and over again. She stared at them for a moment.

"Oh, great. Just fucking great."

*

Christmas, a few years after we met. I was hopelessly in love with her by then, alone, hundreds of miles away in London and feeling as if I was losing control. I phoned her in Berlin - she sounded pleased to hear my voice. I asked if I could visit for New Year's.

"Um," she said. "You know I'm still with – my man. Don't you?"

"I know that," I said. "It's OK. It'll just be good to see you."

I picked up champagne at Zurich and she met me at the airport. We dropped off my bags at her friend's house and we went to a bar for a few drinks.

"Sorry you can't stay with us," she said. "He didn't like the idea. Even though I told him you were gay."

Later, we walked over to her apartment block. At the foot of the stairs, a decrepit-looking man stood holding a bunch of flowers. She beamed and spoke to him in German. In the cramped elevator up, she told me that he was her mother's boyfriend, that he was waiting for her to come down after dinner.

A jolly man - her father - welcomed me into the small flat. In the kitchen, her mother was making goulash soup. Another man was standing in the lounge – mid-fifties, tall and potbellied - and I realised that this must be the Best Friend. He shook my hand. After a moment, he went and sniffed the pot on the stove theatrically, guffawing as he waggled the thick roll of his belly between thumb and forefinger. She went to her room to take a call and we listened to her burbling with excitement as we stood there in silence, sipping our drinks. Her pet rabbit was hopping about in the lounge, and her father scrambled through to pull at its ears, leaving us alone.

There was a photo of her on the wall, taken at her high school graduation. She was sneering at the camera, blonde hair spiked up, all faux anarchy and princess punk. The best friend turned, put his finger to her face, and drew it slowly down her body, lingering. Then he turned back and leered at me.

*

"You really want this to happen, don't you?"

I didn't want to say it, but it was true.

"Right. When the windows blow off and we have no air con or TV for three days you'll be super happy."

She was right. I didn't care.

She glared at me. "This is Florida. Seriously."

"It'll be like our adventure."

She rolled her eyes.

"Oh, sure."

*

The TV showed crowds gathered in the snow by the Cathedral as we sat around the dinner table in silence. The Best Friend was on her far side, and her mother served up the goulash soup as her father squinted at one of the bottles of champagne, twisted the cork and poured it into our fizzing glasses with a chortle. She was wearing a black wool sweater, her blonde hair cut short, and she seemed more beautiful than I had ever seen her before.

We clinked a toast to the New Year ahead, and began to eat our goulash soup. After the bowls were empty, we all stared dumbly at the TV for a while, until her father finally started playing with the rabbit again, chasing it around the cramped room, and her mother took this as an excuse to slip downstairs to her decrepit lover with his wilted flowers. The best friend gave her a private glance. She suggested that we leave now.

Fireworks were exploding all across the night sky as he drove us in his warm Mercedes to the party at the friend's place where I was staying. When we got there, the party had already started, and she came in for a while as he waited outside in his leather seats, the engine running.

A beautiful girl with black hair and a camera around her neck started chattering to me and a cheery guy I assumed was her boyfriend breezed past carrying beers and gave me a knowing wink.

She took me upstairs to my attic room for a moment.

"Please don't fuck her tonight," she said. "Please."

Then she went back outside to her waiting car.

*

The hurricane was travelling at ten miles an hour across the Caribbean Sea – slower than a moped. I pictured Havana being pummelled, the buildings crumbling into mud, the people on the Malecón being hurled into the frothing waves. Katrina had scoured this coastline a few years back and I'd listened to the reports on the

TV as the trucks rumbled past my apartment and tried to write something significant:

The wind that blew in over Lake Pontchartrain,
So dismal and dreary that time drowned itself
Dread and decay where all that remained
In the dawn of the day that the Hurricane made

I hope that I don't grow fat and old and die in Florida, though I probably will.

*

I brought out breakfast – bacon sandwiches with avocado and mustard. On the TV, the animated nebula of the hurricane were still spiralling toward the coast, glowing arrows projecting its path. Later on, I took the hurricane shutters from the loft – mysteriously full of photographs of her mother - sweating as I slotted them against the windows. We drove back over to Safeway to stock up with candles and batteries and water. The day before, gallon jugs had formed great embankments and aisles; now they seemed more like the plundered ruins of some ancient plastic citadel.

Back at home, she sat on the couch, flicking between the glowing spirals and her medical shows. I filled the bath with water, and boiled up three pounds of pasta. Forked it, limp and white, into bowls in the fridge.

*

The night before my flight home, as we sat in the plush darkness of a cocktail bar, I told her that I loved her, that I needed to know whether it was still worth me having hope. She touched the rim of her glass, and told me, seriously, that one day, she thought we would be together. But not yet. That, at that moment, she had two hearts. One, which belonged to her father's best friend. Another, growing slowly, which she thought one day would be mine.

*

Outside, on the porch, we sat smoking, glancing occasionally at the sky.

"You're excited about this, aren't you?" she said. "I can tell."

I was. To be honest, I wouldn't have minded if the world had ended. Mad Max gangs would hurtle down the swampy remains of Daytona Beach on chopped Ducatis. Up the coast, I'd go out in the morning to beach comb, pick raffeta rugs from the shore, scrutinize the flotsam and jetsam of our lost civilization as it washed up on the beach. I'd pick out the bits we could use – the good planks, the abandoned sails and masts. One day a great carved figurehead would wash up on the sand – I'd drag it home and mount it up outside the bungalow.

Those splendid mornings! When the hot and rosy sun would emerge from the sea, brightening the entirety of the sky into blue. My dawn shadow casting across the shore as I walked back home to where she was waiting, my footprints melting behind me in the sand.

The days would come and go. At dusk, I would stroll down to the shore again, fling an ill-woven net into the surf – pull it back, a couple of flapping, floundering fish tangled in its strings. I'd watch the sky bleaken prettily, walk out into the ocean and swim, float, emerge once more, feel the cool wind salting my skin. The sky would become a long smudge of indigo, the silver moon would appear, as suddenly as ever, and roil out across the deep stained sea, pulling the tide in and out, in and out, while faint, far off lightning electrocuted the purple horizon.

I wasn't worried about how we would survive. The Safeway would have food enough for a while – the freezers would keep things fresh until the backup generators went. After that – there were the dry goods, the pasta and such. Then the tins. I could forage for lizards, trap turtles, net fish. We would somehow survive, in the bungalow together. The sun would circle endlessly around us; the vast sky would silently flicker. She would grow garlic amongst the weeds. Every two years, we would have pineapple.

*

The rain came in late that night with a sudden, steady patter. We took all of the blankets from her mother and father's beds, and sat them out in the lounge like two children building a fort. The Weather Channel burbled away as we lay in the blankets and hugged each other. She wondered with a moan why we hadn't thought of the idea before. I slid up her shirt, and she sat on top of me, leaning over. She embraced me with her body, I reached my hand behind her neck. She pushed down hard on my rib cage, protesting.

"You think I'm a fucking high school cheerleader or something?"

I slid away, stung, withering.

We lat next to each other in silence, as the hurricane wandered closer.

"You really want this to happen, don't you?" she whispered.

*

At about one in the morning, a great sighing came from the trees outside. Sudden, violent rain hammered against the house. Air sucked and pummelled at the windows - there was a loud crack, a blast of freezing air and a howling shriek as the first hurricane shutter flew twirling away. The wind hit the window again, hard, the glass shattered - and then it was there in the room with us, like a shrieking witch. There was a vast whump, a bang, and the lights in the house snuffed out like candles. She screamed; the red light on the TV glowed for a second, then faded into blackness. I held her tightly as the driving wind scoured the room, flinging magazines into the air. The storm retarded for a moment, and we sat there in the darkness, a fine, freezing water spraying over us like it water from a sprinkler.

The trees began to roar again and I leaped up and pulled her to her room and we huddled tightly in the bottom bunk of her bed. Then the entire house was being pummelled on each side, slapped by enormous hands, veering and leaning on its shallow foundations.

Even then, as the wall buckled behind me, I could feel her hot body squashed against mine, my hand gripping her breast, the nipple hardening beneath my fingers. I pushed my face into her hair, and could smell the burnt caramel and apricot scent of her skin, the jasmine of her night perfume.

I pulled her as tight as I can, my hand on her ribcage, my sternum pressed against her spine. As the hurricane pounded against the windows, I felt her mouth on my finger, her small perfect teeth against my skin; she bit down as hard as she can, and I could feel the imprints welling there like half moons in my flesh.

*

I was not sure how we slept. But we must have slept, somehow, because when I woke, everything was gone.

I slid out of the bed, leaving her sleeping, and clambered through the wreckage of the house in my boxer shorts. Outside, big, bushy branches had snapped off the palm trees and lay scattered in the driveways. White plastic furniture and tarpaulin had been thrown across the scarred lawns, unripe oranges littering the grass like abandoned tennis balls. Most of the clapboard houses in the retirement community had been blown down, their planks randomly piled against the laurel trees. The wall that separated the little front patio from the neighbour's house had collapsed, and in the parking circle, their cream Mustang lay on its back like an upended beetle.

I picked my way down the path in bare feet. On either side, the houses had been punched in, leaving their contents exposed to the sky – upturned sofas, shattered TVs, PC monitors and old printers. Handicapped toilets lay broken, their cisterns cracked, guardrails unratcheted from the tiles. Wires dangled from the walls, pipes welling fluid into saturated flowerbeds.

Down by the artificial lake, the wooden bridge over the stream had broken off, and was bobbing, half submerged in the water. On the little island, the big willow tree had snapped in two, its branches dangling into the lake. Past the shuffleboard court, the swimming pool was overflowing and tennis nets hung over the fence of the court like ejected spools of film. I stood there for a while, as the sky lightened. I held my breath, and listened. Everyone had gone.

There was a circular flutter in the water. A reptilian spike sliced out of the lake, scaled arms gripped the collapsed side of the bank, and with muscled, determined grace, an iguana hoisted itself up, slipped, then gripped onto the earth with vestigial toes, heaving itself up onto the verge. Its fin erected, shivered, flattened back down again as it clambered up onto the court and splayed itself out there.

The air was fresh and pure. I stood there, on the tennis court, a gentle breeze blowing through the hairs on my arms. The nets shivered. Above the artificial lake, the sky was huge – at its rim, the lilac of dawn glowed steadily brighter, pushing against the indigo of the fading night. The horizon slowly fermented into bands of gold and crimson, and I watched, feeling a great, naked excitement, a startling, limpid beauty rising all around me - high up in the sky, was the silver glint of the morning star . . . In the wreckage of the retirement community, the breeze fluttered and played, and I stood there and watched the sunrise, the first man on earth.

*

Of course.

Of course – it didn't happen like that.

The hurricane was demoted to a Tropical Storm not far from Bermuda. By the time it finally made landfall, it wasn't much more than an infantile Tropical Depression. The Weather Channel was disappointed, but got excited again later about a mudslide in Indonesia, a flash flood in Bangladesh.

*

We sat outside on the porch, the thick, hot night swallowing us. I told her I loved her, that I couldn't carry on living in hope any more. It was about five in the morning by then. The newspaper boy would be getting here soon. She came over, sat astride me, put her arms around my neck. It was quiet.

Later, there was a thump and the shrink-wrapped newspaper slid toward us.

*

I hope that I don't grow fat and old in Florida. I hope that I don't die of cancer. I hope that one day I will find someone that I truly love, someone that loves me back with the same fierce intensity. I hope that we will grow old – and less beautiful – together. I hope that it isn't already too late.

Even if everything in life doesn't turn out like we hoped, then I hope, as the lights begin to go out, that we can just stay indoors, buried in a nest of blankets, together. We'll watch the Weather Channel, wait for the air-con to fail, for the TV to die, as the families of hurricanes crawl in from the ocean.

We'll hug each other as they make landfall. We'll lie there together, warm and placid, as outside, the sky turns black, and the branches begin to quiver.

Low Tide At English Kills
by Ben Byrne

My dreams were drenched pea green, as if saturated with the blood of some mythical creature. The snapping turtles exploded from the poisonous mud beneath Newton Creek and went for the tender white soles of my feet with their razor teeth, again.

In days gone by there were oysters here, two hand-spans wide. Elk came down from the forest at dusk to dip their heads and drink from the clear tributary streams. Water washed in and out – in and out the cleansing salt came. Time and tide flowed up and down, gushed and gurgled, never pausing, never waiting. Why didn't you wait for me?

I was out on a run. The bridge was up over the English Kills, and a boat from the paint factory slid through the chalky green channel below. Through the railings, the water looked dead and inert. A merping siren sounded and impatient engines throbbed as the road began to hum and stiffly reform. Then, in the water, something poked out. A gnarled branch, or a big bloated rat ? But a small yellow eye flicked open on its side – a snout split into two, and the thing gasped like an old man!

I stared at it as it bobbed forward in the water, but it quickly submerged again, leaving a dimpled wake and a bubbly scum on the viscous surface of the water. The trucks in the road began to rumble and smut as the guard rail jerked up – I sprinted away before them down Metropolitan Avenue.

I read that snapping turtles did not make good eating. They looked strange as well, oily green and evil. They had neither the blissful, moronic grin of their cousins, nor the rat-a-tat lute shell. Instead, they had a snaky neck and a slit and rows of sharp, bitey teeth. They looked like nasty bastards, and they were, and they probably tasted like shit. But they were the only edible thing lurking in the sewage and petrochemical murk of the English Kills, and I wanted to kill one, and eat it.

I lived on Paumanok – the Island of Tribute. Tribes once speared the deer that came down to drink here. They shredded their flesh, and strung it out on wicker frames to be dried by the salt wind that blew in from the great Eastern Ocean. They were all now locally extinct, of course – their flesh got shrivelled up in the sun, chewed and digested. It was transmuted into new muscle and sinew – into brawny arms that propelled spears and spells high into the sky, fluttering hands that made sacraments of blood and dirt.

Once, I could have walked into the ocean and strode along the banks of cod! I could have walked across the river to Manhattan – the Place of the Bow and Arrow – upon the backs of salmon. I could have built skyscrapers from the silvery chalk shells of oysters, lined avenues with sheets of glistening fish scale . . .

But the fish have all been vacuumed from the sea now, and the oysters have abandoned their spiny exo-skeletons to the estuarine current. The English Kills that once sparkled fresh and clear into the East River now finds its headwaters in a gushing sewage pipe. Its banks are slick with oil, its toxic waters lurid with chemical run-off and metal contaminate. It is a tarred and stagnant bronchiole within the crippled lungs of the city.

But life still lurks here somehow, unfathomable and unpleasant. The English Kills is colonised by floating scavengers that feed upon sewage, spawn, and baby ducks – soft beaks and all.

I intended to aggress them, with carnivorous distemper. I would hunt here again – I would pay tribute to the ancestors! I would wade waist high into the muddy estuary and writhe with water snakes – I would plunge deep into the cold sound and grapple with hags. I would spear and bleed the snapping turtles that flapped and paddled in the low tide at English Kills – I would trap them and scuttle them, I would spear one's leathery olive armour, and then I would bear it home, blooded and triumphant, and there I would feast upon its flesh.

An appendage is attached to their tongue, I read, it resembles a worm. It slowly extends, and wriggles in sham. The small aquatic fry floating nearby approach – entranced. Then – it furiously flurries and devours them!

Murder police have been known to tie strings to their tails and fling them into the dark canals of the city, following the bubbly beads along the water. Pulling at their leashes, the creatures will swim straight for any corpse that might be decomposing down there in the ooze. They strain for it, jaws akimbo, frantic with the smell of puffy flesh. Just so, the living devour the dead. Otherwise, sewerage will do.

I decided to hunt from the paint factory, with a razor blade tied with twine. Safety blades they call them, though they would prove treacherous to the creature that might try its luck on their intermetallic strips. No other bait was needed, I thought

– confronted with an intruder, such an aggressive species would berserk, unable to restrain itself, even at the cost of its own life.

I ran up through the toxic carnage of Flushing Avenue that night, leaping over the blasted bricks and corroding rails. I streaked past the cold stores of meathooks and carcasses, the barricaded shanties brimming with scrap metal, until, at last, I reached the lonely bridge.

Orange light waggled on the gluey murk of the English Kills. Far away on Manhattan, the lights glimmered from the skyscrapers. I unwound the blade and checked the knot. Then I weighted the twine a yard up from the blade with a key, and flung the contraption over the railing – it plopped into the water, and I waited.

Nothing, that night – and nothing the next, though I waited until the vapours of dawn, shivering in my shorts.

On the third night, I taped the lungs and lights of a chicken to the blade. Within minutes of casting it away, fat bubbles rippled up in the water! I jerked at the string, making it pull through the water – the submariner went into frenzy! The string scripped out through my fingers, tearing off a thread of skin; before the line went taut, and I struggled to hold on as it veered from side to side. I spindled the twine around my arm as I pulled – it was tight and thrumming and horse hairy as I drew him home . . .

Ggggnnnhhh – heave! Splash! There he was! Flapping and grimacing, the twine suspended in the rictus of its gaping mouth. I made a pulley of the rail, and hoisted him up; the stubby flippers became wings, flapping clumsily at nothing as he slid upward through the air. I heaved for one last time, and he clattered over the railing and onto the sidewalk, as I toppled over backwards.

It lay there, inert, faintly rotating on its shell. Its body was dun and slimy, the swallowed bait an angular lump in its curving neck. It was making an odd hissing sound, and a foul smell rose up towards me – sewagey and unpleasant like a chemical toilet. It was clearly disturbed – I would have to make sure that it did not try to harm me.

I walked over to it gingerly – and quickly tipped it over. I straddled the glistening shell, and gripped its thick lizardy neck between my fingers, slowly pulling the hairy twine from its mouth. The blade emerged, along with a fair degree of gunk. I flung the string and bobs away from me, over the railing into the Kills.

Had it already expired? Its yellow eye was open and unmoving. Its mouth was still open, and I could see the rows of sharp, shiny little teeth in there . . .

Then it rattled and I leapt up! It jiggled about madly, spraying a foul smelling liquid that got all over my legs. I wiped at it, but the gobbets were slippery, and I felt suddenly nauseous, and promptly vomited on the creature, as if in revenge.

I caught my breath, and then carefully positioned my open rucksack in front of the animal. I tried to chivvy it inside with my foot, but it didn't move, so I swiftly seized its twitching tail, stuffed it in, and laced the bag up tight. Then I hoisted the rucksack on my back, and bounded away down the avenue toward Boswjick as a full, silver plate moon rose over the distant, glimmering towers of Manhattan.

Bushwick. Boswjick – the 'little town in the woods' in Brooklyn. The woods are all gone now, of course – the trees have been axed down and their roots dragged out of the earth, first by carthorses, then by tractors. Vast megaliths of coal grey stone have been erected in their place, studded with squares of yellow light. As I ran home with my prey on my back, they shook with the sound of drumming, the sky filled with the spotlights of rotorcraft and the shriek and howl of electronic defences.

I couldn't eat the thing straight away, of course. It seemed it had to be purged. I read online that I would have to keep it submerged for several days, change the cloudy water over and over, sluicing away the waste and filth of its innards, until, at last, the water stayed clear. Then I would know that it had been purified, and that it was safe to eat.

When I got home, I heaved it out of my rucksack into the bathtub. It flopped and flibbered on the porcelain, weakly emitting another burst of effluent, so I ran the shower over it, before realising, stupidly, that I would now be unable to bathe in the tub myself. I stripped, climbed on the toilet seat, and traversed out onto the rim of the tub, keeping a careful eye on the beast below for any fast movements. I turned the shower tap with my foot, and sluiced off most of the smelly detritus from my body. Then I hopped onto the floor, pulled the lever for the taps and splashed the bath up a quarter full.

It waited, suspended, lurking in the middle of the tub. Thin threads of blood wavered in the water around its snout, and its yellow eye slowly opened, and closed.

I hit the light switch and ran out of the room, making sure to shut the door firmly.

The next morning, the water was cloudy and noxious again. The creature was on the move. It flapped up to the end of the tub, trying to mount the porcelain slope. It gained a little purchase with its flippers and ascended an inch or so – before encountering the point of gravitational resistance, and in slow motion, pirouetted around and splashed back down into the water. It paddled over to the other end and tried again beneath the taps, but to no avail.

Finally, it gave up, and became indolent again. Gingerly, I

drained the bath. The grains of silt and the gaseous smell slowly dispersed and I refilled the tub with clean, fresh water.

Its shell was clean and vivid now. Fine yellow and brown lines formed concentric shapes on bottle green. I sat down on the toilet seat and observed it as it floated there, unmoving . . .

Was it sleeping?

I slowly reached over and gently touched the shell with my finger. It was hard and soft all at once, just like a baby bird's beak.

Suddenly, its eye flicked open, its neck telescoped around and it snappered me! I whisked my hand back, but the miniature razors sliced away a tiny chunk of fingertip. It flurried feverishly in the churning water.

It bit me! My flesh tasted just like chicken. I held my finger under the running tap as it rotated triumphantly in the bath tub. Unwilling to listen, I clumped up my wound with toilet paper and left it alone in darkness.

After a week, the water stayed clear. All I had to do now was slaughter the beast, and drain the blood from its body. That morning, I went into the bathroom, quickly plunged my hand into the water and seized it by the tail. Its flippers flapped vaguely at the air as I lifted it up. It seemed to have given up the ghost.

In the kitchen, I pulled the thick tail far out of its shell, and positioned a nail at its nub. It gave a faint, half-hearted snap, before I drove the nail clear through the tail and into the wall. A thin, lubricant-like liquid oozed out. Holding onto the rim of the shell, with one swing, I chopped at its neck -

The cloven head dropped into the tray on the floor. The thick neck welled fluid, twitching about like the root of a torn-out tongue.

The head scraped about madly in the tray, still snapping at the air. I stared at it in horror for a moment as its fluids drained away, then rushed to the bathroom and retched into the toilet, over and over again.

It took all afternoon to pick away the flesh and the fat from the shell with my pincers. All the while, the meat seemed to softly shiver and pulsate.

The fat was waxy and yellowish, as if nicotine stained. I laid strips of it in a pan and heated them slowly until they rendered, before pouring out the clear blubbery liquid into a jam jar. I dipped a piece of twine in there, holding it steady until the wax became opaque. Placing the makeshift lamp on the table, I lit the tip with a match. It sputtered, and began to burn with a tall, swaying flame, like a willowy dancer turning slowly on a darkened stage.

I fried onions, and garlic. I put in the chunks of turtle meat, and slowly they began to spatter.

It was a quiet meal, in the end. The flesh was firm, not fishy in the least. But there was an unpleasant aftertaste, a burr at the back of my throat that grew stronger as I ate. Finally, it made me feel sick, and I laid down my fork, unable to finish.

The next morning, I ran along the English Kills to Newton Creek, up the steps to Pulaski bridge where it all oozes out into the East River. The scrapyard before me was piled high with waste, and behind it the glum river and the grey skyscrapers.

I took the shell from my back-pack, leaned over the railings, and hurled it out as far as I could – it spun through the air for a moment, before splashing down into the murk of the creek. As it started to sink, I wondered for a moment if I might suddenly divine some kind of symbols appearing upon it, as the famous Chinese Emperor had once been reputed to have down, but it simply sank and disappeared from sight once and for all. I stood there for a while, as if waiting for something, but there was nothing more to be seen, so I put on my backpack, and slowly walked home in the rain.

I live on Paumanok – the Island of Tribute. Grizzly bears once lumbered in the forests here. They stood in the streams, batting at salmon and biting off their heads. They stood in the shallows and scowled at the eels in the sound.

They are all dead now, to a bear – their skins got peeled off and cured, stitched into thick, cosy blankets to keep men warm in the deep mid-winter nights, when the island creaks and groans as if it will crack off from its moorings, drift away into the ocean and become lost amongst the icebergs.

But out in the night, out in the English Kills, the snappers float, inert and silent in the dark water.

They wait for their blithe prey to pass. Then their tongues extend and flicker.

IN 1992 THE SNES CAME OUT. FOR ME AND MY OLDER BROTHER A RITUAL STARTED.

WE HAD TWO CONTROLLERS, ALL OUR GAMES WERE TWO PLAYER: MORTAL KOMBAT, MARIO KART, ALL BATTLES PLAYED OUT OVER THE WEEKENDS.

"WHY AM I ALWAYS PLAYER 2?" I WOULD ASK.

"WHEN YOU'RE THE ELDEST, YOU CAN BE PLAYER 1."

OUT CAME THE PLAYSTATION, NIGHTS DISAPPEARED PLAYING TEKKEN, WIPEOUT, TWO CONTROLLERS CLICKING INTO THE NIGHT.

THEN THE XBOX, ANGRY YELLS OVER HALO. PLAYSTATION 3, COD, GUNS BLAZING TOGETHER, WIRELESS CONTROLLERS THROWN AROUND. LAUGHS OVER KILLS. I'M STILL PLAYER 2.

PLAYSTATION 4 COMES OUT, CUTE GIRL ACROSS THE COUNTER FLASHES ME A SMILE I HARDLY NOTICE AS I PLACE THE BOX ON THE TABLE.

"YOU WANT AN EXTRA CONTROLLER WITH THAT?"

"NO, I'M PLAYER 1 NOW."

Lazylegs
by Kate Smalley Ellis

I love it when you walk me to the door with no top on. I kiss your lips then both your nipples goodbye. I walk to the tube with bounding steps, smiling.

As I swipe my Oyster card, you feed the cat. I start down the escalator, you get back into bed. I wait on the platform and you turn over. The train arrives, you reach for the remote control. I push onto the tube, you rest your hand between your legs. Sweaty bodies keep me upright, you lie on your back. I stumble into a brief case. You close your eyes. I close mine. You stretch your arms above your head and point your toes. You flick channels, the doors open, I get off the train.

I walk past the crowds, full of sleep and suits, you walk past the sink, full of plates and last nights dinner. I walk past the commute, past the gates, past the exit, on to the street. You scratch and yawn and stroke the cat, he weaves between your just prickly legs, tail pointing towards your blue pants with a hole on the side. I pull your grey jacket tight around me. You fiddle with the fork lying in last nights Korma, all the grease on the surface now, no hiding in the cool air of morning. You scoop a forkful of crispy edged rice into your mouth, you chew slowly, pulling that face you pull when you've just done something you didn't really want to do, the face that you always laugh at on me when I sip the first sip of cider on a hungover afternoon.

I stride up the pavement. The sky is heavy and mauve, coming towards me, just about to split, a threatening smell in the air before the down pour. You are a sloth, chewing slowly now on a chunk of Peshwari, enjoying it's sweetness, thinking it would go well with coffee, knowing we've run out, too lazy to get some. I pull at my black skirt that's supposed to be my smart one but always falls down. You pick at your belly button, skin still warm from bed.

You go to the toilet, place your bottom where I placed mine, you stare at the cupboard that we put everything in, the Hoover spilling out. I push through the glass revolving doors, you hear the kitchen window smash. The cat speeds past the open bathroom door, you stop your pee mid-flow, your stomach lurches. I say good morning to the receptionist, turn to go up the stairs. You stand, slowly, slowly pull up your little blue pants, you stand still, breathing as softly as you possibly can.

All you can see out of the open door is some floor and a stray shoe. You hear footsteps, casual footsteps, confident; footsteps that don't think anyone is home. Strolling through our house like it's their house, peering into our bedroom, looking at our pile of duvet, jeans sprawled on the floor.

Maybe they'll just take the laptop and go, maybe they won't look in the bathroom, maybe they've got a knife? I jog up the stairs and wander to my desk, you stand inert, leg muscles tense. Your sleepy eyes are wide open now. I get to my desk, a post it is on the centre of my screen, I peel it off leaving a dustless strip. You look at the plughole in the bathroom sink, to the world map shower curtain, up at the spider in the corner, searching for an ally, for anything. I place the post it face down on my desk, find my phone and head towards the kitchen.

You hear them rummaging through our clothes, our books. You are partially crouched over the toilet, fearing fully straightened legs may cause a creak in the floor boards or your knees. Your breathing is speeding up. Your brow is beginning to sweat. I fill the water in the kettle, spoon out the coffee. You become aware that your phone is on the bed. You hope the duvet has enveloped it, and hope harder that I don't ring you, that nothing worth reporting has happened at work.

I pour the water into the cafetierre, the too much coffee fizzes under the heat. You scrunch your toes up, tensing them on the wooden floor, the spider abseils down the wall. The cat mews outside, the rummaging ceases, a plug is unplugged, a wire is wrapped and shoved. You hear more footsteps, footsteps made with heavy boots, a heavy person. You smell an unfamiliar smell, someone else's skin, a new sweat. Your eyes search for weapons, goosebumps rise on your belly. I get my phone out of my pocket, think of you at the door this morning, wonder if you're still in bed. You hear the kitchen tap turn on, noisy gulping. I plunge the coffee, pick up my phone, go to my inbox, read your last message, press to reply. Your right leg is beginning to wobble, your nipples are getting cold and hard, you feel very small.

The heating clicks on and you jump, the boiler rumbles into action in the distance. A cup clinks in the sink. I begin to type. You can hear humming in our kitchen, a deep humming, feet shuffling, then footsteps again, getting louder. I can't decide what to write, I put the milk back in the fridge.

You stare down into the toilet, then out of the door. You shiver. I pick my phone up again, decisive now.

I walk to my desk, phone in hand, press send. A bag is zipped shut, there is rustling, the footsteps become heavier, then silent. I sit at my desk, my soft chair squeaks.

You still haven't moved, the silence is broken by a muffled text beep.

'Get up, lazylegs. meet me for lunch?..x'

Great Uncle Ron
by Kate Smalley Ellis

Luce has me pinned down on her bed. My face rucks into the pillow as she tickles her hair along my spine then smears herself down the back of my thigh like a huge slug.

'Are you girls coming or what?'

Her body clamps tight over mine. Breasts to shoulder blades, feet hooked around calves.

'In a minute Mum,' her voice is still croaky.

I twist my head and stare at the door. Through frosted glass I see her mum just two metres away. The arc of her cigarette travels to her mouth and glows orange as she inhales.

'Leaving in twenty minutes, ok? Get downstairs now if you want any breakfast. And wear black.' I can smell her cigarette smoke like she's next to me. 'There's no time to take Chloe home, she can stay here if she likes. Up to her.'

'Ok.'

The door rattles.

Luce's full weight is on me, her lips are hot on the side of my neck.

'Didn't I tell you not to put stickers on this glass?' Her Mum's voice cuts through the door as if it's not there.

Luce bites at my ear, giggles. I concentrate on her bedside table:

on tea cups and chocolate wrappers and a bright red and yellow Mickey Mouse clock whose gloved cartoon hands shake with each tick. Luce pulses her hips into my bum.

I tense everything, try to block out the feeling between my legs. The door hinges creak.

Finally footsteps go down the stairs. I breathe out and Luce laughs into my ear. I can't help laughing too. She lowers the top of her head onto the pillow so her smiling upside-down eyes meet mine. For a glorious moment we're on a level, in it together. This is how it could be. I relax and her body sinks into mine. We fit together, breathe up and down as one.

Then she gets up, shoves my face into the pillow and begins pulling on clothes. I flip on to my back and beetle my legs to pile the duvet on top of me.

She throws her clothes on like a boy, tugging on an inside-out blouse head first then peeling it the right way round over her taut body. Though she's a year older than me, her breasts are neat and self supporting. She doesn't need a bra.

'What you doing?' I ask.

She tugs on a pair of black school trousers and zips the fly. 'Going to a funeral. You're coming.'

'What?'

'I told you.' She didn't.

I prop myself up on my elbow, 'Who died?'

'You can't ask like that. I thought you had manners up in the Manor?'

'I don't live in a man...'

'It's Great Uncle Ron. And I'm upset so you have to come.'

She goes to her wardrobe, grabs out a dress I can never imagine her wearing and throws it at my head. I let my arm drop as if the dress shot me down. My face sweats in the warm dark beneath it. I hear her fumble with shoes on the other side of the room. Then it goes quiet. I want to look to see where she is but don't dare. I want time to stop so I don't have to go to a funeral and pretend to her family we're just friends or the bed roll on the floor is really comfortable.

Slowly the duvet is removed and it lands on the carpet with a soft thud. I wriggle in the new cold, the dress still on my head. She presses the mattress either side of my waist and raises my belly to her breath.

'Luce!' A shout from downstairs.

She pushes on the mattress and snatches the dress from my face. She kisses me hard on the lips then pulls away before my eyes adjust to the light.

'Put it on,' she says, staring at my mouth.

I stand up and slowly squeeze my too big body into its new black confines, Luce watches.

Her Dad's car doesn't have that new plastic smell like my Dad's. There's a collection of old coke cans on the dash and the sour sugary smell clashes with the crammed ash tray. I've never been in a car with Luce before, it's like I'm an honorary member of her family for the journey. Her Dad sings along to the radio in a surprisingly good voice while her Mum does her make-up in the mirror with her mouth open. No one says much. Luce and her brother pinch at each other and push me tighter into the door. I feel sticky. When Luce is close I can smell myself on her. I open my window a crack but it judders noisily so I close it again. It feels like we're going the in opposite direction to my house.

The first time Luce spoke to me was after assembly in my second week. She was behind me and I'd overheard her talking to the boy next to her about how Mr Garnet used the geography store room to suck off Mr Harris and that's why it smelled so bad.

'Slut,' she said in my ear, bumping my shoulder as we filed out, 'I can see your bra through your shirt.'

'Whatever,' I said to her back. She turned and our eyes locked for a burning second then she smiled, flicked me her middle finger and pushed ahead to join the Stair Gang.

People in my year seemed to know who Luce was but hardly anyone actually spoke to her. She has this long face with eyes like caves and lips that are somehow both hard and full. She's shorter than me but stronger, lean like a greyhound.

The next night was Friday and I'd been left home alone with money for pizza and a stack of documentaries. Our house was still full of boxes from moving and the internet didn't work so I walked to the shop.

When I got there, the entrance was surrounded by kids smoking. I recognised a boy from the lunch queue where his friends had dared him to slut drop the vending machine. I kept my hood up as I passed. Just as I was about to open the shop door a scooter came right at me and braked centimetres from my leg.

'What the fuck?' I screamed.

The rider turned off the bike, dismounted and stood up close. After a second they took off their helmet. It was Luce, grinning. Her dirty blonde hair sculpted by the helmet.

'You nearly ran into me.'

'My bike must fancy you, soz'

'Whatever,' I pulled my hood lower.

I had to blink a few times to see properly under the shops strip lights. Luce followed me as I walked past the sweets and crisps to the magazines. I flicked through NME.

'Going up the Downs, want to come?' She grabbed the magazine and flipped pages without reading.

'What's there?' I said, stuffing my hands into my pockets.

'Hills. Should be called the Ups, I guess.'

The helmet she gave me smelled of dirty hair and old cigarettes. Blasting through the dark felt like a forcefield being blown away. I held onto the plastic handle behind me, clenching my fists tight. As we accelerated downhill the air between my chest and her back felt dangerous. One hand at a time I let go of the handle and gripped her waist. She adjusted herself to fill the line of space I'd left between us. I was scared she'd feel my speeding heart through her jacket.

She pulled into a chalky stretch of land on a golf course and cut the engine. We sat hip to hip on a mound of grass and looked over London. It was the first time I didn't miss it. The sky was a dirty orange. The grime from the city risen like grease on an oven hood. I tried to pick out the skyscraper at the top of Bishopsgate to trace the line to my old house. For a long time we didn't say anything but I wasn't bored.

The next morning she left a message on Facebook.

Luce and her brother finally stop bickering as the car crunches to a halt between a battered Transit van and a new Mini. Luce leans across me and pops the door open before the engine cuts. The building in front is concrete and stout with beige columns and purple flowers flanking the entrance. Her Mum says we're late, grabs Luce's brothers hand and leads us in. We walk in silence through a foyer and down a corridor lined with shelves heavy with leaflets, flowers and dust. Double wooden doors lead onto a room packed with dark wooden benches and old people facing a large shiny coffin decorated like a huge cake with flowers and ribbons that looks as if someone might jump out of it and throw rabbits or doves all over us. Luce's parents tip-toe to the front with her brother. She pulls me to the back where it's more empty. There's an old woman further along our bench snivelling into a frilly handkerchief. Her loose body shudders as she blows her nose.

Creases curve over my hips as I sit and Luce's dress digs into my armpits. The backs of my thighs stick on the shiny wood. Luce slumps, legs crossed out in front the same way she does in the canteen ready to trip up year sevens. She hasn't said anything since we got here and I wonder for the first time how well she knew her Great Uncle Ron. I try to catch her eye but her gaze is fixed ahead. It smells the same as the school hall in here: of wood varnish, dust and cheap perfume.

The coffin is the width of a hospital bed. Great Uncle Ron must've been massive. You'd think they could tuck him into a normal sized one so he'd have some dignity in death or something but then people who knew him might imagine his sides had been sawn off to fit, wads of fat lain on top of him like excess steak. There is a blue cloth draped over half of the coffin like a sarong. A framed photograph is nestled in the flowers. He looked like Ronald McDonald without make-up. Pale and menacing but jolly like he could lure you anywhere and get away with it, must run in the family.

Luce's mum scans the crowd to find us. Her coral pink lips are pursed tight, her eyes flit to Luce then linger on me for a second before flicking away. Luce nods as if she understands, her face morphing for a second into something almost kind.

A man comes out from behind a black curtain at the side of the stage.

'I like big butts and I cannot lie' is playing over and over in my head. I can't get rid of it because the man's trousers are stretched tight over a bulbous arse. I have to stop my head from bobbing to the tune.

'I like big BUTTS', says my head.

'Amen,' says the man.

'Amen,' say the people.

And the man begins to mumble the story of Great Uncle Ron's life: He was an absent father, a brilliant teacher and a bad golfer. A tiny hunched lady wearing a flowing black dress and a droopy hat says something about him being a third parent to her, that if it wasn't for him she would have been afloat in the world without a rudder. The woman along the pew blows her nose again.

Frail-looking people who cough and fidget are crammed into the front rows. A hacking cough reverberates around the whole room. Luce is watching them intently like she's making notes, she pretends to look at her phone but I see she's taking pictures.

'GCSE coursework', she explains.

I smile because I don't know what else to do with my face.

This dress is so tight on my armpits that I'm sweating and probably making huge marks that Luce will see when I give it back. I wish I could take it off but my jeans are in her bedroom. If I get Mum to pick me up from here I'll have to explain why I'm at a stranger's funeral and where my clothes are and why I lied to her about being at Ruby's the whole time.

Luce puts her phone in her pocket and drapes her arm over my shoulders. I try to imagine her doing this at school but can't. I shove her arm off. She scowls and rearranges her feet.

It's quiet now apart from the man who is speaking. His small mouth is deep set in his pink chin which wobbles over his tight collar. I wonder if there's a mark like someone's been strangling him with a thick piece of cardboard when he takes it off. I bet someone has been strangled with a piece of cardboard. You could just rip it up afterwards. No evidence.

A square man in a shiny grey suit reads a poem about bogs in a booming Irish voice and I stop hearing because out of the corner of my eye I see Luce put her hand down the front of her trousers. I focus on the stage. The man's gut hangs pregnant over his belt. I imagine it exploding and lumpy custard going everywhere and no one would notice what Luce was doing and I could sneak out and go home and sleep in my own bed and go back to wondering if I'll ever kiss anyone again.

I concentrate on a missed tuft of hair protruding from a crease in a bald head two rows in front. I can still see Luce moving in my peripheral vision. My dress seems to be getting tighter. The man on stage must've said something funny because a woman a few rows in front erupts with laughter. The bench creaks. Luce is holding the service pamphlet with Great Uncle Ron's face on it over her lap. The speaker is saying how the King's Head is never going to be the same without Ron and the crowd groans as Luce grunts. She uncurls her hand from her waistband and wraps it around my face. I inhale and my mouth smiles but I shove her hand away and sink down into my seat and watch the stage. Everyone stands up. If they turn around they'll see my face is guilty red. I slide along the bench away from Luce and run out, crouched down like at the cinema.

A mass of people are outside waiting for the next service. I weave through arms and handbags and suited shoulders, walking fast, heading for the distance. I turn to see Luce skipping out from the crowd like she's just won the lottery. Once I'm past the people I sprint across the graveyard. There's a yellow digger arm poised over a hole ready for the next dead person. I stop next to it. The hole's deeper than it needs to be. There's room for a coffin and for me to stand on top of it. I want to lie down in there, to feel the cool of wet mud sink into this dress and hug me then swallow me up and take me somewhere new.

The sun moves out from under a cloud and everything gets brighter for a second, a puddle of water glimmers in the base of the grave. I hear a crow but when I look up into the tree it's not there. I want to smear my sweaty face clean in the long grass.

'Get in and I'll follow,' Luce smirks between breaths, 'you can finish me off.'

She seems bigger than usual, buoyed up. I want to be air lifted out of her world now, to shatter her control but I can't take my eyes off her face. It's like she's got some magnet in her that sucks my brain in and I don't know if I like her any more but I don't know how to escape either and what if she tells everyone at school what we've been doing? What if she twists it and says I'm a pervert and I made her do all this stuff and she just wanted to see how much of a sicko I was and that I stink and I'm boring?

She's staring into the grave and smiling and I'm scared she's going to push me in. I back away.

She stands up straight and puts her arm around my waist like it's normal, as if we're a couple. I let it lie there. She turns to look at my face. I blink and she's still looking. Her eyes aren't so much like caves any more. There's something else in them, as if she likes looking at me. I look back. Our noses are a fist apart. My lips begin to throb and I have to kiss her and her mouth opens to receive my tongue and it's like there's a capsule around us and nothing else matters.

Back in the car her brother falls asleep and instead of being squashed into the door, I have enough space and Luce allows her body to rest on mine. Her hand slips between our thighs and she leaves it there.

Luce's Mum starts humming along to the radio and I can't help giggling. I think of her wide kind eyes and that soft 'Coo-ee' when she brings us cups of tea and biscuits, offers to make me a bed in the spare room or asks if I like veggie burgers.

'Reckon she'd be humming if she knew I could taste her daughter on my tongue?' I whisper.

LOOK CLOSELY.

YOU TELL ME MY EYES ARE BROWN. IN CANDLELIGHT, YOU LAUGH AND SUGGEST THEY MIGHT BE GREEN. I CLAIM THEY ARE HAZEL.

WE BOTH AVOID THE TRUTH.

IN THE SAFETY OF THE DAY, AS I SQUINT INTO THE SUN, THAT TRUTH IS FAR AWAY. BUT AT NIGHT, AS I LIE IN YOUR BED AND PRETEND TO BE IN LOVE WITH YOU, THEN YOU NOTICE. YOU TELL ME HOW BIG MY EYES ARE, AS I STRUGGLE NOT TO TELL YOU IN REPLY HOW DULL I FIND YOU.

YOU THINK ME YOUR PERFECT MATE. BUT YOU ARE MERELY A DISTRACTION. EASY COMPANIONSHIP. A WAY OF PASSING TIME AND THAT TIME IS NOW PASSED.

SO, LOOK CLOSELY. LOOK TO THE HEART. DO YOU SEE? MY EYES ARE BLACK.

THE EYES ARE THE WINDOWS OF THE SOUL AND MY EYES - MY EYES ARE EMPTY.

THE WINDOWS   LIAM HOGAN

Haar
by Ian Green

The beach was silent, fog drowning all noise and enveloping the dunes and sharp blades of marram grass in its folds. The house was perched just past the high tide line, a simple affair of worn wood adorned with coiled rope and nets and surrounded by row boats in varying states of disrepair. The lonely porch lamp failed to do anything of note, a soft blur of light engulfing the front of the house and nothing else. The boy stood just outside the open door, looking out. He was aware of his breathing, his heartbeat, the blood coursing through his body, the cold of the still air on his bare skin. They called it haar; a sea-mist thicker than any fog that would roll in with the tide and swallow the world. His father was asleep and the house was silent. He closed the door behind him without fuss or noise. The boy looked back, fearful of reprimand or sudden clamour, but stillness reigned. He stepped forward and off the porch, onto the sand.

As soon as his bare right foot made contact with the beach a guttural shriek sounded out from the depths of the night, a bestial scream. The boy's eyes widened, not a sliver of iris visible, only deep black pupils straining to discern something, anything through the dark and the fog. He stepped back onto the worn wood of the porch. His heart was beating so fast it felt like each thump would eventually just run into one long contraction, a drumroll turning to thunder. He held his breath and waited for the scream to come again, for something to come out of the haar and take him into the night. Nothing happened. Eventually he breathed again, great gulps of cold salty air, and he turned back to the house just as the door opened. His father was there. The boy looked up at him, and was afraid.

"What are you doing?"

The boy said nothing, just looked up at his father and tried not to show his fear. His father was big, the way the sea is big. He looked absolute. He was naked, and the boy glanced across his father's bare skin at the tattoos and scars, beautiful women and anchors etched in blue across his arms, the great whale that covered his chest half obscured by wiry hair. The man looked down at the boy and then out into the night. He looked angry.

"Light the lamps and light the fire," he said. He spat into the sand just off their porch and turned to go back inside. The scream stopped him. There it was, again, from every direction, close yet distant, a primordial wail and then... silence. A whimper escaped the boy's thin lips. The man turned back around and placated him, placing his giant hand onto a thin shoulder. Rough skin reassured the boy of his father's unknowable strength. His father would not let anything hurt him, he knew that, but still he could not slow the beat of his heart. They went inside and closed and locked the door.

The boy had lit the lamp on the windowsill and the fire in the hearth by the time his father returned from his room clad in thick wool, his driftwood cudgel hanging from a listless hand. The boy took comfort in seeing its heft and dark sheen, the familiarity of this long heavy wood his father took with him almost everywhere. Once the boy had asked to carry it for his father and within minutes of swinging it his arms were tired. The sea had turned it to something more like rock than wood. The faint light of the lanterns reinforced the boundaries between the fog and the house. The beach was an ocean, their house a lonely and bereft craft.

"Go and get dressed," said the man, and the boy ran to what was his room, all his. It might not have its own window, but he had his trunk and his shells and his bed and the picture of his mother, the only picture of his mother. He dressed quickly and kissed the picture and put it down gently. The colour in the photograph had faded, but he still remembered her golden hair, her pale skin. When he was little she would let her hair spill free and cover him, until all the world seemed to be golden and soft. He could not remember her face beyond what was shown in the photograph. The boy clenched his fists and did not cry and went back to his father and they sat by the fire.

"What was it?"

"The same… *thing*… as before. It does not have a name." The boy's father was staring out of the window, through thin glass into the opaque. The boy knew what it was. It had been years, but he remembered the marks its talons had left on the door. He remembered that the haar pressed tight against the window, the sound of feet running on sand.

"Will it come here?"

"Yes."

The boy remembered his mother, screaming, and then she was gone and only his father remained, holding him back. He remembered her reaching out to him from the haar, being pulled away by hidden hands, and then the screams. He had wanted to run to her.

"I wish mum was here."

His father stood and closed the shutters. He took two spars of wood, one short and one long from the store by the fire, and slowly wound one end of each in tightly bound rags from the sea-chest that sat behind the front door. The boy watched in silence. The man dipped the rags in the bucket of pitch he retrieved from the back porch and then left the makeshift torches leaning against the rough stone of the hearth, just out of reach of the flames. The shutters were all closed, and with the fire rekindled the night did not seem so grim.

"What are they for?"

"This… *thing* does not like fire. When it comes we will light the torches. I will go out and drive it away. You will guard the door."

The boy nodded. "If it will not leave, you must lock the door. Do you understand? If I do not come back, you must lock the door."

The boy did not answer. He went and sat on the floor near the fireplace. It was a rough fireplace, and a rough floor, but the familiar wood and warm haze made him feel secure. His father did not sound afraid, but the boy could barely breathe. If I do not come back, you must lock the door. What would he do, alone? The man sat in his chair and watched the boy. Slowly, he lifted his driftwood spar, worn smooth by tides and wear, and passed it to his son. The boy held it close to his chest. The house was silent, the beach was silent, and the world was mute. They sat until the fresh fire had burnt down to nothing, and the boy was asleep wrapped around the cudgel. The lamp still cast a pale circle of light, scarcely enough to see by.

Just then, when the calm seemed at its most absolute, there was a single knock at the door. The boy leapt up, tears already welling in his eyes. He held the club limply in front of him and mouthed empty nonsense words in his fear.

His father arose with the infinite slowness and grace of a rising tide, and went to the fireplace. He ignored the torches he had so carefully prepared and reached instead for the harpoon that hung above the mantelpiece. It was not a decorative thing; it was a relic of a past life; it had known the flesh of beasts before. The jagged barb glinted in the firelight and the boy's father gripped his harpoon, one hand wrapped tight around the worn leather handle, the other held fast around the metal shaft. The harpoon was taller than the boy. The man held it ready, not to throw but to stab, to gut. He looked at the boy, at the closed door, and then back at the boy.

The boy understood. He held up his cudgel and watched his father. The man went to the door.

"What do you want?" he said. His voice was louder than the boy had ever heard it before. From the other side of the door there came a whisper.

"Please…," a susurrus almost lost through fog and wood. "Please…," the voice repeated, sexless and ageless and pained. There was a noise of fingernails, or talons, gently dragged across the wood of the door. The boy began to cry. He crossed himself and began to silently pray, I wish it was gone, I wish mother was here, I wish it was gone.

"What do you want?" His father yelled. "You took her, it is done."

The boy looked at his father, who swore and reached for the door handle. As the door opened a gust of air blew out the lamp, and there was only darkness and silence. The boy stood swaying back and forth, his hands at his mouth.

He could see nothing.

The sound of a man falling to his knees; the words "I love you," said so quietly by his father in the dark; the sound of meat being torn and of blood spurting over hardwood floors. The boy leapt back and dropped his father's club, flailed in the dark for the torches by the fireplace. He knocked them to the ground with his blind grasping but finally he was holding one, yes. He thrust it into the dead fire and sobbed and hoped and prayed but it did not light.

He was alone in the dark. The boy fell to his knees and wiped at his eyes and listened. He could hear nothing at all, but after what felt like hours, he could see.

The light of the moon came through the window; the haar must have begun its retreat, or a gust of wind had cleared some fortuitous path. Only a sliver of the room was illuminated, a patch of floor between the boy on his knees and the door. He could make nothing of the rest of the room.

A figure stepped forward from the darkness to the edge of that pale moonlight, and the boy thought his heart would burst.

"Mother," he sobbed, as he threw himself forward, and it was her it was truly her. He went to her and she wrapped her pale arms around him, and cascades of golden hair buried him until it seemed the entire world was golden and soft. As he sobbed, she held him tighter and tighter and tighter with her pale arms and her red hands.

Laika
by Ian Green

I wake up sweating and panting for breath and for a moment I'm not in my bed, in my house. For a moment I'm back amongst the scent of citrus and pennies and I can see pale blue eyes. Sometimes the smell is citrus and pennies, sometimes it is worse things. The things that I see before I wake up are worse. There are words for those scenes, but no words I want to use. Eventually, every night, I calm down. Eventually, every night, I go back to sleep.

On the day I find the dog I eat soup for lunch, as I do every day. I alternate between cream of chicken soup, cream of tomato soup, and chunky vegetable soup. When I don't have soup for lunch, it's because something has gone very wrong. At three o'clock every day I eat a tin of sardines in olive oil- I prefer the brand John West, for no real reason. The name sounds reassuring. Every day I unpeel the tin lid with its ring pull and pick up each headless fish with my bare hands and eat it down in three bites. I do this over the sink, so oil does not drip on my shirt. My mother would not approve of this, but she is not here.

Every day after my soup, I read English poetry in the garden. I have six fat books of English poetry. Poetry from anywhere east of Berlin nauseates me, and so I play it safe. After my sardines, I turn on the television and sit and don't think until it is time for dinner.

After dinner I turn on the computer and I browse the internet, looking for distraction. Once a week I order my shopping to be delivered. I have not left my house and its gardens in years.

I am not an old man, but I feel like an old man. In my country if you are my age and you act this way, people know it's because of war. I left my country. I used my father's money to move to a place no one would know me but where I could speak the language: England. I bought a house with a garden deep in the suburbs of London, which was the only city I recognised the name of. The house is simple enough. The back garden has tall wooden fences on all sides and it is there I spend most of my time, when the weather permits. The front garden has a short metal fence at its front and a scrubby lawn. After my soup but before my sardines I am crossing the living room to collect one of the books of English poetry before I retire to the garden, to listen to distant trains and birdsong. English poetry, birdsong, sardines in oil: these are my vices. I glance out of the window and see the dog slumped against my front fence. It looks dead.

I put down the book and swallow several times, and then go to the window. It is definitely a dog, but not definitely dead. I step out of my front door and cross the garden to the front gate and go out and stand over the dog. It is breathing, just, and its eyes are closed. Its fur is matted and I can see the outline of its ribs under the fur like poles in a wet tent, pressing against the skin as if they are about to burst through. On its right front leg are a dozen marks, red and then black at the edges. I know marks like those. Those are the marks made when a cigarette is extinguished slowly on flesh.

I had my own dog, before the war. We were a family, mother and father and Laika and I. Almost every man my age in my country had a dog, and Laika was the most common name. Laika, like the soviet space dog. My Laika was a lithe mutt, brown speckled with white. When I said goodbye to my mother and father and they cried and held me, so proud of my uniform, Laika pressed against my calf and I reached down and touched her face. I don't know what happened to my Laika. As I turned to leave my father pressed a volume of poetry by his favourite poet into my hand, and said "Be brave my son, be good and be brave." He was a romantic.

The dog on the pavement is black, the size of a Labrador but with an indistinct face. No collar. She opens mud brown eyes and stares up at me, afraid. I kneel down and put a hand on her neck. Her tail thumps once and I manage not to cry. Aside from the burns on her front leg I can't see any injuries. She looks starved and scared but she is not dead yet.

"It don't look too well, Mr Mazur, d'you want me to call the RSPCA?"

I haven't spoken a word in twelve years. I don't look her in the eye- if I see a pair of pale blue eyes then the day is ruined for me: I'll retreat to my bed and lay in the dark until I cry myself to sleep. I can't risk seeing eyes in case they are blue. The voice is Mrs Donaldson who lives next door. She came to greet me when I first moved in and I explained with my notepad that I couldn't speak, and had a slight nervous problem and as such could not make eye contact. She waves whenever she sees me in the front garden, taking out my bins. I wave back. I do not know what her face looks like, but she has a plump body. I half turn toward her and shake my head, and point at the dog and then at myself.

"Are you sure, Mr Mazur?" she asks. She has an accent. I don't know where it is from. I nod, and lean down and scoop the dog into my arms. It whimpers, but does not try to move. I take it into the house and Mrs Donaldson disappears somewhere else. I clean the burns on the dog's leg and wrap them in a bandage I find under my sink. She lies still until I am done. I pat her head and she wags her tail tentatively.

You can stay here, I think, *I can give you food and warmth. I can do that, Laika.*

I ordered dog food that night, and dog treats, a collar and a leash and a dog bed and an engraved name tag with my address and LAIKA written on it, and it takes weeks but Laika gets big. I can't see her ribs anymore. Every morning I come downstairs to let her into the back garden and drink water and try to dispel the blue eyes and the lemons and the pennies and the worse things from my mind. One day, I must have ordered the wrong tin of John West's salmon. Instead of olive oil to pleasingly loll on my tongue and coat my mouth, a single slice of lemon sits atop the fish when I pull back the lid. I cry on the floor and you come and stand next to me and the tears seep through the cracks in my fingers and you lick them from the back of my hands and then I am hugging, hugging Laika, sat on the floor sobbing.

I want to say, *how did her hair smell like citrus, how did it smell so strongly?*

I want to say, *I'm sorry.*

I want to say all sorts of things about duty and responsibility and war but I don't believe any of them.

The next day we go for a walk, outside of the garden. I don't know my neighbourhood, but the internet has shown me a map, and the map says there is a park maybe a minutes' walk from the end of my street. We go, and you run and sniff at bushes. The wounds on your legs are scars now, covered in thick black hair. I sit on a bench and close my eyes and listen to the birds and you come back every few minutes and touch your face to my hands. When we go home I have my sardines, and it is past three o'clock. The sun is almost setting. We have dinner together and watch a film about racing cars.

That night I dream about the woman with the citrus in her hair. "Be good and be brave my son," my father said. In the dream I ask her the questions and she answers and I hurt her and I ask the questions again. The cycle repeats, endlessly. Her husband is gagged and bound and crying in the corner of the room. Blood smells like pennies. She smells like citrus. My commander tells me to ask again, to hurt again, to ask again. She is not the only one. It is not the only room where this happens, but I don't dream about the others. I dream about her, and her husband. I dream about washing my hands in the cold water of the old sink by the wall and making eye contact with the man in the mirror, at his crumpled face, at his pale blue eyes.

I wake up drenched in sweat and it smells of citrus and pennies and something is there, on my bed, and I scream and I lash out with a fist, and the dog, my dog, my Laika, whimpers and retreats to the corner of the room.

I am awake. I am not crying anymore. Laika stares at me and I stare at Laika. I go to the dog and I go to my knees and I take her in my arms and bury my face into her fur.

MORE OF UPSTAIRS HAS FALLEN DOWN.

SHE COMES INTO THE KITCHEN WEARING RICHARD'S ROBE. I AM TRYING TO WRITE BUT CAN'T. I LISTEN TO HER EAT.

I LISTEN TO THEM TALKING ON THE TELEPHONE. THERE'S A NEW PLANT IN THE BATHROOM. THE POT HAS CRACKED. I SWEEP UP THE WET SOIL.

HE SENDS HER FLOWERS EVERYDAY. MONDAY TO SATURDAY. ON SUNDAYS HE SENDS A BASKET OF MUFFINS, BREADS AND PASTRIES THAT GO UNEATEN AND STALE. I SIGN FOR THE FLOWERS, FOR THE BASKETS OF MUFFINS, BREADS AND PASTRIES. IF THIS WAS AMERICA, I THINK. IF WE WERE STILL IN AMERICA.

THERE ARE PLACES IN AMERICA, SO FLAT, YOU CAN SEE THE ROAD CURVE WITH THE EARTH. YOU CAN WATCH A STORM COME ALL DAY, AND MOVE INSIDE ONCE IT RAINS.

Pure Fields
by Anna Harvey

The room was white. So white it made Annabel feel sick. Lying on her bed she was saturated with boredom. She had been saturated with coke, now she was saturated with boredom. More like a vacuum actually. Sometimes over the last six weeks she had been able to immerse herself in the emptiness of boredom, floating there: a rock suspended in space. More often, though, she had felt restless, angry with the nurses and family that kept here at the clinic "for her own good", and at seventeen she had no choice in the matter.

She picked over the carrion of her old life: the squat, Jonty, parties, festivals, drugs, sex. It had been wall to wall fun compared to the rehab clinic her parents had locked her up in. For once they had swallowed their bitterness, bile born of an acrimonious divorce, and together contributed their various parenting skills to ruining her life (as usual). In her father's case this was money. He had paid for the clinic and diverted her allowance (£800 a month) into a bank account that her mother now controlled. Her mother's contribution was time. Pretty much constant supervision in fact. Her mother visited her in the clinic every day she was permitted and if Annabel refused to see her, she would sit stoically in the waiting room until visiting time was over, hoping, Annabel imagined, to provoke deep feelings of guilt and remorse in her daughter.

Today, Annabel had allowed her mother to visit, and her mother told her that she was to be discharged in three days time. Her initial euphoria at this news was swiftly drenched when her mother firmly informed her that her new home was to be with her, at the old family home in Hackney, London. This was clearly a cynical attempt to control her life, thinly wrapped in the soft tissue of love and Annabel was swift to shoot down her mother's attempts to convince her otherwise.

When the day came, Jon and Sadie, Annabel's father and mother, collected her in Jon's 4x4. Sadie only ever rode a bicycle, but for once she had to concede that only a 4x4 with tinted windows would do: especially when collecting your drug addict daughter from rehab. In the car, the strained conversation petered out to a thick silence, and they were all relieved when an hour later they pulled up outside a row of terraced houses, some with neat hedges or yucca plants in the front garden, and some with broken furniture packed tightly behind the wall. There was an awkward moment when Sadie asked Jon in, an insulting invitation for an old lion to survey his former kingdom, from which he had been so cruelly exiled. He politely declined and deposited his sulky daughter and her mother (he would never understand her) on the pavement, driving away with a sigh of relief, his duty fulfilled.

Annabel followed her mother into the house, too despondent to protest any more. The house was slightly cluttered but had clearly been tidied for her arrival. Her last visit had been at Christmas (it was now nearly Easter). She had stayed for vegetarian Christmas dinner and one night, which was the absolute maximum amount of time for which she could assume the role of daughter. Her mother's naivety really was mind-blowing, she thought, as she regarded the statue of Buddha that had pride of place in the hall. When Sadie had been mugged once on the way home from work, Annabel had felt almost glad, vindicated that everyone in the world was not worthy of love and compassion. Much to her annoyance though, Sadie had quickly and unwaveringly forgiven her attackers, refusing even to press charges.

"Would you like some lunch darling?"

"Ham sandwich on white would be nice," Annabel poured every ounce of vitriol onto the comment, knowing full well that her vegetarian, wholemeal mother would never have such a thing. Sadie just smiled a little sadly and got some cheese from the fridge.

The days ticked by unbearably slowly for Annabel, so much so that after a week; she began to talk to her mother out of sheer boredom. Also, in the back of her mind she had a plan to feign her full reconciliation to a life of mediocrity, in order to sooner escape, £800 allowance intact, back to the teenage theme park of her former life.

One day, over dinner, her mother made a rather surprising proposal: "How would you like to try horse riding?"

Annabel could think of nothing more ridiculous than herself on the back of a horse and laughed out loud. After a couple more days of hanging around her mother's house however, even the smell of horses seemed preferable to patchouli so she reluctantly put on some old leggings and her cowboy boots and set off with her mother on their bikes across Hackney Marshes.

The football pitches of the East Marsh were dotted with occasional groups of people and dogs, dwarfed by the vast expanse of grass and the giant headless robots that towered above them, carrying electricity to Hackney residents. It was a windy April day and the sunlight was young and sharp, playing on the white wings of the wheeling seagulls and making them shine like silver blades, their calls cutting the air above the faint, low rumble of traffic.

Annabel followed her mother along the side of the canal then they skirted the marshes until they reached the red bridge that crossed the River Lea into the nature reserve. Despite herself, Annabel felt exhilarated by the bike ride; the wind cleared her head, whipping her long auburn hair in and out of her face as the sun gently warmed her milky skin, melting her cares away.

They stopped on the bridge to catch their breath, although only Annabel was panting with pink cheeks, her mother being used to the exercise. Still on their bikes, they held onto the safety rail of the bridge and looked down into the fast flowing water. The bridge was a bizarre structure that had two large semi-circles of red metal extending horizontally but at a slight tilt to the left and right like wings. They were supposed to prevent accidents but had the additional purpose of providing a canvas for local graffiti artists and were covered in tags. Below, in the river, a green mane of reeds bent this way and that, as the water gently pulled them with its flow. The patterns they made were hypnotic and Annabel felt a twinge of loss for her old life. A small voice inside her head was saying that even if she could go back now, it would not be the same – something was lost. This bitter capsule of reality burst in her mouth: her parents had ruined her life forever. She turned to Sadie who was staring at the water, lost in her own thoughts and felt a surge of hate.

"Do you really think that riding a stupid horse is going to make everything ok? Going to fix your broken daughter? Well it's not. You and that loser that calls himself my father have messed me up forever so why don't you just let me go and self-destruct? Then I'd be no more trouble."

Sadie looked at her daughter's beautiful, angry face and was unable to stop the tears that sprang to her eyes. She tried to form the right thing to say but it was impossible, and the seconds ticked by like hours as her thoughts ran frantically down the blind alleys of her mind, trying to remember how to communicate with this young woman she loved so much but could no longer help. In the end she turned away and cycled on towards the stable, blinded by guilty tears.

Annabel was also crying, her 17yr old brain revolving around the disturbing truth that nothing stays the same. The dark, flowing river looked tempting for a moment, as she imagined her mother's devastated face if she saw her daughter floating Ophelia-like in the water. A surge of tenderness tore at her heart and her anger was washed away by forgiveness. Whatever mistakes her mother had made there was never any doubt of her love. Determined to make up for her cruel speech, Annabel followed the path in the direction her mother had gone.

After navigating a gate, she freewheeled down a gentle hill, winding between bushes loaded with creamy May blossom which fluttered to the ground in gentle flurries carpeting the edges of the path with confetti. This all went unnoticed by Annabel, however, as her eyes searched ahead for her mother. She felt a rising panic, similar to her 5yr old self's fear when she had run away in the supermarket and immediately regretted it. All that mattered now was that she found Mum, and she looked desperately for Sadie's red sweater and blonde hair ahead, but there was nothing.

At a junction in the path there was a signpost for Hope In The Valley stables to the right. Through the trees she could see some paddocks with horses in and a series of squat buildings with a tree-lined avenue leading to the entrance. As she cycled closer she saw with relief a flash of red as Sadie waved at her from the front of the building. They hugged and half an hour later Annabel was riding a large, brown horse.

*

As spring turned to summer Annabel spent more and more time at the stables, and after a few weeks Sadie let her go by herself, although she still kept a close eye on her. The horses seemed to calm Annabel and she found their quirky characters endlessly interesting and challenging. She had a natural talent for riding, but what she loved just as much was just being around the horses. Their beauty and strength drew her respect and when they showed her affection, or made her laugh, she felt special and privileged.

One horse in particular fascinated her. Her name was Gwyn, and she was a fairly recent addition to the stable. At first Gwyn wouldn't allow Annabel anywhere near her, lying her ears flat back against her head. In fact, the only person she would tolerate in her stall was a groom called Andreas. Annabel would watch Andreas as he soothed the nervous horse, always so patient and calm. Annabel had never heard him speak and he kept mostly his own company, seeming pleasant, but shy. She knew that he was from somewhere in Eastern Europe and some of the other volunteers (all girls) said that he had gypsy blood in him and was a horse whisperer. Annabel laughed at their wild speculation and dismissed it as schoolgirl fantasy, but couldn't help wondering about him herself.

The more she watched him with the mare, the more intrigued she became with their remarkable relationship. Andreas sometimes allowed her to help him, although he mostly communicated by nodding and smiling, but she did slowly get closer to Gwyn, until one day the horse allowed her to groom her and lead her out to the paddock without Andreas.

Walking with Gwyn down through the avenue of trees to the bottom paddock, Annabel felt a deep sense of contentment. She looked around her at marshes beyond the field, which had sprung to life in the last couple of months with a profusion of grasses, flowers, insects and birds. Every morning and evening, as she cycled to and from Hope In The Valley, she noticed the streams and river were now decorated with yellow iris and sedate bulrushes that grew taller than a man. Children who had collected frogspawn earlier in the year came back in red wellies and shorts to release the little frogs they had nurtured back into the water and pairs of birds fussed around their young, high in the trees, as they squealed for their food. Her daily trips to the stable made her a part of this natural rhythm, and she was carried along on the tide of the changing season. Each day that passed peeled away another layer of her old, chaotic life and new hope was born and flourished among the tall grasses and new leaves.

Annabel's dedication to the stable paid off in more ways than one, in that she was allowed, with one of the grooms, to ride the horses out on the nature reserve. A group of them usually went out on a hack in the evening, when the air was cooler and there were fewer people around. One Sunday evening, she led her horse out to see only Andreas waiting for her on Gwyn.

"Just us today? Where's everyone else?"

Andreas smiled and shrugged, enigmatic as ever. Annabel didn't press the point, as she was secretly glad to have him all to herself for once, hoping she could get to know him better. She mounted her horse and they headed down the avenue of trees at a lazy walk, soon turning onto the bridle path.

In the warm, treacly air little clouds of midges buzzed, suspended in bubbles. The noise of the horses' hooves on the path was regular and rhythmical, although each sound was slightly different: a crunch on gravel, a dull thud on earth, a soft thump on grass. It set a pace that seemed to slow the passage of time, the two horses and their riders in single file moving down the narrow path in the oily heat as if in a dream, stooping occasionally to avoid low branches. After a couple of hundred yards, the path opened out onto the marshes, becoming wide enough for Annabel to draw alongside Andreas and Gwyn. They rode in an easy silence, the grasses waving gently as the riders passed, bowing as gracefully as courtiers, and the leaves in the great trees rustled, whispering to the horses and their riders in a thousand voices as ancient as the earth.

Annabel felt an excitement rising in her stomach, up to her throat and down through her limbs as her hips rocked gently with the movement of the horse. When she was a child, she had loved to read fairy tales, completely losing herself in their magical forests and dark castles. How she had longed then to ride on a white horse next to a handsome prince and have the kind of adventures that always ended happily ever after. Those childish daydreams had made her feel as she did now, and the realisation was making her head spin. She turned slowly to the left and looked over at Andreas' face, serene as always, a still, cool pool of water into which she longed to dive and discover whatever lay beneath. She half opened her mouth to speak but didn't want to break the spell so they continued as they were, joining the quiet of the early evening.

Upon their return to the stable, Andreas dismounted first and held her horse as she swung her leg over its back and jumped to the ground.

"I'm glad it was just us today," he said.

His voice, so unexpectedly close, made her blush with pleasure, but she managed only to stammer, "me too", before he led the horses away.

Annabel cycled home with happiness practically spilling out of her, but it turned to shock as she reached the corner of her street to see a saw a familiar figure waiting for her. It was Jonty, her ex-boyfriend from the squat, and he looked angry.

"Where the hell have you been? You just left, no goodbye, no phone call, no email, nothing. We've been trying to get in touch with you. We were really worried."

Jonty's face was handsome in a child-like way and right now he reminded Annabel of a sulky adolescent.

"Nice to see you too." She smiled at him, refusing to let him dispel the lingering tendrils of her earlier mood. "Sorry if you were worried, but I had no choice in the matter. My parents came and packed me off to rehab. They took my phone and everything. There was no way I could have contacted you."

"You could have just run away." Jonty's face began to soften and tears appeared in his eyes. "I couldn't afford any food or anything. I was going to try to get clean, sort myself out, remember? But you left and my whole life fell apart. Thanks God I've found you again. When can you come home?"

Annabel felt the prising open of that familiar empty hole inside herself for the first time in weeks: the hole that longed to be filled with the substance of oblivion. A yearning for that metallic taste in the back of her throat, the smoke filling her lungs that was stronger than any other desire in the world.

Her hesitation riled Jonty. "What's the matter? We not good enough for you now?"

Annabel replied hastily. She didn't want a scene in the street. "Look, I just need some time to think yeah?" She held out a ten pound note. "You look like you could use a drink. Why don't you treat yourself? Give me your number again and I'll call you later."

Jonty mumbled, "I don't want your fucking money," under his breath but took it anyway and Annabel wrote his number on a scrap of paper from her bag with her eyeliner pencil. As he walked away she breathed a sigh of relief.

The summer languished on and Andreas and Annabel became good friends. He told her about his home in Serbia and his family in Belgrade, the scars of war still painfully visible as he grew up. He said he left because he was looking for something he didn't think he could find there, but he still wondered whether he would find it in London. Annabel hoped that would soon change.

His voice was gentle, with a slight accent, and when he spoke it was as if the words had more meaning than if they were spoken by anyone else: almost as if he was singing without music. He was always calm, though sometimes distant. It was easy to see why he was so good with animals, which he said he trusted more than people.

One cloudy August morning, Annabel arrived early at the stables, about ten to seven. She sat outside, shivering a little in her thin shirt and jodhpurs, when she saw someone approaching from the same path she had come down. The man was shuffling a bit but was definitely heading straight for her, and as he got closer she recognised Jonty. He looked terrible. It wasn't so much his unkempt appearance as his posture that was disturbing. He was twisted and stooped, like an old man, so much so that she shrank back in horror as he approached. As he attempted to smile at her he revealed teeth that were brown and rotting, but it was not a smile with any friendship or warmth in it: it was full of malice. She guiltily remembered the phone call she had never made. This was her fault: how he must hate her now. She felt panic grip her but her only chance was to try to talk her way out of this, as he was now only a few feet away.

She tried to appear casual. "Jonty! What a surprise! How are you doing?"

"Yeah," he croaked, "good, good… um… I er… followed you. Not being weird or anything… Just wanted to like… see you." There was an awkward pause. "So how come you're here then? What is this place? Some kind of farm?" Jonty sniffed and coughed, wiping his nose on the back of a dirty sleeve.

"It's a riding school. I'm working here… well, volunteering." Her voice sounded falsely cheerful and the words hung awkwardly between them. But Jonty didn't appear to be listening and was looking around. Suddenly he took a step forward and met her eye.

"Why didn't you call?" he whined, "You too good for me now huh? Look at you… so fucking fake. You left me; we had plans. I couldn't even afford a fix when you went. I couldn't get clean without help. I couldn't even afford a smoke. We had plans; I'd be alright now but you left me and look what I've become." His face crumpled with self-pity. "You left but you're all right. Look at you. You look fuckin' fantastic. I'm ill but you're like fucking Princess Anne."

Jonty's voice was getting louder and louder as he worked himself up into a rage. Annabel tried to soothe him. "Calm down Jonty, it's not like that. I want to help you out. I could get some cash together and you could get clean like you planned." She fumbled desperately in her pockets and pulled out a note. "Here, look, take this for now." She held out the twenty pound note to him just to try and get rid of him, but this time it wasn't so easy. He snatched it from her hand and began screaming in her face, forcing her back against the locked door of the school.

"You think you can buy me, you think you're so much better than me. You're not and I'll tell you what else: you owe me. We had plans and you're my girlfriend but you just scraped me off like so much shit on your shoes."

Annabel could smell his stale breath and dirty clothes. She had never seen him like this. His eyes were wide and bloodshot and spit sprayed from his lips when he shouted. She realised he probably was ill; seriously ill, and had lost all sense of reason which meant her only option was to run. She tried to dodge sideways but he grabbed her arm. She wrenched away but he caught her again. She began to cry with fear, as Jonty's face set hard like a mask. He wasn't shouting anymore but he was as white as a sheet. In an instant he pushed her hard to the ground as she screamed in terror.

"Leave her alone." The words fell around the struggling pair like rain on a fire. Jonty jumped up as if he had been stung. Andreas helped Annabel to her feet and without thinking she put her shaking arms around his neck and buried her tears in his shoulder. Over her head Andreas stared Jonty in the eyes until he dropped his gaze and shuffled away, muttering to himself.

That night, as she lay unable to sleep in her bed, Annabel listened to the rising wind outside. The unnaturally still air of the day had been disturbed by a series of loud, grumbling thunderclaps that echoed around the valley and now the wind was rising. Rain began to fall, a drop at a time at first, but soon in torrents, thrown against her window by gust after gust of wind. Lightning tore the skies in two, and Annabel went to the window to watch, half excited, half afraid. Below, the street and walls shone like polished, black marble, and the streetlamps weak glare showed arcs of light filled with bullets of water, beating down into the darkness. The longing to see Andreas was almost a physical pain, and she felt this storm might tear her away, house and all, like Dorothy in *The Wizard of Oz*, if she didn't lock herself into his arms again.

Her phone showed 4.30am. She knew that there was a chance Andreas would get to work early to check on the horses because of the storm. Dressing quickly, she slipped out of the front door, quietly manoeuvring her bike down the front steps. Rain lashed against her waterproof jacket, wave after wave, as she rode through the deserted, rain-blackened streets towards the Marshes and a seed of doubt planted itself in the pit of her stomach. Had she imagined his warmth? Maybe he had just been comforting her as any friend would. She could turn around now and wait until morning; see him at the stable tomorrow, and see how she felt then. For all her reasoning she knew that she would not be turning back. There was inevitability about what lay ahead, for better or worse: a fate that must be fulfilled or forever languish on a dusty shelf, unresolved and irresolvable.

She rode over the bridge and onto the Marshes. It was almost pitch black and she hadn't thought to bring a torch. The branches above her bent and cracked in the wind and the rain buffeted the leaves. Twigs and small branches were falling in her path, as the storm stripped the trees of any foliage too weak to hold on. Fear and panic began to creep up around her neck like the hands of a strangler. She was becoming a part of this storm, at the mercy of its elemental caprice, its winds threatening to rip her apart and scatter her to the four corners of the earth.

Ahead, she saw where the path swooped down under the road, forming a small underpass. She struggled to reach this shelter then sank down trembling against the wall while the storm raged around and above. She began to cry, gently at first, one precious tear following another at a stately distance until she couldn't suppress a sob that echoed into the shadows. She couldn't erase the memory of her parent's grim expressions as they had tried to hide their shock at their daughter's ravaged face and emaciated body, and her own feral screams as they bundled her into the car to take her to the clinic.

A loud thunderclap made her jump. She thought of the horses;

she knew they would be terrified. She got back on her bike and rode out into the storm. The sheer power of it made her gasp, but it was only a five minute ride to Hope In The Valley. When she arrived, soaked to the skin, the building was in darkness, but she could hear the horses inside and the occasional shout. The gates to the back were open and as she cycled round to the stalls, a white face suddenly appeared in front of her, almost causing her to fall. It was Mandy, one of the grooms.

"The electricity's down and a tree's fallen onto the roof of the stable block. We need to get some of the horses out. Come and help. It's just me and Andreas at the moment."

Swallowing her excitement at the knowledge that he was there, she threw herself into doing what needed to be done. The scene in the stables was chaos. The terrified animals had to be calmed, but every nerve in their bodies was telling them to panic. The next hour and a half went by in a blur. There was no time to think about anything except the safety of the horses, while the storm blew itself out. Once, Andreas put his hand around her waist to gently move her out of the way, and their eyes met. A moment of stillness descended, then there was the shadow of a smile and he was gone.

When there was nothing more for her to do, Annabel went outside and plumped herself down on the damp grass. Dawn was gracefully withdrawing into a turquoise sky and the sun gilded the edges of the few remaining dark clouds with an intense golden glow. Things that Annabel had known all her life, but never really noticed, the sky, the birds singing, the dewy morning air, now seemed ridiculously beautiful. What was even better was that they would be there again tomorrow, in a world where anything was possible and happiness was here, now. Smiling, she jumped up, took one last look at the climbing sun and headed back into the stable to find Andreas.

Blacklip & Tyrone
by Anna Harvey

From the train window, Tyrone could see into the back windows of the passing houses. Despite the veil of mist on the inside of his glasses, the petty squalor of urban life was all too obvious. Dirty net curtains looked out on neglected gardens with crumbling walls blackened by soot; it was the face of people's lives they hid from their neighbours. The only charm here was the residents' innocent assumption that their smart front gardens preserved a face of respectability, when in fact hundreds of commuters gazed at their secret shabbiness every rush hour.

Tyrone removed his glasses and wiped them on his scarf. He didn't have a ticket as usual and would need all his faculties working at full strength to jump the barrier at Camden Road. He felt a familiar nervousness arising in his stomach, causing embarrassing whining and grumbling noises. He stood swiftly and went to wait by the door, before the attractive girl next to him became an unwilling audience to his stomach's symphony.

An hour or so later he was biting into an egg roll in the café where he was to meet his brother and the angry stomach god was appeased. The fluorescent light was a little too bright. A familiar feeling of unreality began to seep into his surroundings and it occurred to him, as he sat behind the plate glass windows, that being in the café was like being inside a picture on the TV. Tyrone was used to his mind playing tricks in this way. He never talked about it and could control it, in that he could choose how far to allow a hallucination to unfold. It was as if the dream knocked at his mind's door, and if he was bored he would let it enter. Then, when it was no longer convenient, he would show it out and it would politely leave. He watched with mild amusement as the brown and vanilla coloured moulded plastic of the table and chair ensembles began to melt slightly like giant ice creams. The two other customers munched their way through plates of food in oblivious silence with a level of concentration akin to contestants in a game show on the million dollar question, while a tinny radio in the background made loud but incomprehensible sounds.

The door opened and a blast of cold air made him look up and see Blacklip walking towards him. As he weaved through them, the tables and chairs regained their rigid form and all the strangeness disappeared. Blacklip nodded at him with the hint of a smile and sat down. Almost immediately his phone rang and he silently answered it. Tyrone drifted off again but this time his mind was as blank as a contented cat's.

Blacklip had instructions from the boss. They were to go to an address near Regents Park and "collect" a car. Although they had a spare set of keys, it had to be said that this was not a strictly legal operation. The boss's brother owned a garage in Essex selling high-end luxury cars and every so often one would be reclaimed to boost profits. Only the insurance companies lost out so Tyrone felt no remorse.

After Blacklip had had his cup of tea, they walked down into Camden. It was a grey February day and the melting pot of youth culture that had drawn both of them here as disaffected teenagers was nowhere in evidence. Today's youth was presumably on lying on warm sofas in its parents' lounge; too cold for fishnet tights and safety pins today, thought Tyrone regretfully. They crossed the canal and Blacklip flicked his cigarette end into the black-green water to join the plastic bags and takeaway boxes floating there half-heartedly. After fighting their way through the throngs of eager tourists around the tube station they made their way up Parkway and soon the creamy houses of Regents Park replaced the Camden restaurants and pubs, facing outwards and impassive as sentinels.

The residence they were supposed to steal the car from had a conspicuously empty driveway, so they settled down on a bench a little further along the road to wait. After an hour or so the Aston Martin smooched past them smoothly as a ghost bride and after purring in the gravel drive for a minute or so it fell silent. Twenty minutes later, Blacklip had carefully unset the alarm and opened the door. The tan interior boasted thick luxury and creaked indignantly at the grubby, jean-clad bottoms parked unceremoniously on its seats. Unfortunately for them, the owners' daughter chose that moment to look out of the front window, and while she was not unduly concerned, she did shout, "Mummy, why are those men driving our car away?"

They were spotted by the patrol car heading east along the Euston Road and Blacklip felt the adrenaline kick in as the siren and blue light closed in on them through the traffic. Swearing and sweating he did his best to get to the next junction to lose them on the side roads but the traffic was heavy. Tyrone had started making little grunting noises as he always did in stressful situations, rising higher and higher with his panic, as their situation seemed hopeless. The police car was right behind them now and they could both see the pasty faces of the policemen set for the kill. In a last ditch attempt to escape, Blacklip jumped the lights, and as he accelerated down the short stretch of empty road, the sirens multiplied followed abruptly by a loud sound of crunching metal. As they turned off into the relative safety of the Kings Cross backstreets, they saw the pursuit car halted outside the fire station, the front end of it crushed beneath a perpendicular fire engine.

"That was bloody lucky." Blacklip was a man of few sentiments and even fewer words but he always hit the nail on the head.

After that they kept to the backstreets and were soon driving through the eastern suburbs of London towards Maidstone. Night was falling and the motorway was a confusing mass of moving lights. The sun was setting in the rear view mirror but Blacklip was immune to its pink and gold sighs. Even when the clouds were aquamarine with gilded edges he was unmoved. He had no time for beauty and beauty had abandoned him as a man who could not give her the attention she deserved. Predictably, this deep-seated personality failure originated in his early years. He was Tyrone's half brother, brought up in the same house in Hackney with the same mother, but he never knew his father. Tyrone's father was a shadowy substitute for a while but when he faded into the London underworld, Blacklip had stepped into his dirty trainers and from then on he and Tyrone were inseparable.

There were many theories amongst his associates concerning the origin of his name, or rather of the anomaly that had caused the discolouration on his lower lip. One rumour was that he had tattooed himself whilst inside a young offenders' institute, a theory made more believable by the clear evidence of self harming teenage years on the back of his hands. Another theory was that he was stabbed in the lip with a black pen at school in a fight. The black patch was a curious shape, not unlike a manta ray swimming through a pink sea, or a squashed kite flying through rose coloured skies. No one ever asked Blacklip directly because no one dared, except maybe Tyrone but he probably knew anyway.

Tyrone had witnessed most of Blacklip's troubled life: the abuse at the hands not only of his stepfather, but his mother also. The only time Tyrone had seen him cry (though he heard him many times) was when Blacklip had come to his mother covered in guilt-inducing bruises. Often, after a beating from his stepfather, Blacklip would hide away because any appeal to their mother would be met with violent shouting to the effect that *what the hell did he expect if he behaved like that* etc. etc. On this occasion, however, she had abandoned her usual wall of sound tactic. Instead, she had looked into his seven year old eyes and said, "We are born alone and we die alone. I can't help you." After that, Blacklip shut himself away with his pain and his love and neither had reappeared to this day.

They dropped the Aston Martin off in a remote place reached by a dirt track. A dim ramshackle construction, which could have been a hay barn, loomed out of the dusk and they parked in there, swiftly shutting the barn doors before they began the long walk back to civilisation. Once in Maidstone town, they made their way to the Long John Silver where they were to collect their wages and a well-deserved drink or two.

The pub was half full, mostly of office workers looking like oversized school kids playing truant in their crumpled suits and shirts. The dim lighting made the orange pine and swirly carpet a little easier to live with and the heat of the radiators made it positively atmospheric. Rather out of place in the corner was an older man in a camel coat, sitting up too straight and nursing a pint of lager.

Tyrone bought two drinks then made his way to the table where Blacklip was already filling the man in on their close shave. The man's face was set hard as granite but he nodded at Tyrone as he passed an envelope of cash under the table to Blacklip. Then he rose and left his unfinished pint fizzing lazily on the table.

Slowly the pub began to fill up and suits were replaced by more casual attire. Up at the bar, a young girl smiled flirtatiously at Blacklip, her eyes flicking imperceptibly down to the fifty pound note he held. She licked her lips in a parody of seduction and laughed, her pink tongue tucked behind her pearly top teeth.

He bought her and her more retiring friend some drinks and they joined Tyrone at the table in the corner. His tongue loosened by alcohol, Tyrone became quite a charmer and soon even Blacklip was laughing and adding the odd comment. Come closing time Tyrone ordered a taxi to take them all to the room they were staying in for the night courtesy of the man in the camel coat. It was a bedsit in a run down house on the edge of an estate. They had stayed there a couple of times before and it had depressed Blacklip so he opted to walk back and maybe find somewhere else to spend the evening. The pushy girl who had first smiled at him said she would join him leaving Tyrone and the shyer friend the taxi, the bedsit and the next few hours to themselves.

Out in the cold night the streets were fairly empty. There was a waning moon but no stars, only the sulphurous light of the streetlamps. In the window of the take-away customers waited hungrily for their food but the glass that separated them seemed to border a different world, completely foreign to Blacklip. He hadn't really wanted any company, but was too drunk to resist the girl's insistent clamp on his arm. He regretted his weakness now. She constantly demanded his attention, pulling him out of his safe, controlled inner room into her realm of shifting sands. He could feel an ancient beast rising in him, woken from its slumber. She bombarded him with information about herself, and questions, always questions that he was supposed to react to. What with? Desire? Sympathy? Indignation? A laugh? He had no idea. A rising hurricane of confusion blew through his mind and before he knew it the eye of the storm focused itself into an icy fury.

Without thinking about what he was doing he pulled her violently into the doorway of a shop and locked his mouth over hers, as much to shut her up as anything else. He saw the sudden alarm in her eyes as she realised the Pandora's Box she had thoughtlessly prised open was now unshuttable. He held both her arms behind her back with one hand and began to paw her body with the other but she turned her head sideways and managed to let out a scream, attracting the attention of two men on the other side of the road.

Anxious to prolong their evening's entertainment with some kind of sport, both men pricked up their ears, sensing an opportunity for a fight. With a whooping hunter's cry, one of them was on him in seconds. Released from his grasp, the girl shouted curse after curse at him, one minute encouraging her saviours, the next venting her anger. The two men, their kebabs abandoned in the gutter, kicked him senseless then left him where he fell at the edge of the road, his spilt blood mingling with the chilli sauce.

Tyrone awoke with a start. The girl (he had forgotten her name) lay next to him, dark circles under her eyes where her make up had run. He knew without checking that Blacklip had not returned and the sick feeling in his stomach was more than too much to drink. He quickly put on his clothes and left the bedsit, thinking of nothing and following the invisible silken thread that was pulling him with increasing urgency to where Blacklip lay.

The dreamy realm that Tyrone mostly occupied (except when

they were together) was where Blacklip was now drifting. He remained in the road unseen due to the parked cars either side of him and felt no ability to move. He wondered if he was dying. Dying alone. That was what Mum had said. "Born alone, die alone. Born alone, die alone." He repeated it like a mantra in his mind and felt the tears and the pain well up inside him pumping relentlessly towards the surface. But then, as time passed, another memory from his childhood insisted on his attention, pushing out the hurt and replacing it with a feeling he barely recognized.

He was four years old and his mum had been away while he stayed with "Auntie" Mary next door. This wasn't unusual in itself, but when his mother returned this time, she brought something with her. Auntie Mary took him into his mother's bedroom where she sat on the bed in her nightie looking wan. In her arms was Tyrone, newborn and wrapped in a white blanket. The light shone in the window behind her. Although it was only three in the afternoon the golden hour illuminated the room. It kissed the broken MFI chipboard and tired magnolia with benevolent compassion, giving its blessing and making everything blurry at the edges with gold dust. His mother and the baby glowed with Byzantine splendour and the whole world stood still. He approached her slowly but only saw the bundle in her arms. In the folds of white material was a small crumpled face the colour of a mushroom with blue eyes set in it like glass. His face was now inches from the baby's and its eyes widened in acknowledgement. Carefully he turned his head and felt the baby's breath in his ear. Suddenly, it made a cooing noise, and then a gurgle.

A voice from far away said, "Oooooo – he likes you. You're his big brother." But he wasn't listening to that voice; he was listening to the baby's. It was trying to say something. He listened harder.

"Vinnie."

He couldn't be sure. If only it would do it...

"Vinnie."

It did! It said his name. It spoke his name and it was the sweetest sound he had ever heard. Like angels singing.

The scene froze to a tableau in his mind, shimmering gold like in a heat haze and for the first time that he could remember he felt happy. It was as if his life had been eclipsed by a shadow that had just passed on.

In a rush, his mind replayed his life like a speeded up film but not as it had seemed at the time. He saw his hurt and his anger and all the bad things that had happened from the outside and felt a deep desire to help himself. It took him a few seconds to work out what was happening. He was seeing himself through his brother's eyes. Every event in his life where Tyrone was present had seemed to work out in his favour. From narrow escapes to wins on the horses, Tyrone was his lucky charm. He made things go his way, but he had just never realised it until now.

Tyrone was running, searching while his guts were almost bursting with panic. It didn't help that Maidstone had taken on a degree of strangeness. Although the streets should have been familiar, they suddenly looked foreign, and the more he doubted himself, the worse it got. He tried to banish the monsters his mind was creating but this time they wouldn't leave. The shadows looked like people, sinister and watching, ready to trip him up or rob him or worse. His ears began to fill with a strange singing noise that almost formed words but not quite and he could no longer feel his feet.

He could see a cloud further up the road. It was forming slowly and getting larger and denser, like a swarm of bees. He ran blindly towards it, even though it frightened him. A woman crossed to the other side of the road in alarm as he ran up it, his eyes rolling like a lunatic.

At first he couldn't see Blacklip in the darkness between the cars, but he felt he was there instinctively. As he touched his brother's bloody face he let out a sob. His eyes were closed.

"Vinnie," he whispered, his voice caught in his throat.

"Vinnie…………. Vinnie……………….Vinnie."

Tyrone was crying now. He looked around for help but although he didn't remember being on a hill, the ground seemed to fall away like a cliff. He had the feeling they were floating away from the earth. He closed his eyes and clutched his brother's jacket with both hands, the fear of separation cutting through his confused mind. His hand felt a hard lump and he remembered the phone. With a glimmer of hope he opened his eyes, fumbled for the mobile, dialled 999 and blacked out.

At the hospital, Vinnie woke up after a day or so with Tyrone sleepless by his bedside. He had suffered serious internal injuries and his face was pretty mashed up. The brothers barely spoke in the hospital room, their minds too full of the common thought that if they got through this, things would be different. Nursing staff and doctors came and went but Tyrone spent every possible second with Vinnie, willing him better. Spring broke and as the days became lighter Vinnie was able to walk with Tyrone to the small patch of grass at the rear of the hospital with its smattering of daffodils. The day he was discharged, they sat there on the little bench in the sun. Tyrone had found a flat in a village near Maidstone with a workshop underneath; he had been doing some thinking; making some plans; calling in some debts. Vinnie thought it sounded like a good idea, grateful for his brother's lead.

They set up a car mechanic business together in Kent, which

they were to run until they were outrun by old age. In their spare time, they fished at the reservoir or the river, and as the years passed, Tyrone's strange perceptions became less vivid; or maybe he just stopped inviting them in. In direct proportion to their decrease, Vinnie came to love the light at sunset or sunrise, its beauty striking him more and more. The long, slanting rays of the sun would reflect off his brother's fishing rod and break into a thousand diamonds on the water, collecting, and then bursting like stars when the writhing body of a trout broke the surface. The black mark on Vinnie's lip had gone, pummelled out of existence, but no one ever dared to mention this and no one ever called him Blacklip again.

WE LOST MY BROTHER IN A GAME OF HIDE AND SEEK ONE CHRISTMAS. IT'S BEEN FOUR YEARS NOW; WE'VE LOOKED EVERYWHERE.

MY PARENTS TRY NOT TO SHOW THEIR DISAPPOINTMENT IN ME, BUT WHENEVER WE PLAY HIDE AND SEEK NOW THEY ALWAYS GIVE ME A LOOK WHEN THEY FIND ME, AS IF TO SAY, "YOU'VE REALLY LET THE FAMILY DOWN."

HIDDEN CRITICISM   DAVE CLARK

The Boy Who Bit His Nails
by *Max Sydney Smith*

1.

The boy sits at the table, biting his nails. They have finished dinner and his father is talking to his mother.

The boy moves his hand round to bite the side of his thumb. His mother glances over.

"Stop biting your nails," she says.

"Are you listening?" His father doesn't like being interrupted. She drags her eyes back to him.

2.

Who are these people? Let me tell you a little about their lives. The kitchen is on the ground floor of a large, Victorian terraced house in an expensive part of North East London.

On the weekends, the boy's mother and father sit around tables in houses similar to their own, eat organic meat, drink moderately priced bottles of red wine and discuss politics. They discuss the electability of the Labour Party leader and catalogue all the things that are wrong with free schools.

The boy's father is something of a star at these events. He writes for a leading left-wing periodical and is a great talker. He is talking now about his recent article.

"The language of advertising is purely reflective," he says.

He waves his hand lazily in the air. His plump belly rises and falls under his sweater.

"It reflects us back to ourselves as we would like to be. Such that, when we buy, we are buying an illusion of ourselves. And when we consume, we are consuming ourselves."

The boy's mother nods absently. She is thinking about the boy's nails.

The boy's mother is not a star at the long dinner parties of North East London. She is a social worker.

Her job has not required her to cultivate grand narratives of the future of the Left. She has small stories. She has stories about bruised, pale mothers peering round door frames from dark hallways, about absent fathers and forgotten dirty nappies left on the boil. The people in her stories are nameless, because of client confidentiality.

People listen to her out of a sense of obligation. They know they are supposed to care about the people in her stories. They are the *raison d'être* of the Left. But they would rather talk about deconstruction, or what Morales has done for the pueblos of Bolivia. They cannot smell the shit under their noses.

3.

The boy kisses his parents good night. Climbing into bed, he can hear the sound of raised voices. His mother's voice high and fast; his father's deep and slow. He stares into the darkness. He can taste the chalky dryness of his nails.

Don't bite your nails, she said. She should have listened. If she listened, even pretended to listen, they would not be shouting now. Sometimes the boy tried to listen, but his father used words he didn't understand. He never talked about real things. It was always ideas.

His fingers hurt, but he cannot move except to bite. The biting and thinking are locked into each other and he does not have the will to break out. He bites a bit more, and a bit more.

4.

Later, the boy's mother comes to his room and sits on the side of the bed. In the dark, she cannot see what he has done. It is only when she reaches out to touch him that she realises the sheets are wet and something is wrong.

She stands quickly, steps across the room and turns on the light.

The boys head is buried in his shoulder. It is twitching. The sheets are dark red. She goes closer, peels back the sheet and screams.

The boy hears her but does not look up. He cannot.

The boy's father is in the doorway now, holding his toothbrush, blinking, adjusting his spectacles.

"What's the matter?"

The mother does not turn. She is looking at what is left of the boy's arm: the licked clean white of the humerus. She is holding her hand under her nose to hide the tangy copper smell of blood.

The words seem to the boy to come from far, far away.

"He is eating himself," he hears his mother say.

The Heart of Sunday Morning
by Max Sydney Smith

1.

"Jimmy," Omar hisses.

Omar is perched on the edge of the bench. He is leaning forward, drumming his fingertips together.

But Jimmy does not respond. He is sitting cross-legged on the path, gazing listlessly at a couple playing on the tennis courts. I don't know if they are a couple but they look like one: a man and woman, both in their late twenties, both with good skin. There is something uplifting about them, Jimmy is thinking, about the way they have come out at ten in the morning on a Sunday with their rackets and tubes of balls. He imagines tennis is the solution to some problem. He imagines they read about the importance of quality time, of a shared hobby, in a self-help book about relationships. He watches the couple run backward and forward along the baselines. The grunts and thwacks of the rackets as each hits the ball are the only sounds in the park. A relationship teeters on the netting. Love, Jimmy thinks, is hard, unglamorous work. But brave and beautiful work, he thinks, a life's work. Jimmy is a romantic.

I hope you will like Jimmy. I hope you will like Omar too.

Omar is not interested in the tennis players. He simply wants to get Jimmy's attention.

"Jimmy," Omar hisses again.

"Yeah. What?"

"It's winding down here."

This is an understatement. George is lying on the grass in his greatcoat, asleep. Dominik is sitting on the bench, his beard dropped to his chest and Rosa is resting one rouged cheek against his shoulder. They are both asleep. Celia has walked off into the stretch of green to the south of the park to be alone, and is now picking up, breaking and discarding sticks.

This is what happens, Omar thinks, when people take ketamine. Jimmy suggested it. It will help us level out from the MDMA, he said, and Omar wrinkled his nose and entreated them not to take it but they took it. Omar is not a believer in introspection on the weekends, and ketamine is an introspective drug. It is a horse tranquilliser. Not for Omar the deep k-hole, the tunnelling down into his own mind, not for Omar the immobile navel gazing, the silence. Omar prefers the euphoric, tactile high of MDMA, which is why he, alone now, is wide-eyed and jittery with excess energy. Omar wants to be nestled at the heart of a party, and the party is not here.

He looks left and right, up and down the path, quickly. "You wanna go to a party?"

Jimmy blinks.

"Wha? Now?"

"Yeah, now or like soon. I mean we might as well go now."

Jimmy processes this. Slabs of white cloud slide across the rows of low rooftops.

"C'mon. You're still with me, right?" Omar says, "S'dead here, but we wanna dance we want to be around people and there's this party we can go, just the two of us."

Omar does not want to go to the party alone. If he goes alone, he thinks that somewhere between here and Shoreditch High Street station, he might lose his appetite for the party. This is what he is most afraid of.

"Where is it?" asks Jimmy.

"Shoreditch."

Jimmy winces. This is further than he was expecting. It is maybe a thirty minute journey, but this is a long way for someone who is not convinced that, if they try to stand up, they will be able to.

Jimmy is the only one who might be persuaded, thinks Omar. "C'mon," he says. He boogies with the upper half of his body, making little circles in front of him with his fists, like a child pretending to be a train and snaking from side to side. Poor Omar, there is something thin about his energy now.

They have just been to a party. There were fifty or so people in some flat nearby, jostling in the corridors, in the galley kitchen, squashed into window sills. But now they were all gone and it was just the six of them on Hackney Downs, under the sun. Jimmy had not imagined there could be another party. He is suspicious.

"I dunno man," he says.

Jimmy is at the crossover point between being high and tactile and the aching aloneness of the comedown's serotonin and dopamine drought. What he wants is a body to hold. Not any particular body, just some body. Preferably a woman's body, but no woman in particular. Ideally he wants to touch a woman's skin, the soft skin at the top of the arm or the breast or the stomach.

Of course, it is hard to orchestrate this situation without sex coming into it. In Jimmy's experience, by the time he is resting his cheek against the cool of a woman's areola, sex has either happened or there is some expectation that it is about to happen. Jimmy is not averse to this. Not at all. But his actions are not primarily sexual. No, he is not predatory in this way.

But on Wednesday, he will have recovered from his comedown and he would not want this woman around anymore. And next Saturday, it will all happen again. Oh, Jimmy knows he cannot expect this. Being with a woman is not a part time thing, a Sunday to Wednesday thing. He cannot expect this without putting in any of the hard work, and this is why the tennis players, who are working so hard at love, are now making romantic Jimmy feel especially alone.

I like this about Jimmy. I like that he is so clear about what he can expect.

Jimmy looks around at the group. Rosa is with Dominik and Celia is untouchable. She has said this to him before.

"How many people are at this party?" he asks.

"Fifteen or so," Omar says.

"And people are dancing?"

"Probably. Yeah. It's my friend Sean's party."

Jimmy thinks. At worst, he will dance for a bit and then curl up on a couch beside someone, even a guy, which is all there is for him here. And at best, there will be a girl.

"All right," he says, "Let's do it."

Omar punches a fist in the air like a disco dancer.

"All right!" he says.

Omar is happy. He was hoping to end the night at Sean's. Sean is beautiful. All of Omar's other friends seem so straight beside Sean. Even the ones who aren't straight seem straight, too uptight or too crass.

2.

They follow Omar's phone to a nondescript door set into a wall on a side street several minutes walk east of Shoreditch High Street station. The door is open. Jimmy follows Omar in. There is a short, dark corridor which opens out onto a warehouse floor.

They can hear the throb of bass from a door at the back. Omar leads Jimmy between the easels, the large wooden frames for canvases, the paints, a sewing machine, a cardboard box jumbled with cameras and camera bits and other bric-a-brac. Through the door is a smaller room. A man is standing in front of two turntables, between stacks of speakers. He turns and smiles briefly, but does not take off his headphones. Omar recognises him but can't remember his name. They have only ever crossed paths before at this nameless hour of the morning.

Omar looks up. There are feet protruding from the edge of a mezzanine. Sean must be up there, Omar thinks. He is beginning to feel that he might, perhaps, have oversold the party to Jimmy. He dismisses the thought. People make their own fun, and their own choices. Omar is strong like this. It is not easy. I know many people who want to be as strong as Omar.

He climbs the steps. The mezzanine is covered by two double mattresses, upon which are draped a dozen men. Sean is indeed sitting at the far corner. He has one arm round Kieran and one round some man Omar hasn't met before.

"Sean!" cries Omar.

Sean raises a finger and smiles wanly. Is that all I get, Omar thinks, a finger and a half smile? Yes, even strong Omar is a little hurt. So he does what only a certain kind of person would do to save face in this situation: he acts as if the only reason Sean was not more effusive was because he, Omar, was so far away, and he begins to clamber over the bodies towards him.

Jimmy has sat on the corner of the mattress closest to the step ladder, and is observing the group. They observe him. He has already made two conclusions: there are no girls and no one is dancing. This is not a party, Jimmy thinks, this is a gay after-party.

"Hey," he says to a man with a tattoo of a dolphin on his forearm.

The man smiles but says nothing. The man beside him, whose arm is slung across the man with a dolphin tattoo's back and who is resting his forehead on the man's shoulder, looks up at Jimmy for a moment before slumping back. He does not smile. In fact, his eyes are ever so slightly unfocussed.

Jimmy is not aware that his face, too, looks somewhat slack and disorientated. This is partly because the ketamine has frozen his facial muscles but it is also because most of his attention is directed inwards.

He is trying to explain to himself why he does not feel comfortable. It is because he is straight, he thinks.

Jimmy turns the situation around, for this is how he was taught to be liberal. The inverse situation would be for Omar to turn up to a straight after-party: six straight girls and six straight guys, in each others' arms. And that, Jimmy realises, wasn't unusual at all. In fact, Jimmy is pretty sure that Omar had been the only gay person at the party they were at before and there were around fifty people at that party. He was one in fifty! This seems incredible to Jimmy now. There are so many straight people in the world, he thinks.

This is a satisfyingly liberal conclusion, but Jimmy still feels excluded. The problem is that most of the men are not talking, only touching. But why, Jimmy thinks, should he not touch someone? Why does touch have to be sexual? Can it not be, in this instance, simply fraternal? Yes, touch, Jimmy concludes, transcends sexuality.

So lonely, liberal Jimmy reaches out and puts his right hand on the nearest leg, just below the knee and his left hand on the thigh just above the knee. The leg belongs to the man with the dolphin tattoo. The man repositions himself, moving away from the wall and stretching his leg so Jimmy's left hand cannot help but slide further up, towards the man's crotch, and because this man has moved, the man with the slightly out-of-focus eyes is also forced to move, which causes a further ripple of limbs across the mattresses. Because it feels natural now, because he doesn't want to not do it, because the drugs have unlocked in him a desire to touch, Jimmy begins to stroke the man's leg.

3.

This story is not about drugs. It is about love. If this story was about drugs, and you did not take drugs, perhaps you would feel uncomfortable. But that is not my intention at all. No, it is the reasons people take them or do not take them that are interesting. It is the reasons that are universal. Let me explain.

Some people reject drugs on ethical grounds. They say you should not buy them because they are illegal and no one is above the social contract or you should not buy them for the same reason you should not drink coffee that is not Fairtrade, because of the morally dubious nature of the supply chain.

Omar and Jimmy are not ethical people. They are not bad people. Sometimes they give change to homeless men. They do good deeds which fall in their way to do, but they do not go out of their way to be good. I think a lot of people are lazy like this.

Perhaps you are like this. I do not mean to disparage Omar and Jimmy, but they believe in nothing. I understand this. It is hard to see how small decisions impact on larger issues. It is an act of the imagination and of empathy. It is a great act of love. But Omar and Jimmy are not capable of this kind of love.

Other people say it is risky to take drugs. They say Omar and Jimmy take them because they are young men, and like so many young men, they have a diminished sense of their own mortality. Omar's father would often say this to him. It's not that dangerous dad, Omar would reply, it's less dangerous than crossing the road. This, Omar's father would dismiss as facetious and self-serving. It is about minimising risk categories, he would say. Omar's father had worked as an accountant at KPMG for over a decade and knew all about risk categories. Omar's father was right to respond to Omar in this way.

But I do not think Omar believes what he says to his father. I think Omar and Jimmy do understand the risks. Perhaps they are even more aware of their own mortality than these other people. Because why else are they still awake, desperate to scrape every last scrap of excitement from the barrel of the night? Why else are they refusing to give in to sleep, to the little death?

Some people have a more existential problem with drugs. Look at Amelia, for example, who took Jimmy aside at the party earlier.

Jimmy, she said, I liked you before tonight. I liked you when you were that honest, curly haired, Irish boy. But I saw you take drugs and now I think you're a coward. Taking drugs is an attempt to avoid one's freedom and responsibility. It is not only a falsifying rationalisation for one's existence, but also a form of futile hope: for there can be no ultimate fulfilment, no final [lasting] escape from the human condition in this direction besides death. Amelia was a large faced girl, the sort who baked her own cakes, regularly. What

I'm asking you Jimmy, she said, clutching her white wine spritzer, is what are you escaping from?

Jimmy did not know that Amelia had taken a BA in Western Philosophy or that this was almost a direct quote from Being and Nothingness, an essay by Jean-Paul Sartre. He only knew that Amelia evidently had considerably more fire power in this arena than he did. He did not know what to say.

So he tried to touch her. Bewildered, boyish Jimmy reached out and put his hand on the side of her waist, just above her hip and gently, ever so gently, edged her towards him. He-ey, he said, imploringly. But Amelia smiled the way a mother smiles at her baby when it shits into a freshly changed nappy, patient and placating, and carefully removed Jimmy's hand while maintaining as little physical contact as possible.

I think this shows that even honest Amelia was escaping. She was escaping behind all the other stuff that sits between people, the little vanities, the silent, iterative negotiation of what is appropriate, the power plays, all the stuff that drugs clear out of the way. Maybe you would even say that Jimmy is being more honest than Amelia, because both are lonely, and only one is reaching out.

For Omar and Jimmy, for lazy, mortal, honest Omar and Jimmy, drugs bring to the surface an awareness of their aloneness, a hunger for touch, for love. I do not want you to dismiss this. No, I do not want you to be like Amelia and dismiss the lovelornness of Omar and Jimmy as false. It is not as developed as the sober love that brings a couple out to the tennis courts on a Sunday morning but it is just as real. And anyway, Omar and Jimmy do not even know how to play tennis. They are trading in all that they are able.

Maybe when you began this story you thought it was unnecessary or hackneyed or showy to write a story about drugs. Maybe you even thought it was immoral. But now you realise drugs are simply a prop, like tennis. Now you realise this story is actually about love.

4.

"Hey."

Jimmy opens his eyes. Two guys sitting in the middle of the mezzanine have turned to him.

"Hey," he says.

"Do you like to give head or get head?"

"Wha?"

"I said," and the guy leans in closer, "Do you like to give head or get head?"

Jimmy thinks about this.

He had assumed they knew he was straight. He had assumed they had worked it out from the way he dressed, or walked, or the way he was sitting awkwardly on the corner of the mezzanine closest to the ladder. But then, on the other hand, they might legitimately have asked themselves why he was here, sitting beside them, at this hour of the morning, at this particular after-party, stroking the leg of the man with the dolphin tattoo if he was straight. Yes, they might legitimately have asked that.

The best thing, Jimmy decides, is to answer the letter and not the spirit of the question. To answer the spirit of the question would immediately exclude him. They would lose interest. They might, he worries, ask him to leave the party.

"I like to get head, I guess."

"Huh," the guy turns to his friend, "And you?"

"I like to give head," his friend drawls. He does not take his eyes off Jimmy.

The first guy pokes his friend in the chest with his index finger and pouts.

"I am so on your page."

He turns back to Jimmy. They are both looking at him now. Below them, the man with the headphones changes a record on the far turntable.

Jimmy looks carefully at his hands. He concentrates on stroking the ridge of the shin and squeezing the small recesses just below the knee cap. He feels awkward. Poor Jimmy. His notion of fraternal love is perhaps too nuanced for this stretch of the morning.

Why do guys send out such mixed signals? This is what Omar is thinking. He has been out with Sean a few times now and each time they had got on. One time, at an after-party similar to this one, they had really got on.

So when Sean messaged him earlier saying he should come to Shoreditch, Omar had been hopeful. Yes, he would not have admitted it to Jimmy, he had not even articulated it fully to himself, but he had been hopeful.

But now Sean is disinterested. Omar has clambered over and they have not made room for him. He is sat awkwardly in the middle of the circle, facing them. There physically isn't enough room for Omar to curl up beside Sean, not with Kieran sleeping on his right and this other guy on his left, this other guy with the fucking nineteen eighties Doc Martins plus dirty white wife beater look. Who even is this guy, Omar wants to ask.

Omar watches Sean talk without hearing a word. He pictures Sean as a king holding court, a vain, preening king and they are all here for him and he will choose one of them. Omar wants nothing to do with it. He will not wait to be chosen. Yes, Omar is applying his critical faculties, his venom, to Sean. Omar is dismantling Sean to protect himself. But this is the beginning of a lie, because Omar is only here, on the mezzanine, because he wants to be chosen.

He clambers back to Jimmy. There are two men sitting in front of Jimmy, as if in conversation with him, but no one is saying anything. Jimmy looks up.

"Hey Omar. We were just saying" - he gestures to the two men - "about head. Do you like to give it or get it?"

Omar is surprised. He thinks maybe Jimmy is taking the piss out of him. He does not understand that Jimmy is pretending the question is not sexual. Yes, little lies have crept into both of them now.

"Fuck off," Omar says.

They sit in silence for a moment. Omar picks at the bobbles of cotton on the mattress.

"Omar," Jimmy says, "Do you want to go?"

"What? We only just got here," Omar says, but his heart isn't in it.

They look around. There is nothing to hold them here.

5.

They go home in silence. Omar is busy with his phone. Jimmy is sleeping. When they come out of Hackney Central station it feels colder than it was in Shoreditch. The drugs have washed through, leaving their bodies aching and shivering. They feel impossibly thin, as if they might crumple to the pavement at any moment.

They stop beside Hackney Downs.

"Great party," Jimmy says.

"Whatever," Omar flashes him the finger, and grins.

They hug for a long time and then each goes their separate ways, with Jimmy going east into Clapton, alone, and Omar going north towards Rectory Road, alone.

On the tennis court, a couple have paused play. It is not the same couple as the one that was playing earlier, but for the purpose of this story it may as well be. They are standing close to the net, one on each side. The man is gesticulating angrily with his racket. They are both shouting. I do not know what they are arguing about. Then the woman turns away and as she does so she hurls her racket to the floor. It bounces once, away from her, and lands. The man has his hands up in the air. He is still shouting, but his voice is goading now. She continues to walk, but there is nowhere to go. She is held in by the wire mesh fence. This is the toughest part of love. This is the part Omar and Jimmy do not have. They have nothing to hold them in. She reaches the baseline and stops, scuffs her foot, runs her hand through her hair, turns, and begins to walk back.

"MY SON'S LEAVING," THE FISHERMAN SAID. "I DON'T KNOW WHAT TO DO. I COULD GIVE HIM A JOB HERE, A HOME. BUT HE TOLD ME HE WANTS TO LEAVE."

I WATCHED THE FISHERMAN TURN AWAY AND SCRATCH HIS EAR AND HANG LIMPLY AGAINST THE BAR. ABOVE US A DIRTY FAN SCRATCHED THE HEAT. SUNLIGHT DRESSED US IN ALE GOLD.

"YOU COULD VISIT HIM?" I OFFERED.

"I CAN'T AFFORD IT."

THE BARMAN INTERRUPTED US, HIS VOICE BIRDLIKE AND STUTTERED. "I COULD LEND YOU SOME MONEY," HE SAID.

"I COULD NEVER PAY YOU BACK."

"I COULD GIVE YOU SOME MONEY, THEN."

"FROM WHERE? WHAT MONEY?"

THE BARMAN LOOKED ABOUT THE OLD ROOM, ITS RUST-LICKED BARSTOOLS AND MEZCAL AND THE CARAVAN OF FLIES THAT LIVED IN ITS SWEAT. "I DON'T KNOW," HE SAID.

If, Then
by Jo Gatford

The road below looked more like an ejaculation of silly-string than 'ribbons of light' or whatever the guidebook said. The book called the cathedral towers 'thrusting' and the river 'a meandering reflection of the hillside'. What he saw was black and grey and steep and dark. He left the book on a rock and the engine running, digging his hands into his pockets as though he were trying to burrow through to the other side of the world.

He began as long distance drivers do; pulling in at a dirt lay by, groaning at the aches in his lower back, taking two minutes to wander no further than it takes to find a good bush to pee behind. But after twenty steps the moist ground buoyed up his pedal-tired feet and told him to run. The hill dropped down past the gradient at which the highway agency had to stick up triangular signs to warn motorists. The hillside was punctured with rabbit warrens, clods to trip on, undiscovered burial mounds and overgrown fence posts. His ankles squealed in anticipation and dread as his jog-on-the-spot became a forward movement.

In the car, she leaned on the horn, flicked a cigarette butt onto the gravel and yelled something that ended in "-king hell!" but the momentum had taken him and he couldn't stop. He heard other shouts but they were as indecipherable as most of what she said to him lately. He rarely understood what she wanted any more – everything carried some sort of clause or bargain – "If you would only do X then I would feel Y and when you say Z I just want to…" They skirted around each other in the hallway without acknowledgement. They synchronised their turning in bed so as to naturally avoid the drape of an arm or the nudge of a knee against a backside. On the drive back, if his hand brushed her thigh when he changed gear, he apologised rather than adapting it into a squeeze.

His arms stretched out either side of him and his legs moved simply to continue their own existence. He leaned back to try to stay vaguely vertical but the hill took him faster and further and the thuds of his heels resonated the little hammers in his inner ear, blasting his sinuses clear, filling his eyes with briney water until his left shin gave a shotgun rebound and he found himself lying still, face down, his eyelashes brushing blades of grass.

His lungs attempted only to breathe out for a few moments, perhaps with some innate knowledge that inhaling would be infinitely more painful. When he did finally take a breath in, he let it out again almost immediately with a cracked vowel somewhere between an A and an U. Maybe she heard – the horn sounded again. He looked down at his leg, which no longer had the straightness of a leg, and then back, upside down, up at the crest of the hill where she sat parked. She flashed the headlights twice but he had no way to reply aside from another howl.

He waited, trying not to move. The pulsing of his blood around his shin bone, forced through the skin, became the heartbeat of the world, turned the sky blue-pink, the grass into an ocean, the craggy rocks into ancient faces, the towers into jagged knives that sliced into the clouds and let through the glory of whatever lay above. He was unable to doubt anything as he lay there, not God, not her, not fate. The world was simplified into ifs and thens, and he understood her need for balance, for reason, for fairness. He listened for the next 'if'. Either the death of the engine, her approaching feet, her sighing throat. Or the scraping of tyres on loose rock, the silence and the night. It was no longer up to him.

"Have another cigarette," he told the hillside, "Think about it."

Take Off Your Shoes
by Jo Gatford

"It's rude not to," Blake says. "Take 'em off."

I stare at the pairs of shoes pockmarking the sand, at the way the water leaves folds at the shoreline. If I don't look at him he can't land the joke. "Who are they meant to be offending?" I say.

Blake jerks his shoulders up and down. Turns away. The stretch of his shadow against the beach turns him into a praying mantis. He walks slowly through the lines of abandoned footwear and the shade he casts rolls over the shoes in sickening waves. He tilts his face up towards the gaping maw of a cave, twenty feet above the kleptomaniac ocean. The water can't help but take a trophy each time it slithers in towards the cliff: a solitary slingback, an abandoned Timberland, a school girl's patent Mary Jane. A trophy, or maybe a sacrifice.

*

"People come. People listen. People leave," the waiter at the cafe told us. "They hear what they have been waiting for and they know it is time to go."

Blake nodded with mock solemnity.

"To take off your shoes is to feel the movement of the earth," the man replied gently, as if Blake had asked a stupid question.

*

I try to imagine climbing the rocks in bare feet, in wet socks, the sea whipping up behind me, eternity beyond. Did they strip naked, too? To walk into the other place pure and free from worldly baggage? There is no fabric floating on the water. No shirts streaming in the wind, no underwear caught on a jagged edge of stone, no sodden clothing beached like jellyfish. Just shoes in neat rows, equidistant, innocuous, and so terribly empty of feet.

Blake nudges a Brogue that has not been lined up quite right with its bedfellow. "It's like an installation," he says, taking another photo, filling his memory card with low angles and overexposed sunsets and macro shots of shoelaces.

"Pose," he instructs me.

I look to my feet. Flip flops and painted toes. Two moles in a perfect line across the bones of my foot. A habitual click in my right ankle, leftover from a sprain. The cacti prickle of stubble on my shins.

I hear the shutter whirr and resist the urge to kick a pair of slip-ons at him.

*

A bottle of red wine that tasted like bonfire smoke strung itself into the veins of my arms and my chest and my labia when I crossed my legs. I leaned across the tin table and let my foot massage Blake's thigh in a lazy sort of provocation.

"What's inside the cave?" I asked the waiter.

He smiled. Blinked. "No one who has gone inside has ever spoken about it."

"Bullshit," Blake said. "No shoes allowed? Sounds like a cult."

My foot dropped to the floor, heavier than it should have been.

"What happens when they come back?"

The man tidied up our glasses, swiped away a speck of salad from the tablecloth. "Sometimes they don't return at all. If they do, they usually don't live long after."

Blake turned his face to mine and twisted his lips to the side. "We are *so* going tomorrow. Not every day you get to listen to a prophet."

I think I tried to shake my head, crossed my legs the other way, suddenly yearned for coffee. The waiter watched me and nodded just once. "I'll show you on the map."

*

I only brought two pairs of shoes. I wish I'd worn my trainers. Every step scoops the beach inside my sandals and strips away the skin between my toes. The wet sand is cold and shrinks away from our clumsy soles. The cliffside curves above – a wave turned to stone. Blake holds my hand and turns my ring round and around my finger.

The prophet is a bird, the waiter told us, but can change its appearance at will. It can be found perching on a rock that looks like a roaring mouth, and will only show itself to those who truly want to hear the truth. Blake had closed his eyes with a grin, his eyelids flickering down a mental list of all the sarcastic tweets the expedition could produce.

"You've seen one rock, you've seen all the fucking rocks in the world," he says, after we've walked for half an hour, finding no distinction between the pebbles and the merging grey of off-season weather.

"It's quiet though," I say, "No tourists."

"We're tourists," he says.

"You know what I mean."

The coastline veers back on itself, leaving a triumphant thrust of earth layered with strata in twenty shades of red protruding into the bombardment of the sea. "Just a bit further," Blake says, and the wind sweeps my negatives away.

I've never wanted to know who the villain really is under the mask, or how the detective works out the killer's plan, or why people say one thing and think another. I don't want to see around the corner.

We find the rock. The mouth. To me, it looks more like it is screaming. There is no bird. Or, at least, no singular bird. Above the cliff is a swarm. Not a flock. A winding, predatory blackness; a hive-mind of sea birds, thousands strong.

"Listen," Blake whispers. And I listen. He laughs, tweaks the fat at the side of my waist so I squirm. Then: "Fucking hell…"

The shoes begin behind the rock, out by the tideline, bordered with wavering seaweed. Pair after pair in grid-like uniformity, left-right, left-right, one foot, two feet, heels together, toes aligned. They reach all the way to the cliffside and there, as if it has been blasted into the rock by a giant fist, is the cave.

Blake sits on the sand and smokes a cigarette and looks for a WiFi signal, snapping off pictures without more than a glance at his subjects.

I pick up a sandal – white leather and gold buckles, the scent of sun cream and tired walking soles – and put it to my ear like a shell.

*

When Blake looks up again my shoes must be indistinguishable from the rest. Two little flip flops in a field of epiphany.

He calls after me when I begin to climb, but all I can hear is the crowing of so many gulls, fighting for a space to land.

WHEN PEOPLE TALK ABOUT A BEAUTIFUL GARDEN I DOUBT IT BECAUSE MOST PEOPLE DON'T KNOW WHAT THAT MEANS. MY GRANDFATHER REALLY DID HAVE A BEAUTIFUL GARDEN. IT WAS BEYOND THAT: IT WAS EDEN. FAMOUS PEOPLE CAME TO SIT IN IT, THEY HAD FASHION SHOOTS IN IT.

THE LAST TIME I SAW HIS GARDEN HE WALKED ME THROUGH IT. ME, AN AWKWARD, CHUBBY TEENAGER WITH MORE ANGST THAN I COULD HANDLE. I FELT CALM. THE WILLOW TUNNEL ENTRANCE WAS JOINED IN AN INTRICATE TAPESTRY OF HONEYSUCKLE AND SWEET PEAS. THE GROUND WAS COOL ON MY FEET. THERE WAS CHAOS AMIDST THE ORDER: THINGS LOOKED LIKE THEY HAD FALLEN INTO PLACE.

I ASKED HIM ABOUT A GIANT BRAMBLE THAT PEAKED OVER ONE OF THE BENCHES LIKE A WAVE. 'ISN'T THAT A WEED?'

"A WEED IS A PLANT THAT GROWS IN THE WRONG PLACE," HE ANSWERED LIKE AN OLD MONK.

AND I LOOKED AT IT AND I UNDERSTOOD.

In Lieu of a Memoir
by Tadhg Muller

I'd wound up trudging through a bitter London winter as a would-be debt collector for an ailing bakery, run by an ex-model with a heavy cocaine habit who was embarking on her first major literary work, *"Lets Make Cup Cakes, You and Me"*. I was working a seventy-hour week. After three months, the strain was telling. I'd grown detached from my wife, her frustration largely driven by my inability to provide sufficient means for our survival and by my shameless scrounging after other people's money. I'd been evicted from our flat and had taken to parking my sorry arse just about anywhere. In this condition of poverty, isolation and sexual frustration, I'd begun a romantic liaison with a Mongolian pâtissier, an illegal who'd trained in Novgorod, Russia, where she learnt to make the plumpest little pastries. We would fuck senselessly, with her long black hair falling loosely on the flattened and sporadically split bags of flour, which she lay on with her baker's apron rolled up to her tits and her legs spread apart, and me, awkwardly, with my boilersuit undone and tangled around my calves. We would finish and I would dust her generous hips and she would dust mine. There was no kissing, just fumbling and fucking, no goodbyes and no hellos. I'd go home empty and alone, my loins sucked dry, my battered little man incapable of pissing straight. The light would be out, a cold dinner would await me, and I'd hear the echoes of a line from some forgotten epic, recited to me back when the times were good, *He that eats alone, eats his own sins.*

In other words: eats shit!

And shit I ate - the work, the infidelity, the food without substance, the hustling. In the dark, I'd walk my derelict West London flat like some hopeless soldier; like some mercenary tucking my son in. I'd try to sleep but couldn't. Lying there, feeling dirty and ashamed, the only reprieve I could think of was to revive, once more, my stalled literary journey. I began to wonder: Were there other whores like me? Were there other artists who fucked tartars and who bummed other people's smokes, who scrounged around for money and put the heat on desperate men to pay the debts from which they were running? Poverty had made me cowardly. In my fear I'd become everything I hated: a drunk; a cheat; a womanizer; a liar; a thief. So I decided to hunt down my lost companions, my literary posse. And that was how I initiated the so-called North North London Writers' Group and began my own path toward redemption.

My inspiration, the North London Writers' Group (a more respectable fraternity), I located late one night somewhere in cyberspace. Opening up that website, it was as if I'd entered a room without windows, a room without doors. They declared they were "a friendly group of writers." I then read that not everyone could become a member. Their website said places were reserved for "journeymen with publication history" or for those now "seriously pursuing publication." "Journalists" and "MA graduates" could also be admitted. I had no publication history. I was not seriously pursuing publication. I was not a journalist, nor an MA graduate. The bottom line was that this last ditch attempt at locating my own Jerusalem had ended in fresh disappointment that I couldn't bear.

So began my electronic correspondence with that group, leading in turn to other electronic correspondence. It records a very awkward period in my life and so is repeated here *in lieu of a memoir*. And why not? After all, the conventions of memoirs have changed or should change. The old records now are incomplete and fleeting. The new? No longer are they consigned to lost diaries and tattered notebooks, rather they will be found in the trails of impulsive messages darting through cyberspace like the premature ejaculations of a lover.

Sent: 12 November 2010 12.51 am
Subject: A Funeral Note

Hello Victor,

I am an unpublished writer, I am not a journalist, nor an MA graduate. I read the brief outline of your group and it read like an ad for a funeral in the Classifieds. The group sounds like a collection of evangelists, or fascists, or some queer incarnation of the two in literary form, perhaps even a self-help group for arseholes.

I think your membership should only include unpublished dropouts, with current or former vices, little money, not v. much sophistication, and serious time limitations. Perhaps they should even live in extreme circumstances that only allow them to write in the dark (much like the cave painters of old, dripping blood on the walls). And what about single mothers with bold ambitions, who put their children to bed, have a sniff of Vix, and then write erotic novels (roughly a paragraph a night) about literary groups in North London? That could be good. You could meet strictly at dawn?

Anyhow, I have to write my six paragraphs, and rise at 5.15 am. Sadly, for both of us, I do not fit the criteria to join your group, much though I might benefit from it and even enjoy it.

I am thus considering starting the North North London Writers Group. It would be an alternative to the North London Writers Group. It would be based in the West, or the South, or the East, as the North is not on my radar and clearly it's time to move. But, then, there is something to be said about the North North London Writers Group being somewhere other than the North.
Many thanks,
Hans Brady.

There was no reply - a small victory. With haste, I set about sending the above message to a spiritual brother, a fellow dropout I'd befriended in a London kitchen, where we exchanged sordid anecdotes, usually about his escapades with Nothing Hill housewives, whilst he scrubbed dishes. He'd returned to Sydney to "dig in" and pursue his literary career as a crime novelist. As is the way, he was enjoying no success but remained committed. I called him The Poodle, because his prose always spent too long in the salon. It never had a hair out of place. Perhaps that was the secret of his glorious, perpetual failure?

Sent: 13 November 2010 8.40 pm
Fwd: A Funeral Note

Dear Poodle,
I started looking round, out of curiosity, for a writers' group. God knows why! Actually, it's partly because I've decided that if we leave this neighborhood and go either to the south or the east, I'll try and start my own writers' group. I think it will be effective, as I am fairly good at that sort of thing – getting things started!!!
However, this triggered me to look at other writers groups. I could

only find one called the North London Writers Group, I read the criteria to join and realized that for me it was a non-starter. So I felt compelled to write them a email, entitled "A Funeral Note." Having written this, and concluded that it was fairly ridiculous, I realized the only person who would find it entertaining, with the possible exception of Victor, is of course you.
Love Hans.

Sent: 14 November 2010 12.45 pm
Re: Fwd: A Funeral Note

Hansie,
 I like it. I like it, and the funeral note. Sign me up.
The Poodle.
P.S. Could you send me the contacts for the North London Writers' Group? I might email them suggesting a cultural exchange program with the Sydney Chapter of the North North London Writers' Group.

Sent: 14 November 2010 10.22 pm
Subject: developments

Poodle,
 This idea of the North North London Writers Co-op… I am not kidding. I really think I could be onto something. I am going to work on some ads, start posting them across London with my son. I'll create contact details - an email address - and send them to you. You can poster Sydney. Then the North North London Writers Co-op can begin accepting submissions for its first publication of avantgarde writing entitled "Lost Chapters" Each member would

submit one chapter, then we can select a number for publication in a cooperative novel called "74 Hand Jobs". I'd present it to literary agents in London. As for the Co-op, there would be no rules except that before writing we'd have to swear a lot and afterwards swagger a great deal. There would also have to be at least one sex scene every six pages or perhaps every six minutes, as read by the semi- or sub-literate. I feel quite strongly about that. Any member who did not produce a sex scene often enough would have to be expelled. You could do likewise in Sydney – arrange some expulsions. I don't know about government funding but we could only grow bigger + we could only grow stronger. God, we might even make a movie! There are no boundaries, my dear Poodle. There are only the stars!

Hans

Sent: 16 November 2010 12.42 pm
Re: developments

Hans,

"There are no stars."
"I'll find them."

I owe you a serious email and one will come but not this afternoon, nor tomorrow, because I am getting out of here. This place really shits me. I am even beginning to sound like you.

As for the North North London Writers'* Group, I will only say this: we should always feel free to piss on one another, provided that the piss is a good piss, is a happy piss, and occurs outside in the open air, irrigating mutual thought under the stars. (Suggested

new motto: "There are no stars." "I'll find them.")
  In short, I remain,
  Fraternally,
  The Poodle of the North North London Writers' Group
  (But shouldn't it be a Collective?)

Sent: 16 November 2010 12.01 pm
Subject: Bombard the Fuckers

Brother,
  I am happy with the motto but would suggest another:

  "I have been a con, it went wrong.
  I was a fool, I learnt a lot."

  I will get started on the posters.
Hans
*P.S. The North London Writers Club hasn't responded. We
shouldn't stomach that. I will get you their email address, when
we're ready we will fucking strike – bombard the fuckers and tell
them its time they dissolved, its time they went back to journalism.*

Sent: 18 November 2010 1.45 am
Subject: North North London Writers Co-op

Poodle,
  *It's started: I posted a hand written sign outside Ladbroke Grove
tube station at 5.45 am Saturday. It read:*

  No Journalists

No Postgraduates
No White People

The North North London Writer's Co-op

"There are no stars
And we'll find them."
- The Poodle (a founding member)

Fully independent writers group

Contact: Hans at
hjbrady@yahoo.co.uk

Within a day there were three inquiries, one person became a member, another asked: DO you have a problem with white people? I answered that no man was white, the white man was a notion, the white man was the Diablo, incarnation of evil.

I didn't hear back.

Yours,

Hans

P.S. I am having a coffee with Lloyd Vigo next week to talk about writing and to take the Group from two to three members (four if you include the Sydney branch).

P.P.S. According to my wife, my sign was gone by midday Saturday, which is a shame, as she did it, and, well, it looked pretty fucking hardcore.

P.P.P.S. "Bright, bright stars, baby, I can see them."

Sent: 21 November 2010 12.42 am
Re: North North London Writers Co-op

Hans,

Keep after the great white whale of the North North London Writers' Group. There must be at least a short story there. You should write episodically (perhaps by email to a brother in Sydney who promises assistance but never delivers). By the way, that brother in Sydney has reservations about belonging to anything that is called a Co-op as opposed to a Collective. Because IN ANY MOVEMENT THERE MUST BE AT LEAST THE PROMISE OF VIOLENCE, and the term "Co-op" has, he thinks, unfortunate connotations of Wholefoods restaurants in the seventies. Also, that brother in Sydney may be a wanker – indeed he recently posted signs around his desk saying I MUST NOT BE A WANKER –but still he believes the Collective's motto should take the form of a dialogue:

"There are no stars."

"I'll find them."

Which strikes, he thinks, the right note of intellectual courage in the face of grimly declared facts. Also (minor point) that brother would prefer that his name, even his pseudonym, weren't used anywhere, including on flyers in Ladbroke Grove. Why? Just because it's his name, I suppose, and he will attach what statements he wishes to it. Use your own name, or your own nom de guerre, if you have to.

I remain with goodwill,

The (Existential) Poodle.

Sent: 21 November 2010 2.30 am
Subject:

I am writing a short story. It is called: "Not in my brother's name."
Hans.

Sent: 25 November 2010 12.42 am
Subject:

Hans,
  I intend to dedicate my crime novel, "Murder 74," to the North
North London Writers' Group, which will then live on in posterity.
Yours,
The Poodle
P.S. "Murder 74" is set in a retirement village just outside Sydney.

Sent: 25 November 2010 8.45 pm
Subject: News from the Fat Badger

Poodle,
  I met Lloyd Vigo at the Fat Badger. He asked me where the
rest of the group was? I say, "I'm it" and he asks me whether I'm
"having a laugh." I tell him I'm not a fucking comedian. He says
he's written three sci/fi novels:

  1. The Doom.
  2. Lost in Constellation 26, and:
  3. No War Without Charlie

  I say I like the titles. He goes "I brought you a chapter." I take a
look at the first paragraph and tell him it's hilarious, and he asks

me once more if I'm having a laugh? I tell him again that I'm not a comedian. He says: Where is everybody else? And I repeat, "I am it, Lloyd." Then, the whole thing started to get a messy edge, just a bad fucking air. He asks me what have I got to show for it? I say, "Just the odd chapter and some note books." He says again: "Are you having a laugh?" For the third time, I repeat I am not a comedian and I tell him that the meeting is becoming tiresome. He says, "Yes, this is a waste of time, you're obviously a fraud." I tell him I know a good literary group he could join. It's called the North London Writers Group. He says: Hang on, isn't that us? I tell him to watch it, this is the North North London Writers Co-op and he better watch his mouth when it comes to the North London Writers Group. The man has the nerve to ask me yet again whether I'm having a laugh. I tell him he'd better clear out, because quite frankly he's not the kind of person that we're after in the North North London Writers Co-op.
Hans.

Sent: 30 November 2010 12.43 pm
Re: News from the Fat Badger

It has the appearance of the real!
The Poodle

Sent: 30 December 2010 4.30 am
Subject: More from the Fat Badger

Poodle,
I just met Tom Morgan, 19. He saw the ad at Ladbroke Grove tube station and took a month to follow up. Nice guy, we met at

the Fat Badger. Then he asked about the quote on the sign from the Poodle, he said he liked the quote. He asked me what else I could tell him about the Poodle? I told him all I could say is that the Poodle was part of the Sydney wing, though there is already a schism. The Poodle was with the Collective and we were the Co-op. Then he asks wether I have any of your writing, and I say I'm not at liberty to say. The Poodle is the real thing, a kind of one man secret society, and..... well, he gets angry if anyone speaks for him, if anyone makes statements in his name. So I couldn't say anything, except that the Poodle spent some time in the service. He asks if I mean millitary, then says "Afghanistan?" and I tell him not to be so pushy though I knew you'd once travelled over the Karakorum. He asked, "Where the fuck is that?" and I say, "Tribal areas of Pakistan my friend." It went well after that. Tom drank a few pints, then pulled out a joint and suggested we go for a walk.

Poodle, you already have a cult following, and there is a rumour in the London literary underground that you were once a spook running operations across the Afghan border.

Hans.

Sent: 1 January 2011 12.25 pm
Subject: Happy New Year

Hansie,

I have a poem for you to give to Tom. It begins: "I cannot love you." Maybe you should recite it together at the next meeting of the Co-op?

Yours,

The Poodle.

Sydney

"Sire not children by a woman who wears gold"
Pythagoras

I cannot love you

        the rigor mortis of your smile is
a woman with a price on her head and eyes like cash registers
        your lies, your lies, and the bullshit
that follows your skin-deep optimism

I am heading south

       here the sky's great vacancy is a mouth or
an arsehole admiring itself: nothing but borrowed phrases and
slogans in lieu of thought

        your ladies of fashion I cannot tell
from the creatures of the night

So this is my goodbye

At dawn the cathedral I love sails up College Street like a ghost
ship

But you I cannot love

       and the men, Staffordshire Terriers, wear
their flesh like jewellery, or armour, or jewellery and armour, that
late imperial style!

       Sydney your face is fat, it is
fat your face, and pampered, without definition

I am heading south
                    You are a simian circus a screen of anxiety
There is no victory here in the war on excrement

You are slimy as an overripe mango. You are oily as cockroach shit.
You are a total moral and physical dump. Sydney

This is my goodbye.

Sent: 1 January 2011 3.14 am
Re: Happy New Year

You miserable cunt,
We do not respond to poetry submissions.

Sent: 17 January 2011 2.35 am
Subject:

Poodle,
Tomorrow I have a meeting with Jo Fagottini, he deals in
romance, and has a sideline in ripped-off cookbooks. Tom's coming,
too. Then we're all going to drift up to the north, cruise around.
Tom thinks Islington is the best bet. We'll look for a pack of wankers
flicking over their pages, then we're going to try and beat the shit
out of them, let them know whats what. Let those bastards know
that this is serious, that they are rude fuckers for not getting back to
me, those fuckers in the North London Writers Group.
I'm tired brother. More fucking snow, more fucking rice and
pasta, more Spartan living. I need some warm clothes.
Hans

Sent: 18 January 2011 12.36 pm
Re:

*Jo Faggottini? Did you fabricate all of this? I don't mind, but
I'm at the point where, henceforth, my dealings with you will be
conducted via my secretary. His name is Ernst Wanke.*
The Poodle

Sent: 18 January 2011 10.17 pm
Re: Re:

Poodle,
*Like all history, some of it happened, some of it didn't. What
mattered was what was born, what came from it: the North
North London Writers Collective.*
Hans

Sent: 21 January 2011 12.22 pm
Re: Re: Re:

*Don't be slippery. Did any of this take place? Are you still in
London?*

Sent: 21 January 2011 1.25 am
Subject: Confessions of a Drunk, a Cheat, a Womanizer, a
Liar and a Thief

*The meeting with Lloyd took place. Unfortunately, that was it.
There was no more interest. As I told you, the sign didn't last long
on Ladbroke Grove.*
Hans.

Sent: 22 January 2011 12.17 am

Re: Confessions of a Drunk, a Cheat, a Womanizer, a Liar and a Thief

You are, in fact, a bastard.

The next morning I rocked up at the bakery at a quarter to six, still high on the dreams of my encounters with that imaginary body of writers, the North North London Writers' Group, a set of encounters that, I realised, had just come to an end. But, walking the streets, I couldn't escape the feeling that my world, having gone from bad to worse, and then worse again, was about to change once more and incontrovertibly. Yes, it was as if, through my fabrications, I'd shaken off all the cowardice, all the fear, the worthlessness, and isolation that had dragged winter into the pit of my soul. I found my boss in her office. She was at her desk, typing away at the final draft of *"Let's Make Cookies, You and Me"*. She was working hard to meet the false deadline imposed by Penguin. Her radio was blaring 'Billionaire' by Travie McCoy. I picked up a page.

"Still working on this crap?" I said.

She sat back obviously stunned, obviously wounded, but mostly just aware of the truth of my statement.

"You're fired, Hans," she replied.

I nodded, thanked her and walked out, beyond the Tartar who offered me one last smile, then closed the door on that world, a world that was a far greater lie than all the fictions I'd concocted. I didn't know where I was going. It was minus two outside, the air a bitter ice. Yet, inside me, I felt that I was done with being everything I hated. I knew that I was set upon being the person I really was – whatever that is; literature and the power of words? – at any rate, myself. Or as the Poodle had it:

> *"There are no stars."*
> *"I'll find them."*

About a Weapon
by Tadhg Muller

So it turned out Mr. Michael Kelly played golf. The way he hit that Coke can he must have been a real pro. Maybe he played back in Australia. With all the sunshine, and all that space, that would make sense. Maybe all Australians hit a coke can that way.

I had come to play with Ambrose (his boy, no real golfer). The three of us, we went to the park. Not like my park on Telegraph Hill, this park was in Lewisham. A sad kind of park with cans, and bottles, and glass, and concrete, and a playground that was neglected. Empty. Just me on my scooter and Ambrose on his bicycle. I'm pretty crazy. Crazier than Ambrose. That's why he likes it when I come down and we go to the park, and we go sick. And that's how it started… Mr. Kelly on a bench, and me on my scooter.

So I had my helmet on. But not on my head - no. I had it strapped front-on like a visor, me gazing out through the ventilations gaps. I think I looked like an android. Or a robot. I must have looked good. Ambrose and Mr. Kelly were both laughing. Mr. Kelly was laughing hardest. And then the three men walked into the park. And the funny thing was that one of the men, a big man, with a moustache and an Adidas tracksuit, well, he was holding a golf club, a big one. The other two men were drinking beer. Mum would have crossed the road if she had seen these men. The man with the golf club was the boss. He was cleaner and they looked funny together. Ambrose looked at his dad. Ambrose and his Dad spent a lot of time in that park; they spent a lot of time together… Ambrose rode to the other end of the park while the men sat down on a park bench. Mr. Kelly eased back and looked more relaxed than usual. Alongside the strangers he looked sharp, like he might have been a lawyer, or a salesmen, or a detective. He sat there and just smiled. I put my helmet on and started scootering whilst Ambrose rode back. The man with the golf club stood up and walked forward with the club on his shoulder. Ambrose came level to me, breaking on his bike, and looked at his dad. Looked at his Dad as if he were angry, like Mr. Kelly had embarrassed him or done something unforgivable. Ambrose's cheeks were red, what on earth was wrong with him?

Mum always said that Mr. Kelly worked hard, and he was tired. Tired and stressed. The Kellys had a small house and not much money. They were always dealing with the neighbours that complained about the noise of the dog, the noise of the baby, the noise of Ambrose, the noise of their music. They called their neighbour Davy Bottles, which I thought was funny. They called him that because Mr. Kelly didn't like him, and said he was a miserable drunk, always complaining and clinking his bottles in the flat beneath them. I was always careful with Mr. Kelly. Mum said he was a poet… Ambrose said he spent his nights working in a bakery. He wasn't a very big man, but he had eyes like one of those fighting dogs, those dogs that poor people walk around with, alive and hungry, a dog like a knife - as my dad says.

Maybe all poets look like Mr. Kelly. Maybe all bakers too. Those sleepless nights and the time by the oven. 'Crazy insomnia' as Ambrose liked to call it. Whatever it was, the look in his eyes didn't change when the man made a move with the golf club. No, he turned his head to look very carefully. And he nodded when his eyes met those of the man. A long slow nod, like he was half asleep, like they were familiar, and I was sure he had never seen the man. The man with the club was no poet, and certainly no baker.

And then a funny thing happened: the man stopped at a Coke can, he lined it up, he does a practice swing, yells four, and whacks it cleanly, like a real golf pro. And I laughed, and Mr. Kelly laughed, and Ambrose looked at his Dad. He shakes his head, like he knows something that I don't. Maybe they're criminals. The man turns and looks at Mr. Kelly and says:

-Sorry sir...

And Mr. Kelly replies:

-No worries.

And the man walks back to his friends and mutters under his breath:

-He's an Australian.

And I don't know why he says that. Though Mr. Kelly is an Australian, it's not important. No, it's more important that he is a baker, and more important that he is a poet, and that he has eyes like a savage dog when he doesn't smile, and if the truth be told, I'm not entirely comfortable with him. There is something about him, something unpredictable as though he might just decide to walk off and leave everything behind, as though he might just leave us in the park.

The man returned and gave a steady look at Mr. Kelly. He lined up the can once more, and bang! And Mr. Kelly smiles. And Ambrose rides back to other end of the park, and I should also, but I wanted to watch. And the man turns to Mr. Kelly and asks if he can let me have a swing. And Mr. Kelly says:

-Sure.

And I walk over to the man, and Mr. Kelly smiles but his eyes look like the savage dogs, and Ambrose skids up and I can see he is annoyed, and he shakes his head at Mr. Kelly. Ambrose is sure he is smarter than me; he's just like his father. But I know Ambrose is jealous. He wants to have a go. And the man shows me how to swing, and I listen, and he shows me how to hold it, and he holds my hands, and his hands are soft and oily, but he doesn't have the feel of a bad person. The other men put their drinks down, and one turns around and looks around the park. Mr. Kelly looks me in the eyes and nods. As if to say: *Do it. Do it for your own good,* like I am in a movie, and Mum won't understand any of this when I get home, she'll just think Mr. Kelly has been telling us stories, filling our head with...

And then it happens. The man steps back. I swing, and it's heavy and I almost turn three-sixty. And Mr. Kelly cries:

-Look out!

And the man ducks, and I just miss his head with the club. And Mr. Kelly laughs. And the man looks at Mr. Kelly like he is crazy, sitting on that bench like a gentleman. And the man walks away. Ambrose comes and he takes the club, Mr. Kelly tells me to stand back. Ambrose swings, then hands me the club. I guess he's jealous that I swing better.

And then I hear some music, West Indian music like it's Carnival, and the men look around and at the other end of the park as a car pulls in. The big man makes his way over to the car and the two other men look nervous. And Mr. Kelly is standing next to me, and he gently takes the golf club.

-My turn.

The big man pauses and looks at Mr. Kelly. And Mr. Kelly lines up a can, and I stand back. A practice swing real slow and smooth measuring his stroke, and then *POW*. He hits it. And like an explosion the can goes flying in an arc through the air, and the big man, and the men on the bench, and the men in the car, they all stop and stare. And I clap.

-How did you hit it so hard?

-It's all in the hips.

He smiles. And then he walks to the can, and the big man walked to the men in the car, and I look back to Mr. Kelly. And he is just very calmly lining up a second stroke. And he now looks crazy like the Joker. And I can see Ambrose on his bike, near the bench, where his father had sat, and he looks from his father to the men and back again. And I wonder what's going on, and part of me thinks we should have left the park.

As quickly as they came the men get back in the car and drive off. And the big man makes his way across the park. And Mr. Kelly nods as the man draws near. They look at each other and the big man speaks.

-Keep the club, the boys might use it, practise their swings.

And Mr. Kelly doesn't smile, he just looks back. And the man gets his friends, and the three clear out.

And that's when Ambrose messed it all up, just when I thought we might be able to keep the club.

-What were you doing!? Were you out of your mind!? He yells angrily at his dad, almost at the point of tears.

-It was better I had the club.

And I don't get it. I don't get the problem. Why are these Kellys so dramatic? Maybe it's because he's a poet. But what does it matter who has the club? And now I can't have it, says Mr. Kelly. And he does the stupidest thing: He insists on hiding it all twisted in a fence, deep in the bushes, where no one will see it, where it will rust.

And it rusts.

CONVINCED THERE IS A GHOST IN THE DESK DRAWER, CLAIRE HAS STOPPED COMING INTO MY STUDY. SHE STANDS ON THE THRESHOLD, ONE MELTY CRAYOLA IN HAND, SUCKING HER FINGERS ANXIOUSLY.

"YOU CAN COME IN. THERE'S NO GHOST IN THERE. PROMISE."

"WHY DO YOU NEVER OPEN IT THEN?"

HER EYES SWIVEL FROM ME TO THE DRAWER. SHE WANTS JUICE. I SEND HER DOWN TO THE HOUSEKEEPER.

ONCE SHE HAS GONE MY LAPTOP STARES BLANKLY AT ME AT ME. I SPIN LISTLESSLY IN MY CHAIR. THE ROOM STAGNATES. IT IS NOT TRUE THAT I NEVER OPEN THE DRAWER - I DO - BUT ONLY WHEN I AM BY MYSELF. MY EARS STRAIN. CLAIRE'S SQUEALS ECHO FROM THE KITCHEN. THE CLOCK TRICKLES.

I SLIDE THE DRAWER OPEN. SLANTED SUNLIGHT CATCHES ON VARNISH. HER SHOES GAZE AT ME. ONE DOLEFUL EYE WHERE THE BLACK LEATHER WAS PUNCTURED BY GLASS. LACES UNDONE. I CAN'T WEAR THEM, CAN'T GIVE THEM AWAY: THEY'RE CALCIFIED TO THE SHAPE OF HER, SOLES WORN UNEVENLY BY COLLAPSED FOOT ARCHES. CAN'T THROW THEM OUT, EITHER, IN CASE SOME PART OF HER IS STILL WEARING THEM.

THE PARAMEDICS COULDN'T EXPLAIN WHY HER SHOES FLEW OFF. JUST ONE OF THOSE THINGS. THEY SCRAPED THE REST OF HER FROM THE ROAD. WHEN IT BECAME CLEAR WE WOULD NOT FIND HER WEDDING RING, THAT MY OWN BAND WAS ORPHANED, I HUGGED THE SHOES TO MY CHEST. PUT THEM IN THE DRAWER, THOUGHT I'D FIGURE OUT WHAT TO DO WITH THEM LATER.

The Giant Tree
by James King

The hole in the tree was shaped like a heart, not a romantic-shaped heart but a real heart, one with vena cavas and an aorta like he'd read about in one of the old lady's books.

The boy stared at the hole for a good hour until the wet tree trunk upon which he sat began to soak into his pyjamas. This certainly wasn't the longest he'd spent in front of the giant tree, indeed just the previous week he'd spent almost six hours on the same trunk drawing the entire tree on the back of a roll of the old lady's wallpaper using soft pencil grades and smudging the shading of the tree with his thumb, though his art teacher had said not to do this.

He didn't want to draw it this time. This time he was content just to sit and wonder about all of the magic and wondrous places he'd yet to see inside of the giant tree.

*

When the boy was seven years old his friend had told him about all that can be found inside the giant tree: *At the bottom of the hollow tree is a very small room with a very small door, which is perfectly round with a perfectly square door-handle. The door opens inwards so you have to squash yourself to squeeze out.*

The boy's friend was two years older, which was a strange thing when you're as young as seven. He was his best friend, though he wasn't foolish enough to think that the feeling was returned. But the boy was happy enough to simply know his friend and that he was liked by him.

When the boy was eight years old he dared to disturb the old lady in her library to tell her all he knew about the tree. Her face lit up in wonder as the boy spoke and she asked him questions about what else the older boy had told him. But when the boy said he was ready to go inside the tree her face sank, and she shook her head in utter refusal. When he asked the old lady why this was, all she said was: *There are rules about climbing into the tree. You should speak to your friend about them.*

A week after the old lady had forbidden him to climb the tree he found his friend walking in the forest nearby. Resting on his shoulders was a large fur cloak of crimson and cream, with dark spots around the collar. With every stride he took the cloak glistened under the bright sunlight, which broke in beams through the dense canopy of the trees. In his hand his friend held a long, thin knife with a brass handle. The boy ran up to him and asked him about these peculiar objects.

This is the cloak I wear after I go through the door. Sometimes I like to wear it when I come back.

His friend began to cry.

I found the knife at the bottom of the tree resting against the door. I think someone else has been inside.

The boy had never seen his friend cry, but knew, for friendship's sake, that the best thing to do was to sit and listen to him for a while as his friend told him stories from the tree.

He listened for hours as he was regaled with adventures of the people who live on the other side of the round door. They were wonderful tales and the boy loved to hear them, but his mind was plagued by the words of the old lady and the rules she had mentioned.

As night fell they huddled together. His friend was cheerful again, and even when he looked at the knife his face no longer grew sad. The boy asked him about the rules.

There are a number of rules, but I'll tell you the three biggest. Firstly, to enter the round door with the square handle at the bottom of the hollow tree you must bring with you your favourite toy. Because when you go inside you have to leave it with the doorman. He keeps it safe to make sure you don't take anything from the other side of the door that doesn't belong to you. Secondly, there is something inside the tree that judges whether you are worthy to enter. The doorman says the tree has senses, but I think he can see from the other side of the tree who is coming. Then he decides whether you look nice enough to enter.

His friend paused looking for some kind of response from the boy. But his eagerness to learn the last rule had him paralysed with anticipation.

And finally, the last biggest rule: you cannot enter the hole in the tree until you are one-hundred-and-eight months old.

The boy's heart sank. He had just turned eight one month ago and he had to be… nine years old to go into the tree.

*

The boy was now eight and a half, and it seemed as though he had been waiting forever to be nine. But he knew he made the waiting worse by coming to sit on the same trunk every day after school. The good hour had long passed and his pyjamas were now entirely soaked through, so he decided it was time to go home.

In his room the boy pulled off his dirty clothes and threw them to the corner. He lay down on his belly and pulled a large sketchpad towards him. He removed the pencils from his bag and settled in to sketch for the rest of the afternoon. He drew a picture of the giant tree with a man next it. Using a ruler, he measured how many tall men could stand head to toe to reach the top of the tree. Eight and a pair of legs he counted. Next he drew a picture of his friend standing next to the tree. For this he unwrapped the colouring pencils the old lady had given to him for his birthday. He used brown and green for the tree, beige and yellow for his friend and blue and pink for the strange animals his friend had described.

The next day was a Sunday and he was going to meet his friend at the tiny stream near to the giant tree.

The path leading up to the stream was long and winding, *and fraught with danger,* thought the boy. As he skipped along the path, jumping over large stones and fallen branches, he wondered exactly what adventure he and his friend might go on today, even daring to hope, just for a moment, that his friend might invite him into the tree.

As he approached the stream he could hear voices and laughter, and turning the corner around a bush he saw his friend with two others: a boy *and* a girl.

"Hello," said his friend. "These are my friends from swimming club."

"Okay," said the boy. The other boy and the girl nodded, semi-interested.

The boy didn't much like this new arrangement. He didn't recognise them from school, and he'd never been to this *swimming club*. Also, the girl had a rather large mole right in the centre of her chin, which the boy found most displeasing.

The four of them walked through the forest in a three-one formation, and it was perhaps five minutes before one of the three turned around to talk to the boy. "How old are you?" said the girl with the ugly mole.

"Eight...and a half...I am," the boy stuttered.

"You are!" the girl laughed, the other boy sniggered in a rather unpleasant snorting fashion.

"How old are you both?" the boy plucked up the courage to ask.

"I'm eleven, and my brother's ten," she replied with superiority.

The boy thought about this for some time before realising that perhaps a minute had passed and that the girl had turned back to the other two, no longer interested in what he had to say.

All of a sudden he realised where they were. He could see the giant tree emerging into view just over the crest of the tallest hill in the forest. His friend, the other boy and the girl immediately ran up the steep hill, tripping and stumbling on the way. *I don't want them to be allowed into the tree*, he thought in a rush of panic. He sprinted up the hill after them, his legs getting tired halfway. He clambered to the peak of the hill just as his friend disappeared over the other side. He ran to the crest from where his friend had descended and breathed a sigh of relief. Below, riding a large bright red sled, his friend veered down the angle of the hill away from the tree.

"Do you want a go?" said the girl, standing next to him. The boy looked at her but didn't answer.

The other boy jumped into his bright yellow sled and pushed himself over the edge and down the large muddy indent in the hill – perfect for sledding. The girl sat down at the back of her bright green sled and patted the empty space at the front, beckoning the boy to join her. He nestled in between her legs, feeling outrageously uncomfortable, and closed his eyes.

"Here we go," shouted the girl excitably.

The boy felt sick as the sled slowly tipped over the edge, but within six seconds it was over, and laughter rose up to the tops of the trees above as the four of them lay in pools of mud at the bottom of the hill. Opening his eyes his friend stood over him with a grin. His friend held out his hand and pulled the boy to his feet.

The following week the boy took his pencils and his sketchpad back into the forest. Taking his usual detour through the brushwood away from the path he saw, at a distance, his friend. It was late afternoon and the sky was overcast with the threat of rain. The boy didn't call out to his friend because he knew he was heading towards the tree, and he also knew that his friend wouldn't allow him to break any of the three biggest rules. So he thought he'd watch, from afar, to see what would happen once he went inside.

The boy quietly crept behind a large fallen trunk, making sure to obscure everything but the top of his head, just enough so he could observe his friend. Standing between the large roots of the giant tree the boy's friend began to make his ascent. He placed his right hand over a stump where a branch used to be, just above shoulder height, then, placing his right foot on top of the highest root, he pulled himself up so that the stump was now at his waist, and the lowest branch above him was just within jumping distance. The boy watched on as his friend steadied himself before leaping towards it. But, as he grabbed it, his left hand slipped and his body weight pulled heavily on his right arm as it clung desperately to the branch. The boy gasped aloud and immediately, knowing the noise would attract his friend's attention, ducked down out of sight.

He couldn't hear any cries of pain, so he knew his friend had not fallen, nor could he hear a struggle, yet he remained hidden not wanting to be accused of spying by his only friend.

A couple of minutes passed before he plucked up the courage to peer over the trunk. His friend was gone.

The boy waited. For two hours he knelt behind the tree thinking of nothing but the adventures his friend would be having on the other side of the round door.

Time continued to pass slowly. It began to drizzle. Getting tired and wet he contemplated going home, but he was desperate to see his friend come out.

Another hour. Coming from inside the tree a rustling noise grew. As the last drop of rain trickled down the boy's forehead a hand emerged from the heart-shaped hole in the giant tree and the sun began to leak through the dark clouds. Headfirst his friend pulled himself out of the hole and, golden coat glistening in the sun light, he lowered himself down the tree. Several feet from the bottom he dropped onto the highest root and skipped down onto the forest floor. Having knelt down to soften his landing his friend slowly rose. The boy also rose in awe as though everything magical he'd imagined had come to life in that large, glistening, golden coat. His friend turned slowly, holding in his hand a large bejewelled crown. The boy swallowed, and his rain-damped brow began to perspire. *Never in all my dreams have I been friend to a prince*, he thought. He wanted to call out but his throat was swollen and his lips were unable to move. His friend did not see him, he simply turned and walked deeper into the forest with the sun illuminating his every regal step. Just as he disappeared the skies grew dark and the rain started to drizzle once more. *In six months I can climb into the hole, and I too will be a prince*, thought the boy. And for the rest of the summer the boy did not see his friend.

In the time he had spent alone during the summer the boy had taken to crafting his own colourful sled to take to the forest hills.

He had asked the old lady if she could buy him a bright yellow acrylic sled but she had regretfully declined. And when she offered to buy him a new sketchpad he asked instead if she'd let him use her tools to fashion a sled of his own, which she accepted. The boy loved the old lady dearly.

In the fifth week of his summer break the boy carried his wooden sled to the peak of the second tallest hill in the forest, far away from the giant tree. At the top of the hill he lay down the sled and positioned himself in the middle. He placed his feet on the folded cardboard he'd fitted as footrests and gripped the reins at the front. He closed his eyes and shifted his bum forward until finally he reached the edge. A rush of wind peeled the hair from his hot face and filled his ears with a loud gravely roar before he came to an abrupt halt at the bottom. Lying face first on the pine needles and brown leaves the boy laughed. He continued to chuckle to himself for a time until he felt a presence over him. The boy turned over to see a blurry face. He stood, rubbed his eyes to clear his head from the sun's gaze, and looked up to see another boy – the other boy – his friend's friend.

"Hello," said the boy.

"What are you doing?" the other replied.

"I've built my own sled and was racing down the hill."

The other boy picked up the sled and held it against the sun. With his other hand he brought a cigarette to his lips.

The boy's heart started pounding and he looked around to see if they were alone in the forest by the hill. He saw no one, but felt only slightly more at ease.

"Would you like a go?" said the boy, unsure of what else to say.

"No."

The other boy dropped the sled to the ground, pulled a hood over his head, and put the cigarette between his lips.

"Are you by yourself?" he asked through the cigarette.

"Yes," answered the boy, not thinking.

"Good."

The darkness withdrew from the boy's eyes and a white blur filled his vision. Blinking over and over he pushed himself into a seated position. He was on the forest floor surrounded by the broken remnants of his sled. Pressing down on the pain at the back of his head, the boy felt an unusually large lump. After sitting for a moment in utter silence a thunderous rumble began to rise up through his throat and the boy began to cry.

Walking home a breeze began to blow, the sky darkened and what was a fine day had turned into a rain-threatened, gloomy summer's evening. He burst through the door into the old lady's house and ran straight up to his room, diving facedown onto the bed. The rage was building up inside him and he began screaming inaudibly into his pillow.

In the evening the light patter of raindrops hitting the skylight above the dinner table had awoken the boy from his deep thought. It wasn't too dark outside and he thought there must be a good couple of hours light in what remained of the day. The old lady looked at him and smiled. The boy's mouth upturned, but bore no teeth, reluctantly chewing on a spoonful of rice.

"What are the rules about climbing the giant tree?" the boy muttered.

"Well..." she replied, chewing on her dinner, "it's been very long since I was young. I honestly don't remember."

"I'm going to climb the tree tomorrow," he said.

The boy noticed a glint of fear in the eyes of the old lady.

"You're not allowed," she said.

"Why?" he shouted, not in anger but as though he was about to have all the truth revealed to him.

"You're not old enough."

"What's on the other side of the round door?" he said quickly.

But she was silent. She looked at him without anger, without pity, without worry, without any emotion the boy could decipher. He knew that she could tell him if she wanted to, just as he knew she had once been on the other side of the door. For at the base of the giant tree were carved her initials, and the words: *We will return, so long as we are gay and innocent and heartless.*

"Why won't you tell me?" the boy pleaded.

She stared at the boy for the longest time before looking away. "There is no door," she whispered, "there isn't anything inside the tree."

The boy studied the old lady's face, and his heart was broken because it showed no truth. And it was with this lie that he decided what to do.

In his room he filled his bag with used paper, and pencils, and cookies, and pyjamas. He put on his coat and his good shoes and climbed out of the window.

The rain was heavier than earlier, and as he looked up through the trees he could see the largest and darkest clouds forming together to block out the dying light. It was dark in the forest but he knew his path to the giant tree as well as he knew anything.

He came to the tree, and stood at the point from where his friend had climbed.

The boy reached up and put his hand over the stump. With a jump he hoisted both feet onto the highest root and balanced himself. A low rumble filled the forest around him and for the first time he felt afraid. He peered around the tree into the shadows but could see nothing. All around it seemed as though the darkness was closing in, and that even the surrounding trees were lurching forwards. The boy thrust his body upward so that the stump was chest height. He looked up and saw that the nearest branch was just out of reach, even if he should jump, but there was no other path and the heart-shaped hole in the giant tree was all he wanted. He decided to scramble up the slight angle of the tree to the nearest branch, though he'd have only his momentum to carry him, and if he were too slow he'd fall. He readied himself.

Bending his knees and raising his heels the boy leapt up the tree, and the lightning crashed down around him. Blue and red sparks filled the darkness in front of him and he fell far to the ground below. The rain beat down upon him for almost a lifetime until the old lady picked him up. She wrapped him in a blanket and carried him away from the tree.

The old lady tended to his cuts and scrapes before putting him to bed, and after a day or two, the bump on his head submerged and the grazes on his back began to heal. The old lady hardly spoke to him that week, and it wasn't until he tried to leave the house after several days in his room that he realised the extent of his punishment; *you aren't allowed any further than the gates of the garden until I say so*, is what the old lady had said.

It was a week later and a sunny Sunday afternoon. The old lady put on her most colourful dress and a matching cardigan. She laid out an ironed shirt and pressed shorts for the boy and drew him a bath.

"I think you've been in this house long enough, and have been very well behaved," she said in a pleased tone, "and your friend has come home, so we can pay him a visit."

The boy smiled politely. On the surface he'd been obedient and almost sweet for the entire week, but inside he'd been burning with torment. He didn't want to mention the tree out loud to the old lady because he knew she'd offer him no answers. He needed to speak to his friend, someone who wouldn't lie to him.

His friend lived in a bungalow several minutes' drive further from town. Like the boy, he lived alone without his parents under the guardianship of an old man. The old man had a pleasant way and often filled the boy with chewy toffees and glasses of lemonade. The old lady disapproved, but she held a soft spot for the old man. So, that afternoon, the old lady and the old man sat on the porch and drank wine and discussed their readings while the boy and his friend were to play inside.

The boy's friend was delighted to see him. All brown and glowing, his toothy smile was brighter than ever.

"I've been on holiday," he said cheerfully.

"Did you have fun?" the boy asked, not caring for an answer.

And for an hour his friend told him all about his weeks away, and the boy listened out of politeness. But at the end of the story his friend rapidly changed the subject, and to something the boy was most interested in: "...and I said goodbye to my friends and we went to the airport. It was great fun, but I wish you had been there. But maybe in a couple of months we can go into the giant tree together and holiday there. What do you think?"

The boy looked up from his drawings and grinned. "Do you really think I'm ready?" he asked, eager for an answer.

"You've been ready for ages," his friend replied, "but you're just not old enough yet."

"I tried to climb the tree, but it wouldn't let me in," the boy admitted.

"What happened?"

"The sky went dark and the rain came down with thunder, and I was thrown from the tree."

His friend stared in wonder. "I can't believe they'd do that."

"Who?"

"They tell me that the tree can decide who or what is allowed inside, but I don't think that's the truth. I think *they* decide who comes in. *They* decide who wants it most. The tree-keepers I mean."

"But *I* want it most!" the boy yelled, exasperated. "I deserve it. I believe everything you've told me about what's on the other side of the round door."

"That's what I don't understand. I've told everyone all about you, and they should have listened to me. They should not have turned you away because of your age. Not like *that* anyway." His friend had a rage across his face the boy had never seen before.

"Are you a prince?" asked the boy, almost pleading.

His friend shook his head as if to rid himself of his anger. "No. No I'm not."

"But you wore a crown," the boy said.

His friend smiled. "We all wear crowns. Everyone is equal and everyone is a prince or a princess or a warrior or even a tree-keeper. We can be anything we want whenever we go inside."

The boy looked at him confused. "We?"

...and it has the most wonderful streams and rivers, and all the unhappy kids from all the forests in the world can play in them. And everyone belongs. Everyone.

*

Two months into the beginning of the school year the old man passed away, and the boy's friend went to live with his parents in another town near another forest as far away as the boy could imagine. The boy did not go to the tree for the rest of the year.

In school the boy would not do his work, angering all his teachers and damaging their highest of expectations, except for those of his art teacher. At home he drew colourful pictures of hills and streams and rainbows and children, and often the old lady would gaze at them and beam with pride because the boy was regarded as the best artist in the school.

For his birthday, the boy asked for a variety of paints, different sized brushes, and a warm pair of walking boots. He got all he asked for and a warm winter coat to replace the one he'd left on the school bus on the last day of term.

The following day the boy gathered together his coat, his boots, his pencils, his paints, his brushes, some food, some drink, some rope, a torch, and a portrait he'd drawn of the old lady, and he climbed out of his bedroom window and leapt down to the soft blanket of snow below.

The flakes were the largest he'd ever seen. They fell slowly and softly caressed his face. Looking up to the sky, the distant flakes danced together and floated merrily about amongst themselves, and the boy would do his best to watch a single flake from as high as he could see until it fell amongst the camouflage of white on the forest floor. This was his best day.

Beneath the giant tree with the heart-shaped hole the boy stood and smiled. He pulled the rope from his bag and slung it high over the branch closest to the hole. The day was utterly silent except for his movement, until the rumble of thunder could be heard overhead. The boy looked about him for anything moving in the white and saw nothing. The forest rumbled again.

Hand over hand with his feet against the tree, the boy pulled himself up. *Rumble.* Hand over hand, foot over foot. *Rumble.* After a steady climb the boy reached the branch, which was thick enough to sit on, and from there he pulled up the rope and put it into his bag. *Rumble*. He stood up and faced the hole. Both hands clasping the edge he pulled himself up and went head first inside the giant tree before perching himself on the edge of the hole with his feet dangling into the darkness below. He felt around with his feet for a good ledge to put his weight on and slowly began to lower himself. Descending into the darkness he wondered if this was how his friend would climb down inside the tree. *I hope I see my friend.*

He could see nothing in front of him, not even his nose if he crossed his eyes, but he was not afraid of falling, and eventually he reached the bottom. It was soft beneath his boots and warmth filled the base of the hollow. He felt around in his bag and pulled out the torch. He exhaled slowly and, after counting aloud to three, the tree burst into light.

The walls were almost identical all around him, with a dark wood that looked almost smooth. Spread about on the ground were all types of clothes made with all types of fabrics in all types of colours, and tucked into the furthest corner was his friend's crown. Kneeling down he picked it up and a flood of confused emotions began to fill his head. He spun around and was faced with a crudely drawn round door with a faded square handle. The boy's knees buckled and he sank to the ground surrounded by broken wood and dirt and the tiny insects that lived inside the tree. He was still.

At length the boy stirred and sat up. He had felt like crying for the longest time but he did not want to be that boy anymore, and bravery was what he tried to muster. To the side of the door, tucked low and deep into a neatly formed niche, he noticed a small shoebox. He gently pulled it out, carefully lifted the lid, and peered inside. The box was full of paper both old and new with writing and colourful drawings carefully filling each page. The boy emptied the box and scattered the papers all about on the ground. Amongst the pictures were colourful animals of pinks and blues and golden coats and bejewelled crowns and a note. The boy picked it up and read it six times:

I really hope you can enjoy this place as much as I have, and I wish more than anything we could have enjoyed it together. You are my best friend.

Forgetting himself and his bravery entirely the boy began to cry. And there he sat, staring at the words, until his courage finally found him again. And so he turned all of his friend's pictures over and, sitting there for the rest of the day, he drew.

After the Hunt
by James King

After the hunt and his feeding The Creature would spend the black evenings circling the camp, howling at the moon, scratching at his full stomach. These were his formative years, before the hunt had ceased to be as such, before he would scratch his living from dead carcases, rotten trees and beneath rocks. These younger years, and the respective bounty that life offered, were what turned the child into an animal, into the creature, into a stalking death.

At night, beneath the starless sky, he would haunt from the edges of the camp, sitting in the shadows with his tools to hand. He would grind stones to disturb the folk within, to drive away whatever peace they had to alleviate their nightmares. A demon noise with a horrid pitch, like animals screaming before death.

This was his school, his playground and his home. Self-educated in preserving his own life outside of a dying society, he could recall the essential lessons of youth, but even in his self-developed wisdom he would steal from the others; the rusting cups of water and the hanging kills. He would take their tools also, to build his own fires far from the camp where he could spend some time alone. And alone is when he would invent life after the ending, invent the solitude and deluded infinity of the world he knew.

The repetition of light and dark seemed endless; a grey sky

overhead, followed by a black sky with an evanescent glow resting on the edge of the horizon. When The Creature had formed from the child's frame he became more interested in the comings and goings of the campers. He followed them on their hunts, throwing rocks into the distance, breaking sticks on the ground, watching them cower and huddle with their tools clenched weakly in their fists. He developed this game over time, taking the sport to the tops of the dead trees, spitting broken stones from his silhouette, cracking the wood as he taught himself to spring from branch to branch above their heads. When there was nothing to play and his belly was full, when he was tired of torturing them with foul noises, he would kill the skeletal animals that he would find dragging their feet in the unforgiving wild. He would bury them whole.

In a year of particular cold, before the snow came, the camp took up and moved on; a slow convoy moving through the wilderness. The Creature followed, curious in the change, stalking them from afar, unnoticed and maybe forgotten. The convoy was thin, desperate in numbers; maybe three families were all that remained. Relics of an old world. They moved with such apathy it almost encouraged The Creature to develop the taste, he had long since lost it for the animals of the forest. There was no game.

One winter's day a thinning party, in number and frame, moved out from their new home; an abandoned church by an overgrown road. They sauntered into the darkness of the trees to search for dry wood amongst the grey carpet of snow. The Creature stalked them from above, waiting for the smallest to fall behind. Opening her mouth to scream, he stole her voice, seizing her throat between his wretched fingers. It would take her two days to die and a week for him to finish.

His hauntings became more regular. He cherished the narrow eyes that dimmed on the yellow faces of the women, the bravado of the younger men who sat in the window frames of the church at night. He moved noisily in the shadows and watched them cling tighter to their implements of preservation.

That would be the last winter. The weather was relentless in its pursuit of death. The cold took most of them, the hunger taking others, and unnameable diseases felled the rest of the weak. The Creature ventured out, growing tired of their lack of will to survive. These dying souls were lost in the wilderness, not daring to find their way out.

To the borders of the forest he travelled, leaving his instruments of torture behind as markers for any return. He'd find sustenance in the demise of winter, but nothing more. His body now took to decay like the rest of them. He looked for some knowledge of what the others only suspected: evidence that there was nothing human left. He came across the skeleton frames of burnt homes, machines and bodies. The circle had come to the end. There was nothing left but empty spaces and a world devoid of life. His return was certain and immediate.

Through the dark forest he stumbled, beneath a sky lightless in night and day. When he dreamed he put pictures to the convoluted stories that the people had told. He formed images of the muddled words that had created his history and carved the world as he now knew it. He could never know if these images held truth, or whether the words he once heard were a lie.

He returned to the church at dawn. The grey sky cast a cruel light over the torn building, cracked and stained by the irrelevance of sanctity. Hidden amongst the branches of burnt cedar and marking devil images in the fallen ash, he waited for movement.

His breath rose in the morning chill. The shadows disappeared from the ground over the day and began to form anew in dimming light. As darkness came about him he called the cries of an animal, an inviting moan for desperate mouths. But the window frames of the church retained their vacancy.

At dawn the relevance struck him: they had abandoned him, they had cheated his game. He pulled himself from his shelter and scuttled to the gates of the church. He called again. He stood as a man in his rank clothing and moved without noise to the door of the building. A great echoing cry like he had never heard greeted him as he pushed the door inward. Fearing detection, he cowered to the ground. The door rocked gently with a creaking rhythm. He pricked his ears to the noise of a gentle breeze whistling through a crack in the wall. He ran his long nails over the dirt that had settled on the wooden flooring. A wooden beam at the back of the church ached under the weight of something swinging.

Hanging corpses swayed gently. Three figures; a man, a woman and a child, hung like pieces of drab cloth from the beam. Their long hair fell perfectly over their faces, the thin fabric over their bodies dropped neatly to their bare ankles, beneath the cloth their naked bodies drew inwards as though the last remnants of life had been sucked from them. He calculated their death, gently stroking their feet where they hung. What was there now? What would keep him alive? What humanity could provoke any thought within that would allow him to be anything other than mere animal? What was left now that he was the last man alive?

*

I watched the boy play thoughtfully with their bodies, almost animal in his curiosity. His movement fascinates me more than I would have imagined. Watching the motions of another human is something you wouldn't consider missing. But were these other strangers as animal as him? How late have I been? There is skin on their bones.

Following the boy into the forest I never hoped that he would lead me to others. He seemed so alone in the world; his calls to the wild suggesting that he hasn't spoken a word to another human for a lifetime. But he knew where these people were, and his tears now suggest that he hadn't foreseen their deaths.

The boy seems to stalk the corners of this church, as though he's never set foot in a house of stone. He is young enough I suppose to have forgotten the real world. He is leaving the bodies to hang, leaving the church and entering the forest. I have not eaten in four days. I will follow him and hope he returns in time.

He seems to know the forest well, moving with little noise and at pace. He's learned its tricks almost as well as I have. If I can get ahead of him I can anticipate his movements. A hunt without a kill. I want the boy to see me. I need him to talk to me.

I wonder how much this boy can offer me, or whether he can offer me anything at all. He moves like an untrained animal through the dead wood, self-taught, abandoned by the people he shed his tears for. He seems to have a skill that I don't possess: self-sustainability born from his own invention. Those hanging corpses can't have taught him much if they weren't able to sustain themselves within their company. This is why we're the last ones, victorious in survival, he and I.

The boy seems to be sleeping. He has some courage and ingenuity to create shelter. He's survived the harshest times without essential materials: the boots to keep feet dry, the bag to carry the warmest clothes, imperishable foods, water and a home to return to. I am starving, but I could not deny my discovery of human life, even if it took me away from my expedition, where food and salvation remains hidden somewhere in the city. Maybe I will take him there if the weather allows it. Maybe I won't.

I am questioning the last man alive. Time has passed to find that the boy is a hindrance. He offers me nothing but fear and paranoia. His movement and his sensibility have shown a murderous appetite, and his tears will haunt me. I am stronger than he is, he will be easy enough to over-power, but what would I keep him for? Sex? I have past the boundaries of normal desires; intimacy is foreign. Companionship? The boy does not talk, and his potential danger can offer only sport; a game that I imagine he's learned well. Food? That is the answer. But what lies beyond that? How much time, and what to fill it with? What fertility can I provide to birth a year, or perhaps breed a litter of them? How can my mind occupy the room that these years will vacate? What can I fill them with? What ceremonies, rituals or rites will I have to invent? How can I know what I will become if I can't imagine the answers to these questions?

*

The strange man's aged face watched The Creature with a demon's desire. He pulled the long, thin hair away from his mouth and licked his cracked lips. Thoughts of empty spaces beyond the present drew a strange glaze over his eyes and he seemed to stare beyond everything before him. He withdrew the long hunting knife from his bag and stepped out of the shadows, readying for the fifty-yard stalk to The Creature in his lair.

With stealth he entered The Creature's shadow, with the blade by his side dulling out of the light. He drew his hand back to clasp the animal by the scruff of its neck and mumbled a formation of syllables, an antiquated gesture with his impotent tongue.

It was over in an instant: the strange smell of the man had come to The Creature before the shallow scattering sounds of dead leaves across the forest floor met his ears. He swung his demon stones around to the man's face, breaking the skull with surprising ease, and repeating the blows with intrepid precision, leaving nothing but the strange body covered in blood and pulp. A thick smell excreted from the mess. A warm taste was upon his lips. Sustenance given so generously from the wild.

It took a day of exhausting effort to drag the strange body back to the church. He took the hanging family and laid them across the wooden floor away from the fresh kill. He watched them as he ate. He took the stranger's clothing and covered himself for the sake of self-preservation, the new boots fitting his feet quite comfortably.

Before he left the church for the last time he set a fire beneath the beams and then watched from afar as the flames rose high above the trees, an orange glow that fought the dying light of day. At length he drew a final breath at the place of his lasting memories and turned away from the fire, towards the edge of the forest.

IT'S NOT STALKING. NOT REALLY. NOT WHEN THE PERSON YOU'RE LOOKING FOR DOESN'T KNOW THAT YOU'RE LOOKING. THAT'S HOW JENNIE JUSTIFIED IT ANYWAY. THERE WAS A TIME WHEN SHE SEARCHED FOR HIM OFTEN. TYPED HIS NAME ONLINE IN A NOSTALGIC MOMENT, ADDING COMMON PLACES AND FRIENDS. ALWAYS DRAWING BLANKS. ALWAYS WAITING AND WONDERING WHY HE LEFT. IT WASN'T AN OBSESSION SO MUCH AS A CURIOSITY, KICKED OFF BY SOMETHING FAMILIAR. A GESTURE PERHAPS, OR A SMELL. ONCE IT WAS AN OLD LETTER SHE'D FOUND, HANDWRITTEN SCRAWL WINDING ACROSS THE YEARS. THAT TIME GOOGLE SENT BACK SOMEONE'S FANTASY FOOTBALL TEAM.

THIS TIME IT'S TRIGGERED BY A PHOTO IN THE PAPER OF A MAN WITH BIG DARK EYES AND BLACK MOP HAIR, JUST LIKE HE'D HAD BACK THEN. GOOGLE RETURNS A NEW LINK. JENNIE FINDS A HYSTERICAL WOMAN ACCUSING HIM OF DESTROYING HER. SAYING HIS CULT HAD PUT A CURSE ON HER AND SHE WANTED TO END IT ALL. A SUICIDE NOTE. WACKO, BUT SOMEHOW IT RINGS TRUE. THE PLACES, THE HIPPY SYMBOLISM. JENNIE SHUDDERS AS SHE REMEMBERS HIS EXTENSIVE COLLECTION OF CRYSTALS AND BOOKS ON CROWLEY. SHE SHUTS THE LAPTOP.

MONTHS LATER JENNIE SEES A MAN IN THE STREET AND SHE'S SURE IT'S HIM. THE SAME STATURE AND LANKY WALK. SHE CAN'T STOP HERSELF DOING A U-TURN TO FOLLOW AND STARES AS HE PASSES A MIRRORED WINDOW. STILL SHE CAN'T BE CERTAIN AND FOLLOWS FOR TWO MORE BLOCKS BEFORE HE GETS ON A BUS. HIS EYES LOCK ONTO HERS AS IT DRIVES PAST.

Wildlife Nuisance
by Mat Woolfenden

My wife and I, we have everything we need in our attic flat: a bathroom, a bedroom, bed, telephone for the takeaway and a cat. That morning Raffles returned with a swollen cheek. I knew the culprit was our neighbour at the back, it was his bee hive in that garden. Already I had studied the pensioner for a good couple of weeks. Something about his stoop, the creepy smile spread above his chin; a face that spelled retired war-criminal, or a school teacher, to my mind. I did not trust him at all. I had watched his shuffle. He had carried the mis-directed post in his arms, brought it to our front door, all the way down those stairs. Yes. Saliva clung to his denture's plate.

"Thank you," I think I said, that one time in my pants.

His garden, their garden: well, you people look for yourselves, over the fence, even back then everything appeared too perfect: rose bushes lined the borders by a swing for tiny children, trees, real fruit on those branches. The white wooden box, the bee house sat atop of its frame, a mere fifty yards from my bathroom sky light. I owned a .22 air rifle, and perched upon the lavatory seat, I exacted my revenge, call it a natural justice with the pellets. Or a "restitution fuzzballs," like I said it to them all.

For your information, I am an enthusiast with the rifle, collect

269

three varieties of the ammunition: spiked tipped, the traditional dumdum greys; the others with the pretty directional feathers for a long distance kill. But collateral or not, it had been the most satisfying of mornings shooting bugs, like our hypermarket drive the Tuesday before really; a matter of stopping distance, but in military terms. One shot dropped a single bee. I shall never be, heh heh, exactly sure of the individual miscreant as regards the pussycat's face, but my sights were upon each and every one of them, determined, as I was, to maintain civilian order. You fuck with my cats; rather:

"Whilst my felines are disturbed, I shall man the sniper's perch," I cried, and waved my fist from our loft extension.

After a couple of beers, and a sandwich, I recounted the bee business to my wife. She was vague with a magazine in hand and a duvet to spine, though finally roused, appeared more interested in my memoirs on the laptop. I am a writer, you see.

"Pervert," she called me, "your fantasies over giant women, they are revolting."

She said all this, my little wife who spoke.

"The bees," I said, and then more conciliatory: "Cakemix, how can you say such a thing? No, the Gaia Slut Giant to whom you refer, she is a fictitious being. Shall I write another story tomorrow, my love, call it the Dynamo Dwarf Sexual Subservient, in a tribute to your stature? Don't worry your pretty...head, I am writing it now."

She said nothing more to me, but just to be sure, I swung the boot, "She will be blonde, like you are," I said, "at the moment." Heh, heh.

I kissed her, flicked to the YouTube in our bedroom paradise for reassurance from Metallica. Still, thinking about it all, she drove me into a new horrible mood with her filthy talk about my giants. I was a woman-altered beast once again, and resorted to picking at the special fingernail, rubbed this stubble on my face. My eyes poked between these fingers before you now, yes. The bed top became like a raft, my despair, rest home of the mis-underrated male. Surely, surely all X-factor type opportunities were lost to me.

I sat-up, looked through the window at the front. The sky dripped white and the seagulls taunted me with their musical song of happiness.

"Fetch the air rifle," I said, 'I'll show parasites who is the Daddy in Brighton and Hove.

"One shot," I said.

My black shadow inspired suburbia. I cried "death to the gulls" out of the front window, fired that first shot, and listened to the deafening silence. The pellet ricocheted from the lamp post. Smoke whispered from my muzzle. I re-cocked, squeezed and the seagull crashed, dead in the road.

I fingered my piece, my delicate curl, a digit on cold metal, "another one bites the dust." I commanded an excellent regime. "Look honey, seagull corpses spread across your bonnet." I told her, "do me a favour, go clear them up."

"You killed them, you go outside," said my wife. "Anyway, too late my lover, there is a policeman, looks like he is doing it all for you."

"Where is he? I shall put on some trousers." I said. "Watch this." Again I drew back the sheet at the window. "YOU WON'T GET ME COPPER!" I cried.

My voice wiped every smile off all of their faces, yet even with the trousers on I needed to slash. The sound in my ears rang an emergency tingle,

"an ambulance for the bees?" I said and handed my rifle to my assistant wife, stepped manfully through to the lavatory. I saw the bug. He crawled around the white porcelain. I maintained a steady stream, and pissed him to death, but with his screams a pair buzzed through the high window. I staggered off guard, and then swiped wildly with the arms. The trajectory of the bees climbed to the rafter, they gained height. I stared but was blinded by the sunlight and crashed back into the sanctuary. More bees buzzed through the frame. There were a dozen bees in our bunker. We maintained control of the situation.

"The spray" I screamed.

There were many matters to resolve: two policemen by the bonnets. One lifted the seagull, flapped a limp wing, confirmed the casualty.

"This is our revolution, soldier," I said, smiled to my confederate woman, "bring me the cutlery drawer, a newspaper, barricade the bedroom with your shoes. And stick on my Johnny Cash."

The Crass Gang
by Mat Woolfenden

Crass levered a double mattress - up, on to his red car's roof. The overhang swayed: a fresh haircut for the old car, and together, old man and old mattress enjoyed the mile driven past shutters of the estate's arcade, and beyond towards a shiny town centre.

Crass, a week of stubble spiked over cheek, indicated at the new roundabout, swung left, drew the car gently to kerbside. He wobbled from his driver's seat, rested at the bonnet, and stared over the road, watched in wind, the shambles, the shame of a disgraced family; a family as they emerged from a regional police station.

Unsteady in her gait, the mother tottered through swing doors.

"A woman," Crass shook his head in pity.

A woman catching tears in a tissue, and with that same hand, she clutched her cheap fur coat, grasped it tight against the windpipe. Behind her, bowed, shaven, shuffled a lad dressed by the state. Complimentary – were the blue sweat pants, and free like him was the indispensable grey sweatshirt of honour.

"Filth, you bastards," Crass cried as charity. Stony tears leaked. Grit littered the cheek of a man stood alone aside his motorcar, "Why, you ruin lives," he said, and punched his palm, railed in defiance of the law. "Time to make my stand," he confirmed, and reached a shaky claw to the hatchback's boot. Those fingers untwisted a jerry-can's lid, poured a last gallon of petrol over that once comfortable bed. Mattress sagged, saturated in fuel; a rooftop haze shimmered. Petrol vapours filled nostrils. Crass inhaled anew, deeply, a man in flu treatment, maybe. Below him, the engine groaned - despondency. He lifted the house brick from the brake pedal, flicked the wheel on a Zippo lighter with his thumb

Eyes shone lightning, he flamed at the teeth, spewed the brass lighter on to the mattress. Blazing, his vehicle rumbled across the road, its hair on fire, and smashed into divisional police headquarters at five miles an hour.

"So?" said Crass, "next time," he said.

Silence radiated man's impotence. Glass only tinkled at the reception desk. Then a more satisfying smoke billowed from the doorway. Civilians – that mother, that poor child wearing his sweatshirt, they rushed to their own vehicle's safety, to spread word of victory.

Compatriot Stan arrived at the rendezvous. A younger man, boyish bulk graced upon scooter, he greeted Crass, used the tradition of shoulder's thump.

"Nice work, uncle Crass," he said.

"Our Ed should be out in a minute or two," his uncle replied, and he coughed.

A crowd of community support officers, police women, cop cleaners trampled out, through the car park gates, some with ears applied to telephones, others, the chubby palms raised as if in flight from Argos. Over the way, Stan tried to padlock this new, liberated scooter to a lamppost.

Crass staggered down the adjacent grass verge, rolled a cigarette, reached into his companion's discarded satchel, withdrew two delicious Polish beers. Stanley was now, like Crass, comfortable on the grass, enjoyed the view.

"Toast," he said.

"Lend me your lighter, sonny," said uncle Crass. Guts laid over grass, our man, our Crass held a pair of rockets in his fist. Fuses lit on his fag end's sparkle, he dipped fireworks into beer bottles, celebrated with a yelp. Rockets whizzed towards the copshop, skittered, sparked again, over the high windscreens of the paramilitary automobiles. High specification alarms wailed from the building, and away, behind them all, came the high screams of the sirens. Overhead - insurgents felt the whirr, the wind of a helicopter's rotor tickle across the back of their necks.

"Let's catch the bus," said Crass.

Confined in a barren cell, 'Ed' enjoyed the distraction of the alarm, only between temples. Many hours Ed contemplated a decent suicide in demonstration of his liberty, yet, as always, lumpen authority confounded schemes. Keys rattled in the door, a Groupon security fellow flicked a hairy chin.

"Up," he said.

Ed rose full height, imposed, a smart prisoner in a blue paper suit.

"Turn around," said the guard, and handcuffed Ed's shoulders tight against the blades.

"You are a fucking cunt," said Ed, elucidated emotional fragility.

"No chat, big man. Step outside, stick on your shoes," said the guard tormentor.

Hunched, by no means submissive, Ed waded past the vast octagonal control area, surveyed the empty booking suite, grimaced at the sight of this fortress of plexi-glassed repression. In strength, it loomed over individual convict bays, and the lino floor with which he, Ed was familiar to taste. He followed in a:

"Stop, now follow me," the growl of the Groupon man. He unlocked a door. The guard's boot twisted on a lino square, he squeaked. "Stop," he said, and paced around behind the prisoner. They continued on, through the cold antiseptic dungeon. Sound echoed, a florescent medley of whines in their ears, all unlocked, all irritating in the extreme. With his overtake, the guard tooled one more door. One more big key turned in a wide padlock.

They reached the yard, tasted smoke in the air. Officers jogged to their cars. Cops pulled strides to waistline, discarded pasties, crusts, coffee; gathered, at a run, body armour, tazers and hats. The pair stepped, one shackled, the other in shirt sleeves, beyond the commotion of vehicles revved in spaces, and approached the custodial transportation lorry parked in the end space. Ed leaned against brickwork, exhaled.

"Get up," said the security man who turned, un-padlocked the back doors, pushed, with his fist, the right wing. It swung wide, the axle groaned as if in her military orgasm. The dull guard grinned for memory's pleasure - Barbara, mother's carer in the year of '97, riverside car park encounter. Then startled almost, he remembered himself anew, spun to face his charge. Ed swung from waist, full tilt, head-butted the smaller man a force - hard, down, into the face.

The skull cracked on concrete, leaked to guttering. Topside, the spoon-dented cheek had split, wept teeth over the beard groomed in round globules of blood. Ed smiled, fresh wheeze hissed through bubbles at his enemy's nostril.

"Prick," said the prisoner, the decorator in a paper suit. Crouched low aside the bleeding man, his tissue groin ripped, and balls liberated in pendulum, swung through cold air. Still, the key-ring dangled from the other man's belt. Ed fell on the man, swallowed almost, the key-ring, tugged from lips; stood with great effort, ripped the keys from trouser loop. He turned, saw a fellow prisoner. The convict squealed from the van's interior.

"What are you doing, Crazy Edwin?" said the coiled and probably innocent felon.

Ed grinned, the keys revealed in his mouth. He spat his collection through the feedbox shutter.

"Sort me out," he said, turned his back to the convict now pressed against the crosswire frame.

Uncuffed, Ed rubbed wrist on palm, bent aside the guard one more time, swiped the kapo's van key from top shirt pocket. He spat on waxen features, raised himself on knuckles, slammed the rear door of the van, the axle groaned again. Within three strides the escapee arrived at the driver's window. Security cameras observed a white van throttle carefully out of the gates of the station jail.

Crass flashed his bus pass at the bus driver, climbed the spiral towards his favourite back seat experience. A teenager sat there in the most insolent way; telephone plugged to an earpiece, his mouth open to tune:

"Baby, my baby ape," he sang, wore soft fabric, condition ruined when Crass hoisted mobile from lap, and dropped it out of the window.

"Up, you little fucker," he said.

Worm with hands, knees affixed to worm skin - the boy crawled away from Crass and the more slack-jawed Stanley. He knew his place in their bus theory, and for a while the righteous rocketeers relaxed on the long bus-bench, made the journey through their home city. Smoke of their cigarettes drifted over black combat jackets. Stan squinted, used the blade of a carving knife and he scooped soil from under fingernails,

They disembarked outside the bookmakers. Idiot shoppers paraded in the way. Insects sniffed for their crisp packet deals, their pizza boxes piled for a pound. And kerbside, a white security van purred, the wheels settled over yellow double lines. Three militant, independent confederates of a new Albion Dixy were at last reunited. Without break of stride, heads nodded the stiff recognition, passions appreciative to sacrifice, a shared endeavour is the struggle for anarchist justice through crime.

Ura!

Narrative distraction, reader, please;

Stan shoved a grandmother by the shoulders. She had fussed in his way, spilled tartan trolley past his tattoos, and from kneecaps the old lady scooped apples, a broken pair of spectacles, into her belly.

Urban guerrillas marched inside the bookmakers, beyond the fruit machines, beyond the desperate crowd of low-life. Men fiddled with pencils at individual troughs. Crass approached the window of the principal ledger. Behind glass, a beautiful Latvian chap studied medicine on his Kindle.

"Excuse me, please," said Crass. "I dropped my benefit book, laddy. I dropped it right down there, chump."

The bright youth hopped from the stool, untwisted an armoured door, proffered assistance for the older gentleman. Indeed, he stepped through the door, and the bone of Ed's paper-suited elbow greeted his chin. A weighty boot see-sawed upon an Eastern European chest.

"Mate," said Ed. "Rest a while, maybe I'll smear them bol-lacks away?' he said. 'See carpet squares, eh, son?" he smiled again.

Stan, then Crass almost, rushed the door, crashed past to the back room of the bookies. Manageress wore a tight 'azure' suit, she would say, but only howled when Crass found her counting money.

He attacked her in a snarl, grabbed the forearms. Stan, gliding behind the swivel-chair, held his long knife against her throat. She shivered, plain features wobbled: a pullet's crop, bulbous neck exposed under light bulb. In gurgle, exertion, she pointed to a grey cabinet, the finger nicotine-stained.

Upon Channel seas, the plastic seating, stacked in the corner of the rear passenger deck, caught in wind, tumbled over sole, Crass selected a recliner from amidst the disgraced pile, and bow-legged, staggered towards a rear-rail. Fresh air jostled him bodily, here on the deck of the Mont St Michel, operated by Brittany Ferries. At last, amongst civilised company Crass savoured a tin of Special Brew on his lips, relaxed in a chair, relished the sight of white cliffs disappearing from his life forever. Seagulls squawked, white water churned at the prow. Aside him sat compatriots. All three men wore a selection of Lycra: tops, shorts. The new racers, their bicycles, stored securely below decks, earlier wheeled from the front window display of Halfords on the high street.

"Seven thousand," said Edwin, cash removed from his shorts and for now held in his fist.

"Where are we going, Uncle Crass?" said Stanley.

"First stop is Turkey for a suntan," said Crass, "and then boys, swing north. War requires our skill sets."

"You're not wrong," said Ed. He lifted his tin, "here's to killing Russians."

"Ukraine?" said Stan.

"Scotland," said Crass, "Aye."

BIOS

Will Ashon is the author of two novels, *Clear Water* and *The Heritage*, both with Faber and Faber. He is also the founder of Big Dada Recordings, a record label. His most recent project was the micro-fiction collection, Shorter, published as a phone app. He is currently working on a non-fiction title about counter-culture, Enclosure, magic, mad dogs and Epping Forest.

Peter Higgins was born in Dewsbury and has been living in London since 1994. His short stories and articles have appeared in *Tales of the Decongested*, *PenPusher* and *Litro*, and in *Open Pen* twice. His situation comedies won the second prize in the world-famous Sitcom Trials two years in a row.

Darren Lee lives in London and has had work published in *Transportation: Islands and Cities*, *Storgy*, *Londonist* and in the *Scaremongrel*, *Fugue*, *Lover's Lies* and *Fifty Stories For Pakistan* anthologies. Several of his stories have also been performed on stage at the *Liars' League*.

Xanthi Barker's fiction has appeared in *One Throne*, *Cadaverine* and the Arts Council funded anthology *Things That Have Happened*. She recently completed an MA in Comparative Literature at Goldsmiths University. Currently she is writing a novel and teaching kids.

Ben Byrne was born in London, studied drama at the University of Manchester, and later worked in San Francisco, New York and Tokyo as a brand consultant, musician and film maker. His first novel, *Fire Flowers,* was published by Europa Editions in 2015, and his short fiction has featured in *Litro* and *Writer's Hub*.

Kate Smalley Ellis is a London-based writer, bookseller and recent Birkbeck MA graduate. She's currently working on her first collection of short stories. Her short fiction has been published in *Open Pen*, London/Tasmanian anthology *Transportation: Islands and Cities*, and *The Mechanics' Institute Review*.

Ian Green is a writer from Northern Scotland. His short fiction has been performed at *Liars' League London*, *LitCrawl London*, and the *Literary Kitchen Festival*, and published in *Open Pen*. His work can also be heard on *The Wireless Reader* literary podcast and will feature in the upcoming short story anthology *Broken Worlds* by Almond Press. His story *Audiophile* was a winner of the BBC Opening Lines competition 2014, broadcast on BBC Radio 4.

Anna Harvey is a prolific consumer of literature, music and art. She has been described as an all round Renaissance woman (amongst other things). Anna fell in love with Open Pen's pastel shades after finding her story on the cover of Issue Two, and saw an opportunity to nurture the magazine in a blossoming literary scene in East London, where she likes to sit in the pub by her house, writing stories and exchanging pleasantries with the local patrons.

Max Sydney Smith was born in 1986 in London. His work has appeared in the literary magazines *Structo*, *Open Pen* and *Shooter* and the flash fiction app Quick Fictions. He is currently working on a novel detailing the life and opinions of a Greek communist.

Jo Gatford wants to live on your bookshelf. Her debut novel, *White Lies*, was published by Legend Press in 2014. You can find her short stories and flash fiction in *Aesthetica*, *Litro*, and elsewhere. She lives in Brighton where she wrangles two insomniac children and writes sweary social media content for rude cartoonists.

Tadhg Muller is a London based expat Tasmanian. Muller's fiction has been published in *Open Pen, Skive, Griffith Review,* and *Island,* whilst his poetry has been published in *The Cannon's Mouth.* Muller is currently putting the finishing touches to a novel, his first.

James King lives in London where he works in TV listings. While he looks back at his first story 'The Giant Tree' with mixed feelings, one thing for which he is forever thankful to the story and *Open Pen* for is how they rekindled his desire to read and write short fiction, without which his creative outlets would be restricted to work and shouting curses at footballers.

Mat Woolfenden was raised in the Netherlands, Iran, North Devon, married in Walthamstow and retired to Brighton at the age of 42. He may be an acquired taste, an eccentric voice, yet Matthew perseveres in prose. To date, Mat has been published in *Hobo Pancakes* (USA) and *Wasafiri.*

Sean Preston is the editor of *Open Pen.* He was born in East London, where he lives, now by the river.

N Quentin Woolf is a contributor to *Open Pen,* author of *The Death of the Poet* (Serpent's Tail), and the voice of *Londonist Out Loud.*

Paul Ewen is Francis Plug, the author of *How to be a Public Author* (Galley Beggar).

The microfiction pieces were written by:

Mazin Saleem	Matthew Cutler
Lisa Fontaine	Dave Clark
R.M. Clarke	James Vella
Jamie Collinson	Rhuar Dean
Piers Pereira	Jasmin Kirkbride
Liam Hogan	Katherine Vik

NOTES

"Smoking in the Library" by Peter Higgins first published in *Open Pen Issue Ten* (December 2013)

"The Grudge Elephant" by Darren Lee first published in *Open Pen Issue Four* (February 2012)

"Love in the Time of Ketamine" by Xanthi Barker first published in *Open Pen Issue Five* (May 2012)

"Inherent Sick" by Jamie Collinson first published in *Open Pen Issue Five* (May 2012)

"Waiting for a Hurricane" by Ben Byrne first published in *Open Pen Issue Fourteen* (May 2015)

"Player 2" by Piers Pereira first published on the *Little Printer Open Pen* publication (January 2014)

"Lazylegs" by Kate Smalley Ellis first published in *Open Pen Issue Four* (February 2012)

"Haar" by Ian Green first published in *Open Pen Issue Nine* (August 2013)

"Of All The Bras In All The World" by Matthew Cutler first published in *Open Pen Issue Ten* (December 2013)

"Pure Fields" by Anna Harvey first published in *Open Pen Issue Two* (June 2011)

"Hidden Criticism" by Dave Clark first published on the Little Printer Open Pen publication (August 2012)

"The Boy Who Bit His Nails" by Max Sydney Smith first published in *Open Pen Issue Thirteen* (February 2015)

"An Ecstatic Lightning of Strange Birds" by James Vella first published on the *Open Pen* website as part of the series *Devoured Further*, a follow up to the short story collection by James Vella *Devourings (Wounded Wolf Press)*.

"If, Then" by Jo Gatford first published in *Open Pen Issue Eight* (April 2013)

"In Lieu of a Memoir" by Tadhg Muller first published in *Open Pen Issue Six* (September 2012)

The poem "Sydney" from Tadhg Muller's 'In Lieu of a Memoir' was written by his brother, K. Muller.

"The Giant Tree" by James King first published in *Open Pen Issue One* (April 2011)

"Wildlife Nuisance" by Mat Woolfenden first published in *Open Pen Issue Thirteen* (February 2015)

All other pieces are published here for the first time.

THANKS

Open Pen and *The Open Pen Anthology* has been:

Sean Preston, Anna Harvey, Josh Hollwey, James King, Liam Kelly, Piers Pereira, Josh Neal, Barry Rogers, Helen Rogers, Joe Johnston, Nicola Day, Patrick Smiley, Menna El-Guindy, Kate Smalley Ellis, N Quentin Woolf.

We owe our thanks to:

Adam Luria, Anna Jean Hughes, Ariadne Godwin, Arthur Jeffes (of The Penguin Cafe), Bare Fiction Magazine, Bobby Nayyar, Brick Lane Bookshop, Carrie Kania, Charles Hollwey, Dan Coxon, Elliot Egerton (Bang On!), Gareth Marshall, Giulia Ferrazzi, Ian Gittins, Jamie Collinson, João Cerqueira, Joe Borges, Julie Orsatti, Karen King, Kirsty Cook, Kit Caless, Lisa Goll, London Writers' Club, Lotte Daley, Mariam Gouverneur McKeown, Martin Hutchinson, Mateusz Odrobny, Maximus Boethius, MG Paterson, Olga Preston, Owen Jones, Phillip Clement, Sebastian Sandys, Stacie Dexter, Tamara Vos, Tania Hershman, The MODO guys, Will Ashon, Darren King, Elaine Peace, John Muller, Anahied Luria, Laurence Dorman, Carolyn Gindein, Steve Fiori, Chris Jarvis, Gretchen Heffernan, Rupert Dastur, Omar Rafique, Louis Harber, Pippa Hennessy, Alasdair Tod, and Kara Gerrie.

Extended thanks to the high-heeled Anna Harvey, my second-in-command and a true-blue. And to Helen for putting up with me.

Open Pen has been a pleasure and constant source of distress. The distress is worth it.

Sean Preston
Editor-in-Chief

You write to be read, of course.